"He's not exactly Winnie the Pooh," Nick whispered nervously.

"He's going to love you," Carly whispered back. "Hi, Attila," she called to the bear. "I've brought someone to meet you."

Attila grunted, then fixed Nick with a glare that didn't look even remotely loving. Not that he really wanted the bear's love. He'd be happy if it just didn't eat him!

Carly rubbed the big bear's nose, then said, "Attila, that's Nick. I want you to go and say hello to him. *Two feet.*"

Standing up, he looked like an enormous sumo wrestler in a fur coat.

"Good boy," Carly said. "Now go say hello."

Attila gave a little snort and started toward Nick, who swallowed hard. "Hello, Attila."

The bear eyed him for another second, then took a final step forward, wrapped its arms around him and began squeezing him to death.

Dear Reader,

In Tinseltown, *Wild Action* would be pitched as a romantic screwball comedy: Dirty Harry meets Gentle Ben.

Of course, hero Nick Montgomery meets a whole lot more critters than just Attila the bear when he inherits half of an animal talent agency. And in the beginning he doesn't have a clue how to deal with any of them.

He also doesn't have a clue how to deal with his newfound partner, Carly Dumont. But that's what makes the romance fun.

As an animal lover, I found this book a delight to write. It's not often that my research involves something like visiting an animal ranch and being licked by a bear, but the research for this one did. (And yes, bears' tongues really are warm and smooth. For some reason, I was expecting them to be rough, like a cat's.)

At any rate, I hope you enjoy reading about Carly, Nick and the antics of the animals in the Wild Action agency.

Warmest regards,

Dawn Stewardson

WILD ACTION
Dawn Stewardson

Harlequin Books

TORONTO • NEW YORK • LONDON
AMSTERDAM • PARIS • SYDNEY • HAMBURG
STOCKHOLM • ATHENS • TOKYO • MILAN
MADRID • WARSAW • BUDAPEST • AUCKLAND

ISBN 0-373-70748-7

WILD ACTION

Copyright © 1997 by Dawn Stewardson.

All rights reserved. Except for use in any review, the reproduction or
utilization of this work in whole or in part in any form by any electronic,
mechanical or other means, now known or hereafter invented, including
xerography, photocopying and recording, or in any information storage
or retrieval system, is forbidden without the written permission of the
publisher, Harlequin Enterprises Limited, 225 Duncan Mill Road,
Don Mills, Ontario, Canada M3B 3K9.

All characters in this book have no existence outside the imagination of
the author and have no relation whatsoever to anyone bearing the same
name or names. They are not even distantly inspired by any individual
known or unknown to the author, and all incidents are pure invention.

This edition published by arrangement with Harlequin Books S.A.

® and TM are trademarks of the publisher. Trademarks indicated with
® are registered in the United States Patent and Trademark Office, the
Canadian Trade Marks Office and in other countries.

Printed in U.S.A.

To John, always.

With special thanks to Janet Howsam and
Norman Phillips of the Northwood Buffalo and Exotic Animal
Farm in Seagrave, Ontario, for giving me a special tour and
patiently answering my "bear" questions. I hope all my
Ontario readers come to visit you.

Blackie edged farther out on his branch.

CHAPTER ONE

Where There's a Will, There's a Way

"GOOD CAT," Nick said, reaching the top of his ladder and swinging onto a main branch of the towering maple. "Good cat."

From above, Blackie peered down with a little cat smirk. Nick took that to mean the beast was contemplating one of its higher-and-higher routines, and the prospect made him swear under his breath.

He wasn't a superstitious man, so it didn't really bother him that Blackie made a point of crossing his path on a regular basis. But this trick with the tree was damned annoying—especially since he knew the cat would eventually come down on its own. At least, that's what the several cat owners he'd asked had told him.

Unfortunately, his next-door neighbor didn't believe it. Even more unfortunately, Hilda was eighty-three years old and Blackie was the most important thing in her life.

Nick swung up onto a higher branch; Blackie twitched his whiskers and glanced skyward.

"Okay, here's the deal, cat. You stay right where you are, and I'll let you out of this with all your nine lives intact."

Blackie edged farther out on his branch to consider

the offer. Nick climbed another foot or two, then tried a quick grab.

The cat managed to hiss, lash out with a paw and scramble backward all at the same time.

Nick checked his hand and saw the beast had drawn blood. Thus far, it was definitely winning this round, so he fixed it with one of his best cop glares. "I'm warning you, I've been up all night and I'm in no mood for your games. I need sleep, not exercise."

Blackie made a low growling noise and arched his back. Nick muttered a few ungentlemanly words in reply. He'd spent the past fifteen hours convincing an escaped con to release his hostage, and he'd done a far better job of negotiating with the man than he was doing with Blackie.

Of course, the con had spoken English. The cat only spoke Meow.

He considered that for a moment. Then, telling himself nobody would ever know, he stared Blackie straight in the eye and hissed loudly.

The cat blinked, looking startled. He recovered in a second, but not before Nick made another grab— and this time lucked out.

Gingerly pulling the squalling animal to his chest, he pinned it with one arm and started back down the tree, thinking that if anyone ever tried to give him so much as a pet rat, he'd take off on the dead run.

"Oh, thank you so much," Hilda said as he reached the ground and handed Blackie to her. "I don't know what I'll do after you move."

"Well, with any luck your new neighbor will be a tree climber, too."

He listened absently while Hilda promised him freshly baked cookies, wishing she hadn't reminded him he was being evicted. He'd been renting this place for six years and he'd be happy to stay for six more. But when an owner decided to sell, the tenant generally had to go.

Once Hilda finished thanking him, Nick escaped into his house—grabbing the morning's mail from the box and riffling through it as he went.

There was the usual junk, a couple of bills...and a letter from the firm of Evans, Broderick and Rowan, Barristers and Solicitors, in Toronto.

Staring at the return address, he wondered what a law firm in Toronto wanted with a police detective in Edmonton, Alberta. None of the possibilities that popped into his mind appealed to him.

He really *wasn't* a superstitious man. But he'd seen bad news come in threes often enough to figure there just might be something to that one. And right now he was at two and counting.

First there'd been the bombshell that he'd have to find a new place to live—which he still hadn't managed to do, even though time was getting awfully tight.

Then, just last week, the best partner he'd ever had announced he was taking early retirement at the end of the summer. So this letter...

Hell, the way things were going, he was probably being sued. Ripping the envelope open, he unfolded the letter and began reading.

Dear Mr. Montgomery,

   I am writing to inform you that your late father's brother, Augustus Montgomery, passed away on the second of July.

Nick paused to glance at the date on the letter. It had been written on the sixth, ten days ago. Canada Post must have routed it through the Northwest Territories.

Picking up where he'd left off, he continued reading.

His last will and testament names you as his only living relative and the sole beneficiary of his estate, which is primarily comprised of a rural property in Ontario and a company that operates under the name of Wild Action.

Please contact my office at your earliest convenience so that we may proceed with transferring legal ownership of these assets to you.

My direct line is (416) 555-1711.

Yours truly,
William Brown, LL.B.

His heart beating faster than normal, Nick tried to decide whether he should be feeling sad about Gus's death—finally telling himself there was no reason to.

After all, he'd never even met the man, and he'd certainly never heard a good word about him. Much the opposite, in fact.

During his younger years, Gus had worked in the family business along with Nick's father and grandfather. Then, one day, he'd vanished, and the others had quickly discovered he'd embezzled a small fortune from the company and left them on the verge of bankruptcy.

Gus had never been heard from again, and it was surprising he'd even known he *had* a nephew. So why hadn't he left his estate to a friend? Or to charity?

The obvious answer was that he'd felt guilty and was trying to make restitution. Unless...

Nick skimmed the letter once more, warning himself not to get too excited until he had a few more details. According to the stories his parents used to tell, Gus had been a practical joker as well as a thief. Which meant he could be reaching out from the grave to play a final joke—by leaving Nick property that was worthless and a company mired in debt.

There was an easy way to find out, though, so he picked up the phone and dialed Brown's number, glancing at his watch as he finished. With the time difference, it was already past noon in Toronto, but hopefully the man took late lunches.

"Mr. Brown's office," a woman answered.

"Yes. My name's Nick Montgomery. Mr. Brown asked me to get in touch."

"Well, he's in court all day today. But if you'd like to leave your number, he'll return your call tomorrow."

Nick swore to himself. He didn't want to spend the next twenty-four hours wondering exactly what was what.

"Are you familiar with the Augustus Montgomery estate?" he tried. "Could I ask you a couple of questions about it?"

"I'm afraid I wouldn't have any answers. I'm just filling in for Mr. Brown's secretary while she's at lunch. But if you'd like, I could ask one of the other lawyers to speak with you."

"Great. That would be terrific."

He waited for what seemed like forever—imagining how happy this call was going to make his long-distance carrier—until a different woman came on the line and introduced herself as Linda Weaver, one of Brown's associates.

"I've pulled Bill's file on Mr. Montgomery," she said, "and I'll try to answer your questions. What would you like to know?"

"Well, at the risk of sounding mercenary, is there even a ballpark figure on the value of the estate?" He waited again, this time listening to the soft rustle of shuffling papers.

"Not that I can see," she said at last. "Bill would probably have a pretty good idea, but I'm new to the firm. I don't know much about any of his clients."

"So...for all you know the property could be a marsh."

That elicited a laugh. "I wouldn't think so. There's a house on it. That's where your uncle lived. And let's see... It's a hundred acres in all, about an hour's—maybe an hour and a half's— drive from Toronto."

Nick could feel his excitement growing. Even if it wasn't much of a house, a hundred acres near Toronto had to be worth something.

On the other hand, what if the company was in the red? Was that where the joke came in? Was he liable for a stack of debts?

"And what about this Wild Action?" he asked. "Is it a money loser?"

Linda rustled some more papers, then said, "No, the financial statement shows it as profitable—with revenues of more than a million dollars last year."

A sudden buzzing in Nick's head made him afraid he'd misheard. "More than a million?" he repeated.

"Uh-huh, a million and ninety-one thousand, to be exact."

Dollar signs began floating in front of his eyes. That was definitely a go out and celebrate with champagne kind of number. But what sort of business were they talking about?

When he asked, Linda said, "I'm not sure. It's a private company, so there's no annual report. But the name sounds awfully familiar. Just hold on a second. I'll ask someone else."

Nick heard her putting down the receiver. Then there was a murmur of female voices in the background. Eventually, Linda came back on the line, saying, "We're pretty sure it's a brand of casual wear. You know? Something like Northern Adventure or Rough and Ready?"

After profusely thanking the lawyer for her help, Nick hung up, his mind reeling. He told himself to calm down, that he didn't really believe in omens any more than he believed in superstitions. But wouldn't *anyone* take this as a sign from the gods?

For the past year or so, he'd been running on empty. He'd joined the force when he was only twenty, and after fourteen years he'd seen enough of the seamy side of life to last the rest of his days. On top of which, the bureaucracy on the job was getting more and more intolerable.

He wanted out, wanted to get a private investigator's license and set up his own agency—the sooner the better. Some days, it was all he could do to keep from walking into the staff sergeant's office and quitting.

But he'd been holding himself back because he hadn't managed to save anywhere near enough money. Now, the money was magically there. Or would be, as soon as he sold that business and the land.

For a minute, he sat mentally reviewing his case-load. There were no serious loose ends that demanded that he tie them up personally, which meant nobody would really care if he left on short notice. So that was what he was going to do. The idea felt right, and he'd never been a man to delay acting once his mind was made up.

Reaching for the phone again, he pressed redial. This time, he made an appointment to see William Brown at two o'clock the next day.

After that, he booked an obscenely early morning flight to Toronto—with an open return date. He had no idea how long transferring legal ownership would take. Plus, he'd need a day or two to get the business and property listed for sale.

Finally, charged with exhilaration, he left for head-quarters to turn in his badge.

AS THE ELEVATOR CARRIED him up to the law offices of Evans, Broderick and Rowan, Nick was still trying to shake the uneasy feeling that had been nagging him since yesterday.

An hour or two after he'd walked out of head-quarters, he'd realized he should have asked Linda Weaver about Wild Action's *profits*, as opposed to revenues, before he'd gone ahead and quit. After all, aside from his meager savings, those profits were all he'd have to live on until he got things sold.

But his brain hadn't been firing on all cylinders during their conversation—partly because he'd been dead on his feet and partly because her revenue figure had pretty much stopped him cold.

The elevator slowed to a halt and its door slid open. Telling himself yet again that any company earning more than a million dollars a year had to be making substantial profits, he strode across the waiting area to the receptionist.

"Mr. Montgomery to see Mr. Brown."

She gestured toward a hall. "Straight along there. It's the last door on the left."

"Would you mind if I left my suitcase out here?"

"Not at all."

Parking it near her desk, he straightened his tie and headed down the hall.

To his surprise, when Brown's secretary ushered him into the inner office, there were three people waiting for him—two middle-aged men and a great-looking woman who couldn't be more than thirty.

"Mr. Montgomery, I'm Bill Brown." The man behind the desk rose. "Okay if I call you Nick?"

"Sure."

"I'd have known you anywhere," Brown added as they shook hands. "You bear a strong resemblance to your uncle."

Nick simply nodded. His parents had told him that years ago, and right now he was more interested in hearing who the two in the visitors' chairs were. The man might be a lawyer, an associate of Brown's, but the woman wasn't.

She was wearing a casual dress, minimal makeup, and her dark hair was hanging loosely down her back. She definitely wasn't a big-city professional. So who was she and why was she here?

When no logical answer came to mind, his anxiety level began edging upward.

"I'd like you to meet Carly Dumont and Roger Harris," Brown said.

Nick nodded an acknowledgment, then looked at Brown once more.

"Please have a seat, Nick."

Casually shifting the remaining visitor's chair so he'd be able to keep an eye on everyone, he sat.

"We were just talking about your being a police detective," Harris said. "It must be interesting work."

"Some days yes, some days no." Nick left it at that. There was no reason to update total strangers on his job status. Not when he'd rather find out what was going on here.

"Carly worked for your uncle," Brown offered. "She was his right hand at Wild Action. Roger is her lawyer."

"And her friend, I like to think," Roger Harris added. "Just as I was Gus's."

Ignoring Harris, Nick focused on Carly Dumont, anger starting to simmer inside him. His brain was working just fine today, and he didn't need any more clues to figure out exactly what the story was. This woman intended to contest Gus's will.

He glanced at Brown again, wondering if she had a legal leg to stand on. But he'd be damned if he'd ask with her sitting there listening.

"I'm afraid I have some bad news," Brown continued. "I only learned about it this morning, when Roger called me."

"I see. And I assume it involves Ms. Dumont?"

"Yes, it does. It seems your Uncle Gus had Roger prepare a new will a year or so ago. A more recent one, I mean, than the one in my files. I've had a look at it, and there's no doubt it's valid. And under its terms, Gus's estate is to be divided between you and Carly."

Nick willed Brown to grin and say he was joking. Instead, Harris cleared his throat and said, "Bill, perhaps you'd better make clear *precisely* what the will states."

"Yes, of course. I was just getting to that. Nick, the division isn't fifty-fifty. Your uncle left forty-nine percent of his estate to you and fifty-one percent to Carly."

Nick could feel himself starting to grow numb.

"I'm sorry this is coming as a shock to you," Carly said quietly. "But until last night, I didn't know about it myself."

"You see," Harris explained, "my practice is in Port Perry, which is the closest town to your uncle's property. That's how we knew each other. And when Gus had me draw up the will, he said he didn't want Carly to know she was a beneficiary while he was alive."

"But he died on July second," Nick managed, his voice sounding more than a little strangled. "That was more than two weeks ago."

"Yes. I only learned about his death last night, though. I'd been out of town."

"And I'd called Bill right away, because he's the company lawyer," Carly put in. "Gus's *only* lawyer, as far as I knew."

"As far as I knew, too," Brown said. "Which is why I didn't hesitate about contacting Nick," he added, glancing at Harris and looking darned put out that Gus had gotten himself a second lawyer.

"Any of us would have contacted the beneficiary

right away," Harris told him. "In any event," he continued, focusing on Nick, "as soon as I got home and learned Gus had died, I advised Carly of the existence of the new will."

"I tried to reach you this morning, Nick, after Roger phoned me," Brown said. "But you must have already been on your way to Toronto."

Their explanation complete, the other three sat watching him while he sat trying to think straight. But he couldn't think past the fact that fifty-one percent of the estate belonged to Carly Dumont. And a controlling interest would give her the right to call the shots.

He looked at Brown. "You said this other will is definitely valid?"

"I'm afraid so."

"Then why didn't Gus tell you about it?"

"There's no law that says he had to. Or maybe he meant to and forgot. He tended to be absentminded."

"But definitely of *sound* mind," Harris said quickly. "No doubt about that. He was sharp as a tack, right Carly? And he seemed in good health, too."

She nodded. "He was just fine on July first. We went to a Canada Day party and he was dancing up a storm. But..."

Pausing, she wiped away a tear. "I don't know whether it was too much sun or all the exertion or what, but he wasn't feeling well before he went to bed. And in the morning... When I tried to wake him, he was gone."

"A heart attack in his sleep," Brown elaborated.

"You tried to wake him?" Nick said. "You mean you lived with him?"

"Uh-huh. For twelve years."

Nick gazed at her, wondering if his parents had known that Gus was into cradle robbing along with all his other sins. Then he forced his thoughts back to the problem at hand and tried to convince himself this wasn't a total calamity.

After all, it was only half of his inheritance that had vanished overnight, whereas Gus's new will might have left *everything* to Carly. Besides, with any luck, his forty-nine percent would be more than he needed.

Glancing at her again, he forced a smile.

When she tentatively smiled back, it made him feel a little better. She seemed like a reasonable woman, so how hard could it be to work things out?

Carly felt herself starting to breathe more easily. She was still up to her ears in problems, of course, but at least Nick Montgomery wasn't turning out to be an additional one.

On the way here, she'd let her imagination run rampant, picturing him as an enormous dragon who'd kill her by breathing fireballs when he heard he was only getting part of the estate.

In reality, he was a good-looking man—with a very nice smile and rugged features that made his appearance decidedly masculine. And even though he was clearly upset, she couldn't see any homicidal impulses dancing in his gray eyes.

"Let's lay our cards on the table," he said, leaning forward in his chair and meeting her gaze. "I have absolutely no interest in the fashion industry, so the best thing all around would be for you to buy me out."

She glanced at Roger. When he seemed as puzzled

as she was, she looked at Nick once more. "The fashion industry?"

"Yes. I wouldn't know a fashion trend from a snowplow, so—"

"Wait. You mean you've been thinking that Wild Action's in the fashion business?"

"Ahh... You're saying it's not?"

"Nick?" Bill said before she could answer. "There are so many movies shot in Toronto that it's known as Hollywood North. It masquerades as New York, Chicago, Detroit, you name it."

"It's cheaper to film here because of our low dollar," Roger added.

"At any rate," Bill continued, "Wild Action is an animal talent agency that supplies animal actors."

Carly watched Nick digest that information, feeling distinctly sorry for him. His expression said he'd just as soon have inherited half a leper colony.

"Do you know much about animals?" she asked when nobody else broke the silence.

"I see a lot of the neighbor's cat," he muttered.

She glanced at the scratch on his hand. It made her suspect he and the cat weren't the best of friends.

"Actually, when I was a kid I used to spend part of the summers on a ranch," he went on. "So I know something about horses and cattle. That's really it, though. But I guess it doesn't matter what kind of business it is. Your buying me out is still the simplest way of settling things."

"Yes...it would be. If I had any money."

"Well, there must be money in the company, so if we—"

"No, I'm afraid there's not," she interrupted, hoping the fact wouldn't reflect too badly on Gus. There probably should have been a lot more money than there was, but he'd always said money was for spending.

"But if it's profitable..." Nick said. "I don't have that wrong, too, do I? I was told it was."

"And it is. It's just not *very* profitable. We have a lot of expenses."

"What? More than a million bucks' worth?"

"Well, Gus was always trying to expand and improve. You know, replace old equipment, upgrade the facilities. Just this spring, we built a big new aviary for the owls."

"We have owls," Nick said dully.

"Uh-huh, and some other birds of prey. At any rate, between improvements and the day-to-day expenses... The bear's food alone costs over a thousand dollars a month."

Nick's face went pale beneath his tan. "A bear? What kind of bear?"

"Oh, just a little black bear."

Roger snorted. "You call Attila little? Hell, Gus told me he was pushing six hundred pounds."

"Well...yes, I guess he *is* on the large side for a black bear," Carly admitted, wishing Nick wasn't looking more upset by the second. "I just meant he's not a grizzly or anything *really* big."

"And his name's Attila?" Nick said. "As in Attila the Hun?"

"Yes, but he's actually a sweetie. His only drawback is that he *does* eat up a fair bit of the revenue."

"So to speak," Nick said dryly.

"Yes...so to speak." She smiled, surprised he could joke under the circumstances.

He eyed her for a long moment, then said, "Do we own a swamp full of alligators, too?"

She eyed him back, not entirely sure whether she found his sense of humor amusing or annoying. "If a movie's set in a swamp, nobody's going to shoot it in Canada," she said at last. "So having alligators would be rather foolish. But getting back to the point I was making, the bottom line is that there's no money. The company's entire cash reserves would barely buy you a ticket home to Edmonton."

Nick rubbed his jaw, looking even more unhappy. "Then do you know anyone who'd be interested in buying my forty-nine percent?"

She shook her head.

"I expect finding an investor would take time," Roger said. "People are leery of getting into minority ownership positions. Besides which, Wild Action isn't exactly your run-of-the-mill sort of business."

"What about mortgaging the property?" Bill Brown suggested.

Roger gave him a quizzical glance. "It's already mortgaged to the hilt. Did Gus forget to mention that, too?"

Carly glanced at Bill, wishing Gus had kept him better informed. The man was obviously not pleased that Roger kept handing him surprises.

"We took out the mortgage when we had a chance to buy a new trailer for Attila," she explained. "We desperately needed one to get him to shoot sites, but it cost a small fortune. And Gus said that as long as we were taking out a mortgage anyway, we might as well make it big enough to build the new aviary and fix up a few other things.

"But look," she continued, focusing on Nick,

"I'm really sorry things aren't the way you expected them to be. I feel badly about the whole situation."

He exhaled slowly. She couldn't feel anywhere near as bad as he did. But it wasn't *her* fault there was a new will. And he'd *known* bad news came in threes, so if he'd used his brain, he wouldn't have been so damn quick about quitting his job. Then this situation wouldn't be such a disaster.

"Nick?" Brown said. "Lawyers are always coming across people who want to invest in a business. So if both Roger and I keep an eye out, sooner or later we'll find someone to buy your share."

Sooner or later. Nick had no doubt it would be later rather than sooner, and what the hell was he going to do in the meantime? Or maybe he should be more concerned about what was going to happen to the company in the meantime. Carly might have been Gus's right hand, but that didn't guarantee she could run things herself.

"Carly?" he said. "Are you going to be able to manage the business on your own?"

She shook her head. "I've found a high school kid to help out for the moment, but I'll have to get somebody who knows more about animals. And hopefully has a head for business."

"Absolutely," Harris agreed. "And fast. You couldn't possibly handle everything yourself even if you didn't have the Get Real people practically on your front porch."

"The Get Real people?" Nick said.

Carly looked at him as if she couldn't believe he had to ask. "Get Real Productions. An up-and-coming player in L.A. Gus landed us a film contract not long ago—for a film directed by Jay Wall, no less. And Get Real is providing the financing.''

Nick nodded. He didn't have a clue who Jay Wall was, but he could do without another of Carly's ''Did you just crawl out of a cave?'' looks.

''They've already been filming in Toronto for a week,'' she went on. ''So any day now, Jay's going to decide he wants to start shooting the wilderness scenes.

''This was supposed to be our big break,'' she added. ''Gus said that if a director like Jay Wall was happy with our animals, the sky would be the limit. But now...''

''But now?'' Nick prompted, the uncertainty in her voice making him nervous.

''Well, it's still the limit. And this movie will really help with the bottom line. Gus negotiated a great fee for the animals, *plus* Jay's doing a lot of the shooting on our land and we'll get paid for that. So Wild Action will have cash in the bank—assuming things go well.''

''You mean we won't get paid if they don't?''

''Well...if we don't fulfill our end of the contract... If the animals didn't perform well enough or something.''

''Is that a real possibility?''

Carly shrugged uneasily. ''I'm afraid that with Gus gone there are some problems. And if Jay *doesn't* end up happy, not getting all our money for the film wouldn't be our only worry. He's the type who'd go out of his way to ensure Wild Action's name was mud.''

That possibility was enough to make Nick break into a cold sweat. He owned forty-nine percent of land that was mortgaged to the hilt and a company that might self-destruct if Carly didn't please some hotshot director.

If that happened, forty-nine percent of Wild Action would probably be worth about a dollar and a quarter.

"But if you *do* make Jay happy?" he said.

"It would open the door to more Hollywood deals, and Wild Action would have so much money coming in that you wouldn't have to look for a buyer. I'd be able to buy you out in no time."

Which meant, Nick realized, the only intelligent thing for him to do was help make Jay Wall as happy as hell. And if that required a stint of playing zoo-keeper...

The prospect sure wasn't appealing, but it seemed like the only sensible solution. Of course, he had to move at the end of the month, but he could always get some of his buddies to put his things in storage for a while.

"How long will this movie take?" he asked Carly.

"It's hard to be sure. When Jay's on location he shoots every day—assuming the weather's right for the scenes. But the animals don't always cooperate, and without Gus...

"But if things go right, they shouldn't be filming on our property for more than a month or so."

Nick nodded, his decision made. He could stand anything if it was only for a month or so. Besides, he assumed that if you weren't pretty hard-nosed, those Hollywood types would walk all over you. And after a couple of looks into Carly's big brown eyes, he figured she was about as tough as a marshmallow.

"What if I stuck around for a while?" he suggested. "As a working partner. That would get you through this movie and let you look for someone to hire.''

"You could do that? What about your job?"

He shrugged. Damned if he was going to admit he'd been such an idiot yesterday. "I'm sure I could work out some kind of leave."

"That would be ideal," Harris said. "Having someone with a vested interest helping out."

"Why don't you see about it right now," Brown suggested, sliding his phone across the desk. "I'd feel a lot better if I knew things were arranged."

Nick desperately tried to think of a reason for *not* seeing about it right now, but no divine inspiration came. So either he had to admit he'd quit his job—barely two seconds after saying he could take a leave from it—or he had to pick up that phone.

"Well?" Brown said.

Wishing to hell he'd been thinking more and talking less, Nick reached for the phone, punched in his own number and had a brief conversation with his answering machine.

"Done," he said, clicking off. "I can take up to six weeks."

The sick-looking smile Carly gave him said she wasn't exactly thrilled about that—which he found darned irritating.

She needed help and he was offering to help her. Of course, he'd be looking after his own interests as well as hers, but that wasn't the point. The point was that instead of being grateful, she looked as if she were racking her brain for some alternative solution.

"Is there a problem with this idea?" he finally asked.

Carly hesitated. There were several problems with

it, but she did need *someone*. More specifically, she was pretty sure what she needed was a man with a deep voice. Like Nick's. And her odds of getting anyone else on short notice...

She just wished she weren't certain Nick would have a fit when he found out what he'd have to do. It was hardly a matter of helping out with horses and cattle.

"No," she said at last. "There's no problem. You just took me by surprise."

"Fine. Then it's settled. I mean, I'm assuming there's a spare bedroom in the house?"

"Ahh...yes, of course. It has four bedrooms." She reminded herself Nick was a police detective, which surely meant he wasn't into rape and pillage. But that only alleviated one worry.

The scratch he was sporting hardly boded well for his ability to work with animals—in which case he might turn out to be more of a liability than an asset.

Just for starters, what if Attila didn't like him? Or what if Nick was too frightened of the bear to try working with him?

For a moment, she considered telling him that was what she *really* needed help with. Then she decided she'd better save it for later. Nick obviously expected her to say something, though, so she asked if he knew anything about the movie industry.

"No, but I've always been a quick study."

She managed a smile.

He gave her a warm one in return.

Roger and Bill were positively beaming.

But if the three of them figured this was such a great arrangement, why was her intuition saying it had all the makings of a catastrophe?

CHAPTER TWO

Close Encounters of the Furry Kind

WHILE SHE WAS ATTEMPTING to get them out of downtown Toronto, Carly got lost so many times Nick stopped counting.

Instead, he started thinking that if she proved to be as good at running a business as she was at navigating, he'd made a wise move by deciding to stick around and keep an eye on his inheritance.

Their conversation was interrupted every time she pulled over to check her street map, which made it awfully disjointed, but by the time they found the Don Valley Parkway and were headed north, she'd managed to tell him a little about most of the animals they owned.

To his relief, the bear was the only potential man-killer in the bunch. Aside from Attila, there were the birds in the aviary, a couple of ponies named Paint and Brush, a parrot called Crackers and a few cats and dogs.

Oh, and she'd mentioned rabbits, as well, but they didn't sound like much work. They wandered around loose, so it was only a matter of giving them food and keeping an eye on them. Similarly, Rocky, the trained coon, did his own thing at night and slept on the porch roof during the day.

Actually, Nick had assumed there'd be a lot more animals than there were, but when he told Carly that, she gave him a sidelong glance and said, "Trained animals all need to be worked with or they don't stay trained. That's where the *agency* part comes in. We have a lot of animals under contract that are owned by other people. Everything from lizards and snakes to tigers and an elephant."

When she lapsed into silence, he immediately started thinking about the bear again. "This Attila," he said. "How did you end up with him?"

"He was orphaned by a hunter—would have died if we hadn't taken him in. He'd either have starved to death or been eaten by an adult bear."

Bears didn't exactly sound like charming animals, but Nick kept the thought to himself.

"So Gus and I bottle-raised him," Carly went on, "until he got too big to live in the house."

"Ahh. And he doesn't mind being in a cage now? All by himself?"

"Oh, he's not lonely. Bears aren't pack animals, so he'd be on his own in the wild. And he doesn't live in a cage. Gus didn't believe in caging wild animals, and neither do I."

"You mean..." Nick cleared his throat uneasily. "You mean, he wanders around loose? Like the rabbits?"

"Well, no. He'd find some of the other animals just too tempting, so he's got a fenced field—with a pond to swim in and a bunker Gus built him for hibernating. We call it his cave."

Nick nodded, wishing it was January instead of July. He'd be a lot happier if Attila was hibernating, because he had a horrible feeling a fence wouldn't stop a six-hundred-pound bear that really wanted out of its field. But maybe it was declawed and detoothed and whatever.

When he asked, the look of utter horror on Carly's face told him there wasn't a chance. And he'd lay odds it was *his* forty-nine percent of the beast that included the claws and teeth.

Apparently, Carly did mind reading on the side, because she said, "There's nothing to worry about, Nick. Attila's a real pet."

He nodded, but it was tough to get his head around the idea of a pet that weighed as much as three large men put together. "So...you're not nervous working with him?"

"No, not at all."

Without a doubt, that was the best news he'd heard since he'd learned they *had* a bear. He had every intention of doing his share of the work for the next few weeks, but he'd be drawing the line at Attila. And that meant it was a darn good thing she had no problem with him.

Carly drove a little farther up the parkway, breathing a sigh of relief when she spotted the exit sign for the highway. She'd missed it more than once in the past and always had a devil of a time making her way back.

"I guess you've noticed I don't have much sense of direction," she said, pulling onto the exit ramp. "But I'll be okay from here."

"Good."

"That's how I ended up with Gus," she went on when Nick said nothing more. "It was because I got lost."

"Oh?"

"Uh-huh. I grew up in Kingston, which is where my parents still live. But after I finished high school I had a chance for a summer job in Toronto, and I took a wrong turn on the way there."

Nick eyed her for a minute, making her wish she'd kept quiet. Everybody had faults, though, and surely he couldn't think that having a poor sense of direction ranked right up there with pulling wings off flies.

"Isn't there a major highway that runs between Kingston and Toronto?" he asked at last.

"The one we're on now," she admitted. "But I guess I wasn't paying attention and zigged when I should have zagged. At any rate, the car I'd borrowed quit on me, so I walked down the nearest side road until I reached a house—which turned out to be Gus's. And when we got talking, he mentioned he'd been looking for someone to help with the animals."

"Then you just moved in with him?"

Nick's tone made her look at him. Surely he didn't think...

Just in case he did, she said, "I assume you didn't mean *moved in* the way it sounded. I was an eighteen-year-old kid and Gus was fifty-nine, so there was certainly nothing like *that*."

"No. No, of course not."

"Everyone who'd ever worked full-time for him lived in the house. It only made sense."

"Right. All I was thinking was...most eighteen-year-olds wouldn't have buried themselves out in the country. It couldn't have done much for your social life."

The remark made her smile. Her mother had been worried about that from day one.

"It was worth the trade-off," she said honestly. "I

love working with animals—it's not really like working at all. So even though I'd only intended to stay through the summer, I ended up never leaving. And Gus gradually became like a favorite uncle to me. He was the sweetest man in the world. It's too bad you didn't get to know him.''

''I had no chance to. He cut off contact with the family before I was born.''

She didn't reply for a moment, trying to decide if Gus would have minded her explaining things. Finally, she said, ''He never intended that to be forever, you know.''

''No?''

''No, he assumed he'd eventually be able to cope with seeing her again.''

''Seeing who again?''

Carly glanced across the van once more, her heart sinking when she saw Nick's puzzled expression. Surely she hadn't put her foot in it, had she? ''Your parents must have told you what happened,'' she tried tentatively. ''*Why* Gus left Edmonton.''

''Well...yeah.''

Nick sounded as puzzled as he looked, which meant she *had* said the wrong thing.

''Actually, my parents told me all kinds of stories about Gus, but I'm not quite sure which one you were referring to.''

''Oh. Well, if you're not, then they didn't tell you everything. So I should have kept quiet.''

''Why? I can handle whatever you were going to say. So who did Gus think he'd eventually be able to cope with seeing again?''

She stared ahead at the highway, not wanting to answer the question. But what else could she do?

Making something up wasn't an option. She hated being lied to, so she never lied to anyone else unless she felt it was *really* necessary.

"I guess it doesn't matter much at this point," she finally said. "But Gus was in love with your mother."

"What!"

"It's true," she told him gently. "They both were. Both Gus and your father. And when she chose your father, she broke Gus's heart. That's why he left town.

"But he assumed that after enough time had passed he'd stop caring. I guess he never did, though. Then he learned your parents had died. I–I'm sorry about that."

"Thanks," Nick said, hoping she wouldn't pursue the subject. His parents had been gone for five years, but he still didn't like to talk about the crash.

They'd taken up their Cessna knowing a storm was closing in. And ever since, he'd wished he'd objected more strongly to the way they flew regardless of the weather. Not that they'd have listened, but still…

"Gus always kept in touch with a friend in Edmonton," Carly continued. "Which is how he knew about their accident. And about your being a detective and all."

Nick nodded, then sat staring out at the passing countryside, his thoughts returning to the story Gus had told Carly.

He'd certainly been a sly old fox, because the *truth* was what Nick's parents had told him. There was no doubt about that. From the day his grandfather discovered that Gus had made off with their money, he'd never even allowed his elder son's name to be spoken in his presence.

But Gus had obviously reinvented his past, making it tragically romantic—which certainly fit with everything Nick had ever heard about him.

Glancing across the van, he eyed Carly for a minute. In the bright sunlight, he could see there were pale freckles scattered across the bridge of her nose. Between that and the way the air conditioner's breeze was playing with strands of her hair, she seemed a lot younger than she had in Brown's office. Younger and very innocent-looking—the kind of woman who aroused a man's protective instincts without even trying.

Not that she'd aroused his. The only reason he was hanging around was to protect his *own* interests. Hers simply happened to coincide.

"What *did* you know about your uncle?" she asked.

He hesitated, then said, "I guess not as much as I thought." For half a second, he'd considered telling her the truth. But since she'd cared for Gus, it would only upset her—assuming she'd even believe it.

And she likely wouldn't. If she'd worked with him for twelve years and referred to him as the sweetest man in the world, he must have really cleaned up his act.

"You obviously didn't know he'd gotten into the animal-actor business," she said. "But you'll get a kick out of hearing how it happened. Initially, he won a share of Wild Action in a poker game."

Nick grinned. That sounded more like the uncle he'd always heard about. He'd bet Gus had been cheating, too.

Carly looked over at Nick once more, thinking that while he was smiling might be a good time to bring the conversation back to the subject of Attila. But when she tried, she couldn't make the bear's name come out, so she said, "Then, eventually, Gus took over the entire agency. It was a smaller operation in those days, and it wasn't doing very well, but he'd discovered he was good with animals. So he bought a big piece of property and began gradually attracting clients."

Focusing on the road ahead once more, she told herself she was a chicken. And that she was going to have to tell Nick about the problem with Attila *very* soon.

But maybe it would be better to wait until they got home and he'd unpacked. And it would probably help to give him a stiff drink of Gus's best Scotch first.

"What's this movie we're involved with?" he asked after she'd turned north onto Highway 12.

"It's called *Two for Trouble*. And it's basically about two ten-year-old boys who take off from summer camp and get lost in the woods. That's the part of the film Jay will be shooting on Gus's...*our* property. A lot of it's forest."

"And the stuff he's shooting in Toronto?"

"Oh, those scenes are supposedly in Manhattan. And the summer camp's supposedly in upper New York State—but they'll actually be using Camp Run-a-Muck, near Lindsay.

"At any rate, the opening scenes in the city show the parents getting the boys ready for camp. The adults are the name actors—Sarina Westlake and Garth Richards. You know them? She looks a lot like Meg Ryan, and he's the Latin-lover type."

"Uh-huh. I know the two you mean. They're married in real life, aren't they?"

"Yes. But in the movie they play single parents who fall in love while they're helping search for their kids."

Nick waited for Carly to go on. When she didn't, he said, "That's it? That's all there is to the plot?"

"Well, Jay's the kind of director who improvises, so I expect he'll add a few extra wrinkles during the shooting."

"Or maybe a *lot* of extra wrinkles? I mean, it doesn't exactly sound like a box office smash."

"Let's just hope it is, because Gus held out for a small percentage of the profits."

"Oh? How small?"

She held up her hand with her thumb and forefinger a fraction of an inch apart.

"Oh," Nick said, looking disappointed.

"He did really well to get anything. In any event, the movie might turn out to be a lot better than the story line sounds. I've read the script, and there's pretty good adventure and drama, what with the boys in a woods full of wild animals."

"And Attila's one of the wild animals?"

She nodded but didn't elaborate. It really *would* be better to leave any further discussion of that until later.

"We're almost home," she said, pointing toward the township sign and changing the subject.

"Township of Scugog," Nick read aloud.

"In Ojibway, it means 'muddy, shallow water.'"

"Ahh."

When he seemed content to simply watch the passing scenery for the remainder of the trip, Carly let her thoughts drift back to the meeting in Brown's office. Nick had taken the bad news a lot more coolly than she would have. But she had a horrible feeling he wasn't going to be even half as cool when it came to Attila.

Turning onto the Sixth Line, she decided it might be smart to give her new partner *four or five* drinks of Gus's best Scotch before they talked about Attila.

WHEN THEY TURNED ONTO the gravel road that Carly said led to the house, Nick could see she hadn't been joking about a lot of their property being forest.

Huge trees overhung the road on either side, with only the hydro poles and power lines to indicate this wasn't really the middle of nowhere. Then the road curved and they were at one edge of a fifteen-or twenty-acre clearing with the house ahead in the distance.

Built of gorgeous old fieldstone, it had white gingerbread trim on both the second-story gables and the overhang of the porch. He was just about to comment on how nice it was when four large gray blurs appeared from nowhere and streaked toward the van.

"Wolves?" he said anxiously. "You didn't tell me we had wolves."

"We don't. Those are the dogs. We took them because they looked so much like gray wolves, even as pups, but they're actually half husky and half malamute.

"They're perfectly safe. They don't even bother the rabbits," she added, giving him an amused glance as she pulled the van to a stop. "Their names are Harpo, Chico, Groucho and Zeppo. Collectively, of course, we refer to them as the Marx brothers."

And Uncle Gus, Nick remembered someone once mentioning, had been a huge Marx brothers fan.

"I said *we,* didn't I?" Carly murmured with a sad little smile. "I wonder how long it'll take before I stop doing that."

She got out of the van and hugged each of the dogs in turn. Then they rushed around to the passenger's side and stood eyeing Nick through the window—drooling as if they were looking at lunch.

Checking them out from up close, he wondered if Carly was certain they weren't at least *part* wolf. They were one hell of a size, and he'd never seen any other dogs with those sinister-looking yellow eyes.

Telling himself they weren't a whole lot bigger than the German shepherds the police used, he opened his door and climbed out—the heat and humidity hitting him hard.

It had been hot in Alberta, but that was a dry heat. Ontario was at least as hot and sixty times more humid.

He cautiously extended his hand and let the dogs sniff it. Despite their appearance, they seemed friendly enough, so he risked taking his eyes off them long enough to get his suitcase and jacket from the back.

"I thought Dylan might still be here, but his truck's gone," Carly said. "The high school kid who's been helping out," she explained.

Nick nodded, then gestured toward the wooden building with the wired-in open area that stood maybe sixty yards away. "That's the new aviary you mentioned?"

"Uh-huh. Attila's field is at the bottom of the hill beside the house, and the little barn you can see is where we feed the rabbits and stable the ponies. But let's save the grand tour until after you unpack and change. And then maybe you'd like a drink. There's some Scotch that Gus used to say was smooth as silk.''

Glancing at his watch, Nick discovered it was only four-thirty. He'd been up for so long it seemed later. ''It's a little early for something as strong as Scotch,'' he said, ''but a cold beer would go down fine.''

They'd just started for the porch when a tremendous roar rattled his eardrums. He stopped dead, the hairs on the back of his neck standing on end. Carly and the dogs continued along as if they were deaf.

''What the hell was that?'' he demanded, hurrying to catch up.

''What was what?''

''That noise.''

''Oh, it was just Attila welcoming us home. He must have smelled us.''

''From this distance?''

Carly gave him another amused look. ''Bears have an incredible sense of smell. They can scent things for miles. But he won't mind if we don't say hello until later.''

Nick looked in the direction of the hill, half surprised to see the ground wasn't vibrating. The last time he'd heard anything that loud he'd been in Costa Rica, watching the Arenal Volcano spew fire and boulders—and that had made him a little nervous, too.

Following Carly the rest of the way to the house, he did his best to relax. After all, she'd told him she was perfectly fine with the bear, so there was no reason she'd need any help with it.

He just wished he didn't have the sense there was something she *hadn't* told him.

CARLY CHANGED INTO SHORTS, then went back downstairs and chatted with Crackers while she made a jug
of iced tea. The parrot loved company and was paper-
trained. So, years ago, Gus had built a big solarium-
type addition to the kitchen, and Crackers was pretty
good about staying in it.

"Treat!" he demanded as she stirred the tea.

She cut him a wedge of apple, then poured herself
a glass of tea and put the jug into the fridge, lingering
in front of the open door and thinking how heavenly
the coolness felt.

The house was too old to have central air, and Gus
hadn't liked air-conditioning anyway. He'd always
said that even window units were for wimps, so she'd
learned to live with the hot, muggy spell that inevi-
tably settled in during July. But she'd far rather live
without it.

Hearing footsteps on the stairs, she dug a beer from
the back of the fridge and reluctantly closed the door.
When she turned, Nick was standing in the kitchen
eyeing Crackers.

"Is he usually out of his cage?" he asked.

"Uh-huh. He really hates being in it during the
day. But he stays in it at night. I think he worries that
one of the cats might try a sneak attack while he's
asleep."

"Would they?"

"I doubt it. And if they did, they'd regret it. Big
macaws have incredibly strong beaks. He could amputate a man's hand. But he wouldn't," she added
quickly. "He loves people."

Nick nodded, although he didn't look entirely convinced. Then he glanced at the beer she'd forgotten
she was holding. "That looks good."

"And you look like a cowboy," she said, handing him the bottle. "You also look even more like Gus. He always wore jeans and boots."

"Must be one of those things that run in families." Nick twisted the top off his beer and took a long, slow drink.

Watching him, Carly felt an unexpected twinge of attraction. Oh, she'd realized earlier what a good-looking man he was. But it had been an in-the-abstract kind of awareness, because he hadn't struck her as her type.

Not that she exactly *had* a type. As she'd told him earlier, living out here meant her social life had never been exactly hectic. And there'd been nothing about any of the few men she *had* gone with over the years that had made her think they were Mr. Right.

When Nick lowered the bottle, she reached for her glass of tea and said, "Let's sit outside. Maybe there'll be a breeze."

She gestured him to precede her, letting her thoughts drift back to where they'd been. Whatever her type was, Nick Montgomery wasn't it. His hair was far too short for her taste, and in his suit he'd seemed too...*civilized* was the word that came to mind.

Although now, she had to admit, with those hip-hugging jeans and his T-shirt clinging to every muscle, that wasn't true anymore. But Nick was her temporary business partner, and she'd be a fool to even think of him in any other light.

He'd only be here for six weeks, tops, then he'd be heading back out West. Or maybe he'd be gone a lot sooner. For all she knew, he might be out of here ten minutes after she told him about the problem with Attila.

She followed him outside and they sat on the porch in silence for a minute—until one of the cats stalked by to check out the company.

"His name's Blue, and he's been in quite a few commercials," she offered. "That's mostly what Wild Action has done until now. Commercials, some work for television, the occasional documentary and one Canadian feature film that opened and closed the same week. I don't think they even bothered making it into a video."

"So *Two for Trouble* really is your...*our* big chance."

She nodded, aware that this was the perfect time to speak up—while he was contemplating how important the movie was to them. All she had to do was think of the right words.

When Carly lapsed into silence, Nick sat casually looking in her direction and not letting himself stare at her long, tanned legs. It was tough not to, though. They were such great legs they'd stop traffic if she ever walked down a city street in those shorts. And as for that little sleeveless blouse...

Earlier, she'd looked the picture of innocence. And she even *smelled* innocent—like prairie wildflowers. But in that outfit she looked sexy as hell. And it had him imagining all sorts of things that had nothing even remotely to do with their business partnership.

Shifting his gaze from her, he told himself he'd have to be careful while he was here. She had an easy manner he found appealing. And when you added that to the way she looked... Well, he'd just better watch himself.

He'd had his share of relationships with women, but none of them had ever felt as if they might last forever. And he sure didn't want to find himself in one that *did* feel right when the time and place were entirely wrong.

His life plans didn't include either animal actors or rural Ontario. All he wanted was enough money to go back home to Edmonton and set up his agency.

"Nick?"

When he glanced at Carly again there was a tiny drop of perspiration on her throat, trickling ever so slowly toward the V of her neckline. As hard as he tried, he couldn't keep from following it with his eyes.

Finally, it disappeared beneath her blouse, but by then he was following it with his imagination.

"Nick, there's something we have to talk about."

He looked up quickly, feeling like the proverbial kid caught with his hand in the cookie jar.

"We have a bit of a problem with Attila."

Aha! His imagination instantly shut down and he switched into cop alert. He'd *known* there was something she'd been holding back about that bear, and her expression told him it was more than a *bit* of a problem.

"Did I mention that he's the star of *Two for Trouble*? The animal star, I mean?"

"No, I think you just said he was in it."

"Oh. Well, he is. The star, I mean."

Nick waited for her to go on, doing his best to hide his annoyance. But he'd bet that she'd been intentionally avoiding talking about the bear—that she'd been waiting until she got her newfound partner out here, away from civilization, before she hit him with whatever this problem was.

"You see," she finally continued, "the boys' encounter with Attila is a really pivotal scene in the movie. And there'll be a lot of earlier shots of him— foreshadowing the encounter."

"I see. And the problem is...?" he asked, bringing her back to the important issue.

"Well, Attila hasn't been himself lately. I know he misses Gus, but from our point of view... The problem is that he's taken to only doing what I tell him when he feels like it."

"Because he's in mourning? That's bear behavior?"

"Well, I'm sure missing Gus is at least part of it."

Nick uneasily thought back to something she'd told him in Brown's office—that if Jay Wall wasn't pleased with their animals, the agency's name would be mud.

"If missing Gus is only part of the problem," he said, picking up on her last words, "what's the other part?"

"Well, Attila always worked better for Gus than he did for me. So I suspect he considers me just a backup trainer. And now he's acting like a child who's trying to see just how much he can get away with."

"But if he worked better for Gus, then the two of you must have done things differently. Why don't you try doing everything exactly the way he did?"

"I already do. We always used the same tone and commands and hand signals. You have to with animals or they get confused. So there's got to be something else involved. Maybe something as simple as the fact that Gus was a lot bigger than me.''

Nick eyed her, doubting she'd weigh a hundred and fifteen pounds sopping wet.

''Or maybe it's that bears find a deeper male voice more authoritative.''

''That's a fact?''

''No, it's just a possibility. Nick, the only real facts I have are that Attila responded better to Gus and that right now I can't count on him to listen. So I can't help thinking…''

Carly paused, then the rest of her words came rushing out all at once. ''It would make a lot of sense to try another man working with Attila. Ideally, one who resembles Gus. And if you wore some of Gus's clothes, his scent would even be mingled with yours.''

Nick simply stared at her, the words *you* and *yours* flashing like neon signs in front of his eyes.

She gave him a weak smile.

''Oh, no,'' he said at last. ''Absolutely, unequivocably no. *You* are the one who bottle-raised that bear. *You* are the one who figures he's a pet. *You* are the animal expert here.

''*I*, on the other hand, don't know a damn thing about bears except that they can kill people. Plus, I'm a complete stranger to him—one he outweighs by more than four hundred pounds. I'd have to be out of my tree to try working with him.''

Carly gazed at her sandals for a long minute, then finally shrugged. ''I didn't really think you'd like the idea.''

Nick resisted the urge to tell her she was the queen of understatement.

"I just..." She shrugged again, looking at him this time. "I guess it was a dumb suggestion, even though he really *wouldn't* hurt you. We've done all kinds of shoots with him, and he's never tried to harm anyone. And I'm so worried that if I can't make him cooperate for Jay, and the agency ends up going down the tubes because of it... Well, I'm worried about what would happen to the animals if I couldn't keep things going. Especially to Attila. It would be incredibly hard to find him a good home."

Nick shoved himself out of his chair and began pacing the porch, thinking he was insane to even consider her idea. But if Attila didn't perform, Jay Wall would bad-mouth them. And if that led to the agency going bust, there'd be no income to pay the mortgage—which would mean they'd lose the property, as well.

Still, he'd rather face a man pointing a .350 Magnum at him than get within mauling range of a bear.

"Why don't we give Attila a little more time," he finally suggested. "Maybe he'll come around."

"Or maybe he won't."

Turning away from Carly, Nick stared out across the clearing. He had no job and not much money. And if they blew this chance to establish a Hollywood connection, he'd probably have no inheritance to speak of, either.

But at least he'd still be alive, rather than—quite possibly—bear breakfast. That was certainly an important point to consider.

He weighed the issue for another minute, then took a deep breath and said, "You're *positive* he's never tried to harm anyone?"

"PUT THE HAT ON, TOO," Carly said. "Gus always wore his hat."

Nick took the cowboy hat off its peg and slapped it on his head, even though he knew damn well Attila wasn't going to think he was Gus. Not for a second.

Clothes don't make the man, the saying went. And the fact he had on a pair of Gus's jeans and one of his shirts wasn't going to fool a bear any more than it would a person.

"Good," Carly said, eyeing him approvingly. "If you look and smell like Gus, it's bound to help."

That, Nick knew, was not a fact. It was merely another of her possibilities, and he didn't like them any more than he liked her.

Maybe she'd initially seemed to be a nice woman, but first impressions could be wrong. And in this case there was no 'could' about it. That easy manner he'd liked had been hiding her true self—a manipulative woman who'd maneuvered him into doing this. And he hated being either manipulated *or* maneuvered. The problem was, he suspected he'd hate a life of poverty even more.

"Ready?" she said with a bright smile.

"Dying to meet him," he muttered, hoping the remark wouldn't prove prophetic. "But if he hurts me, I'll be voting to turn him into a bearskin rug."

"He *won't* hurt you," Carly said for the millionth time.

Picking up the pail full of raw, boned chicken, which she'd told him was the bear's favorite treat, Nick followed her out the back door.

As they walked down the hill toward Attila's field, he tried to convince himself it was only the heat that had him sweating buckets.

Every instinct for self-preservation was telling him to turn around and run, and the farther they walked, the harder it became to keep putting one foot in front of the other.

Raising his forearm to his nose, he sniffed the sleeve of Gus's shirt. He didn't smell a damn thing, but Attila would. Carly had said bears had an incredible sense of smell. So Attila would smell Gus's scent, but he'd know Nick wasn't Gus. And he'd think...

What if he thought this guy who smelled like Gus was trying to put something over on him? And what if it made him mad as hell?

Nick wanted to ask Carly about that, but his heart was suddenly in his throat, making it impossible to speak. He could see the bear now. It had spotted them and was ambling in the direction of the fence.

"Hey, Attila," Carly called.

The bear plonked down on his haunches about ten feet away from the gate. The next thing Nick knew, he and Carly had reached the fence.

He tried not to look at Attila while she sorted through the keys on her ring. Instead, he gazed at the pond, then eyed the hibernation cave. But despite his best efforts, his gaze was drawn back to the bear, and all he could think about was how damn big it was.

"Poor baby looks a little unkempt because he's molting," Carly said, sticking a key into the padlock.

Nick nodded, but he was far less interested in the condition of the bear's fur than he was in the fact that its thick claws looked about a foot long. And its teeth were undoubtedly even bigger and sharper. The only small things about Attila were his rounded ears and beady little eyes.

"He's not exactly Winnie the Pooh," he whispered nervously as Carly opened the gate.

"He's going to love you," she whispered back. "Just follow me inside and put the pail down for the time being. He knows he doesn't get the chicken until after he's been good.

"Hi, Attila," she added to the bear as Nick set the pail beside the fence. "I've brought someone to meet you."

Attila grunted, then fixed Nick with a glare that didn't look even remotely loving.

Not that he really wanted the bear's love. He'd be happy if it just didn't eat him. After all, Carly had admitted she couldn't really count on Attila to listen to her at the moment.

"Now, I know you're probably feeling a little uneasy," she said, glancing at Nick and slipping into her queen-of-understatement routine again. "But just try to remember everything I told you. Especially that you should never excite his predatory instinct by running."

With that, she slowly walked over to the bear and scratched him behind the ear.

"You still okay?" she asked, looking at Nick once more.

"Sure," he said. In truth, of course, he was as far from okay as he could ever remember being. He couldn't keep his eyes off those claws, and he couldn't stop thinking a scratch from them would make one of Blackie's feel like a pinprick.

Carly rubbed the bear's nose for a minute, then said, "Attila, that's Nick over there. I want you to go and *say hello* to him. *Two feet.*"

The bear glared over again. Then he pushed himself up onto his hind feet—sending a rush of utter terror through Nick. Standing up, he looked like an enormous sumo wrestler in a fur coat.

"Good boy," Carly said. "Now go *say hello*."

Attila gave a little snort and started toward Nick, stopping a couple of feet away. Nick stood stock-still, even though the urge to run was almost overwhelming. In his cowboy boots, he was well over six feet tall, but the bear's eyes were level with his. And it was so close he could smell its earthy scent and hear it breathing.

"Nick?" Carly whispered. "Say hello to him."

He swallowed hard. "Hello, Attila."

The bear eyed him for another second, then took a final step forward, wrapped its arms around him and began squeezing him to death.

CHAPTER THREE

Boys Will Be Boys

"CARLY, I can't breathe!"

She was so thrilled to see that Attila liked Nick, his words didn't register for a second. Then she realized Attila was getting carried away with his bear hug.

"Attila, *enough*," she said. When he didn't stop, she felt a flutter of concern. An enthusiastic bear was hardly the same as an enthusiastic puppy. "You tell him, Nick," she quickly suggested. "*Enough* is the command, and be firm."

"*Enough*," he said, sounding more strangled than firm.

Miraculously, Attila grunted and backed off. Dropping to all fours, he began snuffling the leg of Nick's jeans.

Carly almost jumped for joy. If Attila was going to listen to Nick, things just might work out.

"He obeyed you!" she said excitedly.

"Obeyed me? He practically killed me!"

"No he didn't. He was being friendly." And she was *so* relieved. She hadn't told Nick about the phone call, because she hadn't wanted him feeling even more stressed when he met Attila, but now she could.

Before she had a chance, though, he took a backward step and said, "Listen, if that's his way of being friendly, I sure as hell don't want to be near him when he's being grouchy. This isn't going to work, Carly. We've got to figure out some way of making him listen to you better."

"Give him his chicken."

"What?"

She pointed at the pail. "Give him his chicken or he *will* be grouchy."

Nick grabbed the pail, then turned back toward her. "I just put it down in front of him?"

"You could. But if you feed him by hand, it'll help the two of you bond."

"Bond? Did you go deaf in the past minute? I said this isn't going to work. I'm not...*comfortable* close to this animal. You're going to have to handle him."

"Nick, do you want Jay Wall to be happy with us or not?"

"Of course I do. I just don't want to work with a bear."

"Well, it could take months to figure out how to get him to listen to me better. And the chemistry's obviously right between you two."

"No. It was right between him and Gus. I'm wearing Gus's clothes, remember, so it's his scent on them—his chemistry. And what happens after they get washed?"

"Well, maybe there are enough of his things to last through the filming."

"Not a chance. His closet's practically empty. And after I wear something once or twice, there'll be more of my scent on it than Gus's. How will Attila take to that?"

Carly told herself he'd be okay with it, but she knew it might be a problem.

"Maybe the scent's not really important," she said hopefully. "Maybe it's your deep voice Attila responded to. I mean, he did what you told him even though you didn't sound very authoritative."

"What do you mean I didn't sound authoritative? I've been *trained* to sound authoritative. And the bear listened, didn't he?"

"My point exactly."

Attila woofed; Nick's gaze flashed to him.

"He wants his chicken."

As Nick looked down at the pail, then back at her, Carly prayed he wouldn't simply turn and walk away. But she could hardly blame him if he did. Wild Action might mean everything to her, but it meant little to him. And even though she was certain Attila wouldn't harm him, *he* obviously wasn't.

"Nick," she said at last, "I know how much I'm asking of you, but if you'll try working with him I'll be right there every minute. And... Look, I hate to put even more pressure on you, but Jay called while you were changing into Gus's clothes. The cast and crew will be arriving before lunchtime tomorrow. And the way things stand, your working with Attila is the only hope we've got."

NICK HAD WASHED HIS hands half a dozen times, but he could still smell the raw chicken on them. He could also still feel Attila's smooth warm tongue licking them.

But hell, while he'd been feeding the bear he hadn't been sure how much longer he'd *have* hands, so maybe he should count his blessings.

Of course, tomorrow he'd be right back in the lion's den—or the bear's field, as the case might be— even though he was probably insane to be going along with Carly's plan. He looked across the kitchen to where she was stirring the spaghetti sauce, wondering exactly how she'd convinced him to do something he *seriously* didn't want to do.

Then he recalled how her smile had lit up her entire face when he'd agreed to try working with the bear. It was, he'd discovered, a very dangerous smile, because it made him feel strangely warm inside. Which, in turn, made him tend to forget all about her negative qualities.

Obviously he was going to have to be even more careful around her than he'd realized.

"That salad almost ready?" she asked, glancing over.

"Uh-huh."

"Almost ready?" Crackers repeated from his perch in the solarium.

"Yeah, almost ready," Nick told him, thinking the house was *very* full of animals. He'd probably hardly notice the three cats if they were the extent of the menagerie, but he'd be a while getting used to those huge Marx brothers flopped all over the floor. And to a big blue bird that talked. Especially when Carly'd said it could amputate a man's hand.

Every time he looked at Crackers, he found himself wondering if he should find a pair of heavy work gloves to wear while he was here. Between that beak and Attila's teeth...

"There's something I've been forgetting to ask you," Carly said.

He looked over at her again.

"You don't have any orange clothes, do you?"

"No, why?"

"Oh, I just wanted to check. Fruit and vegetables are okay, but for some reason anything else orange makes Crackers a little nutsy."

When she didn't elaborate, Nick decided he didn't want to know what a macaw did when it got nutsy. So, instead of asking, he began mentally running through the list of Attila's commands and hand signals once more—feeling as if he were cramming for finals. In the past couple of hours, he'd learned enough about bears to fill an encyclopedia on them.

The entire time he'd trooped along with Carly, helping her tend to the outdoor animals, she'd told him about bears' behavior in general and Attila's behavior in particular.

Then, while they fed the dogs and cats, she'd drilled him on the commands Attila responded to. Or maybe *was supposed to respond to* would be a better way of putting it. He was still far from convinced the bear was going to obey him. And if he inadvertently did something that made Attila angry...

Forcing that thought from his mind, he glanced at his watch—and then at the phone on the counter beside him.

Before he'd left Edmonton, he'd told his ex-partner that he'd be home in a few days. But now that he wouldn't be back for weeks, now that he was going to need Ben's help getting his things moved out of his house, he wanted to let him know as soon as possible.

He looked over at Carly once again, thinking how Ben always yelled into a phone, then thinking about the extension he'd noticed when he'd glanced into her bedroom.

But he'd feel funny asking if he could go use it. And since he never seemed to be in the kitchen when she wasn't, he might just as well phone Ben right here and now. No matter how loudly he talked, Carly was hardly going to hear him from the other side of the room.

"Carly? Would you mind if I made a long-distance call?"

She smiled. "You don't have to ask. It's half your phone."

He reached for it, dialed and got Ben's wife, Ida.

"Nick!" she greeted him. "You're back already?"

"No, I'm calling from down East."

"Oh, well, it's good to hear your voice. But you could have knocked me over with a feather when Ben told me you'd quit. I mean him putting in for early retirement is one thing, but you just walking away at your age..."

"Yeah, I guess it surprised a lot of people." He glanced uneasily at Carly, but she didn't seem curious about what had surprised people.

"That must have been some terrific inheritance you got."

"Well, I'll tell you all the details once I'm home. But right now I'm using someone else's phone, so is Ben around?"

"No, he had to go down to Lethbridge for a bit. Something came up there about a case he worked on years ago. Want me to give him a message?"

"Yeah. Please. I'm going to be stuck here for a lot longer than I figured. And I don't know if he mentioned I've got to move at the end of the month, but—''

"He sure did. That sort of thing should be against the law, you know. Those landlords get away with murder."

"Maybe. At any rate, I need a huge favor. If he could get some of the guys to help move my stuff out and put it into temporary storage..."

There was a silence at the other end, which probably meant Ida was wondering why he didn't spend some of his terrific inheritance on hiring a moving company. But all she finally said, was, "Sure. I know he'd be glad to help out."

"Great. My next-door neighbor has a spare key. I'll call and tell her what's happening."

"Okay. And give me the number where you're staying in case Ben needs to ask you about anything."

"Sure."

After he'd given it to her she said, "Now don't you go blowing your entire fortune on those fast eastern women, eh?"

"No, I won't. And thanks, Ida."

As he hung up, Carly said, "I couldn't help overhearing."

"That's okay. It was my partner's wife I was talking to."

Ex-partner's, an internal voice of truth corrected him. But the phrase had slipped out easily. He hadn't *really* started thinking of Ben in those terms yet.

"But you have to move?" Carly said.

"Uh-huh."

"And you said temporary storage. So you don't have a place to move *to?*"

"No. I was looking for another house, but I hadn't found one yet."

"And despite all that you stayed here?"

He merely shrugged, then changed the subject by saying he had to call his next-door neighbor to let her know what was going on. He quickly dialed Hilda's number, thinking that the last thing he wanted was to get into a discussion with Carly about why he'd stayed.

Normally, he was a pretty honest man, and at the moment his conscience was telling him to straighten her out about his newly unemployed status. But she'd think he was an idiot for quitting his job so rashly. And since he'd be out of her life again in only a few weeks, there was no real reason she had to know.

Besides, telling her at this late date would be a little tricky. She'd been sitting right there when he'd phoned and supposedly arranged for time off.

When Hilda answered, he explained that he was going to be away for longer than he'd expected and that Ben would be looking after moving his things.

"Well, don't you worry about your mail," she said. "I'll keep taking it in. But what if there's anything important looking? Or letters? If there are, I should forward them, shouldn't I?"

"That would be great," he told her, although he doubted there'd be anything except junk mail and bills.

He gave her the address just in case. Then he hung up, tossed the salad and carried it over to the table. Carly dropped a handful of spaghetti into the boiling water, then came and sat down across the table from him.

"I want to say something," she told him after a moment.

"Say away."

"I want to tell you how much I appreciate your helping out. Aside from anything else, I know this has to be vacation time you've given up to stay here. And the fact that you're willing to inconvenience your friends to help me..."

He smiled uneasily. There was gratitude written all over her face, and his conscience started in on him again. He really *should* tell her he wasn't quite as terrific as she figured, that he was motivated by a lot more than a desire to help her.

But before he could make himself say anything, she went on.

"And I can imagine how nervous you must be about working with Attila."

"I'm sure that'll fade." Unless, of course, the bear did something to make him even *more* nervous. Or to make him dead.

"I'm sure it will, too." Carly gave him one of her terrific smiles. "At any rate, I just wanted you to know I really appreciate what you're doing—especially when keeping Wild Action afloat can't mean anywhere near as much to you as it does to me."

He managed another smile of his own, but keeping the agency afloat meant a whole lot more to him than she realized. It would keep him out of the poorhouse.

WHEN HE'D PHONED YESTERDAY, Jay Wall had told Carly he'd be arriving with the cast and crew well before noon. By eleven-thirty, sitting on the porch and still waiting for them to appear, she was a nervous wreck.

She glanced over at Nick, who was reading her copy of the *Two for Trouble* script, and reminded herself that his morning session with Attila had gone fairly well. But that was no guarantee things would go smoothly during the shooting. And if they didn't, Jay would want her head on a platter.

She'd never met the man, but Gus had. He'd spent a week in L.A., working out the details of the contract with Jay and the producer. And he'd come home referring to the wunderkind director as "that obnoxious young snot."

According to Gus, Jay was charming one minute, explosive and demanding the next, and drove everyone he worked with crazy.

He was also, she knew from the phone conversations she'd had with him, extremely annoyed that Gus had had the audacity to die before *Two for Trouble* was in the can. And he was *not* pleased that he'd be stuck working with the "understudy," as he'd called her yesterday.

Sight unseen, he'd decided she was second rate. "You're certain," he'd demanded, "the bear's performance will be up to scratch if *you're* working with him?"

Naturally, she'd assured him it would be, but she suspected he'd have tried to back out of their contract if he'd been able to line up another trained bear on short notice.

"What's with this scene where Attila chases the boys?" Nick asked.

"Oh, that's the pivotal one I mentioned yesterday."

"No, I mean what's with him *chasing* them? You

told me people should never run away from bears. You said it excites their predatory instincts.''

"Well, the boys won't *really* be running away from Attila. I know the notes call it the scene where he chases them, but Jay will do separate takes of them running and Attila running. Then they'll edit the sequences so it *looks* as if he's chasing them.''

"Ahh."

When Nick went back to his reading, she sat watching him, still not quite able to believe that he was actually helping her. Of course she realized it was to his benefit, as well as hers, if things worked out with Jay. But most men would never have stayed when they'd been in the midst of looking for a place to live.

Even fewer would have agreed to work with a bear, no matter how much it might prove to be worth to them financially. Especially when they already had a good job. Which added up to the fact that she felt very, very grateful. And despite her resolve to keep their relationship strictly business, she was aware of feeling more than simple gratitude.

As hard as she'd tried to fall asleep last night, she'd lain awake for a long time, extremely conscious that Nick was in the bedroom right across the hall—and that both their doors were open to allow what little breeze there was through the house. Then, at breakfast this morning, before he'd shaved, it had been impossible to ignore how sexy he looked.

Just as she was ordering herself to think about *anything* other than him, he tossed down the script and glanced over at her. "Here they come.''

Trying to quell a fresh surge of anxiety, she rose and looked across the clearing. Sure enough, there they were, just rounding the curve in the road.

Three black stretch limos led the way, followed by a convoy of trucks, trailers and RVs that would be home to the cast and crew while they were on location here.

The noise sent the rabbits scurrying under the safety of the porch, and in the house the Marx brothers began barking. They hated being shut inside, but she couldn't chance letting them out until everyone was safely parked. All in all, there was such a commotion that she half expected to see Rocky Raccoon peering down from the porch roof—even though it took a lot to rouse a coon from his day's sleep.

"Looks like an invasion," Nick said.

She glanced at him and forced a smile, hoping he couldn't tell how nervous she was. It would do nothing for his self-confidence.

The trucks began turning off into the field where she'd told Jay to set up camp, while the limos pulled up in front of the house.

The third one had barely stopped before the back door flew open and two boys leapt out.

"I guess those would be our ten-year-olds," she murmured as they headed for the porch.

"Hi, I'm Kyle," the blond one said, grinning at her. "And this is Brock," he added, pointing at the dark-haired one.

Brock produced a grin of his own.

"Well, hi. This is Nick and I'm Carly." She glanced at the two frazzled women who'd hurried after the boys—their mothers were on location with them, she knew.

"They've been sitting in the limo too long," one of the women said. "Would you mind if they looked around a little? Burned off some of their energy?"

"We'll keep an eye on them," the other woman promised.

"Sure. Go ahead. Just don't let them stick their fingers into the aviary."

By the time Carly turned her attention back to the limos, the drivers of the remaining two had opened the back doors. A couple of men were getting out of the first one, while Sarina Westlake and Garth Richards emerged from the second.

Carly focused on Jay Wall, whom she recognized from Gus's description. Of average height and weight, he had long dark hair pulled back into a ponytail, a scraggly beard and wire-rimmed glasses. His clothes said he wasn't a man who dressed to impress—tattered jeans, a T-shirt with *Two for Trouble* printed across it and a bright orange baseball cap pulled on backward.

Luckily Crackers couldn't see him from the solarium, but she made a mental note to mention the bird's little color quirk the first chance she got. Some of the cast and crew were bound to end up in the house, so they'd all have to be warned.

Glancing at Nick, she whispered, "The one in his early thirties is Jay. And I think the midfifties one must be the producer, Brian Goodfellow."

"You're sure *he's* not the director?" Nick whispered back. "He's got that pear-shaped Alfred Hitchcock look."

"Well, despite that, he has to be the producer. Get Real Productions is his company."

"Carly, darling," Jay said, heading for the porch as the limos started back down the drive. "Finally, we meet in person."

Reaching her, he took both her hands in his and

stood beaming at her so warmly that, if she didn't know better, she'd have thought he was positively dying to work with her. For a director, he made a great actor.

"This is Brian Goodfellow," he added, releasing her as the short, rotund man joined them on the porch.

"Goodie," he said, nodding to Carly. "Everyone just calls me Goodie."

"And our stars..." Jay paused and made a sweeping gesture toward them.

Sarina and Garth nodded from the drive, then went back to whatever they'd been talking about.

"And this," Carly said, "is Nick Montgomery, my new partner in Wild Action."

"Oh?" Jay extended his hand to Nick, his expression saying he didn't like surprises.

"Nick will be doing most of the work with Attila," she added.

"Oh?" Jay said again. "Do you have a lot of experience with bears, Nick?"

"Actually, most of my experience has been with cats."

"Big cats, he means," Carly said quickly, shooting Nick a look that said this was no time for humor. "Lions, tigers and panthers mostly, right?"

He grinned at her. "Right. But Attila and I are good buddies," he added to Jay.

Before there was time for anyone to say another word, a child yelled, "Jay? Look what we've got!"

Carly turned, then froze in horror. The two boys had come around the side of the house—Kyle with Crackers on his shoulder.

"We went in the back to get some water," he said

excitedly. "And all I did was say hi to him, and he hopped right on me."

Behind the boys, their mothers appeared, both wearing "Aren't they cute" expressions. A split second later, Crackers noticed the orange baseball cap.

He shrieked. Carly dove at Jay.

"Shee-it!" he said, ducking to avoid her hand.

She still managed to grab the cap—but only an instant before Crackers swooped through the air and snatched it from her. Landing on the porch railing, he sat bobbing his head up and down, the cap's bill securely in his beak.

"Awesome!" Brock said. "Can you make him do it again?"

"Sure," Nick told him. "Want to see him do it again, Jay?"

The director glared at him. "I hope you're a better bear trainer than you are a comedian."

Smoothing his hair, he looked at the mothers and snapped, "Keep those kids away from the animals, understand?"

When they nodded in unison, Jay turned his glare on Carly.

"I'm so s-sorry," she stammered. "It's the color orange. It sometimes makes him freak out."

When Jay glanced over at Crackers as if he'd like to wring his little feathered neck, Goodie said, "You're lucky he didn't sink those claws into your head. If he had, I'd be starting to believe this movie really *is* jinxed. But come on, let's go make sure all the equipment made the trip safely."

Jay nodded, then looked at Carly again. "Goodie and I will be back after we've had lunch. I'd like you

to show us the bear then. And you think you can keep
that parrot in a cage for the duration?''

"Well, the bird likes his freedom," Nick said. "So
we're not going to coop him up in a cage for a month
or more. But all you need to do is tell everyone not
to wear orange.''

"Or maybe we could see if the chef has a recipe
for parrot cacciatore," Jay muttered.

IT TOOK AT LEAST fifteen minutes for Carly to get
Crackers back into the solarium—by which point the
baseball cap was in shreds.

Nick had hovered nearby while she'd coaxed and
cajoled, but he wasn't nearly as much help with the
bird as he was with Attila. She probably shouldn't
have told him Crackers could amputate a man's hand.

Just as Crackers finally flew onto his perch, the
phone began to ring.

"Don't you move," Carly said sternly, pointing her
finger at him before she reached for the phone.

"Hi, darling," her mother's voice greeted her.

"Oh, hi, Mom, What's up?"

"Nothing much. I just wondered if you'd heard
exactly when your movie people are arriving.''

"Actually, they got here about half an hour ago.''

"Oh, good. And is everything going well so far?''

"Everything's just fine.'' Except for the fact that
Attila might not perform for the camera and an un-
nervingly attractive man was living in her house. Not
to mention having an entire horde of people setting
up camp in her field and a parrot who'd come close
to scalping the man who could make or break Wild
Action.

"Well, I won't keep you, dear. But we were curi-

ous about what happened when you met with the lawyers. How did that nephew of Gus's take to learning
that he'd left half the estate to you?''

"Ahh, he took it pretty well." She glanced over
and saw that Nick was still hovering. "Actually, he's
going to be staying here while they're shooting. He's
helping out with Attila."

"*Really*," her mother said, packing about thirteen
questions into one word.

Carly had no desire to answer even one of them
with Nick standing there listening, so she said,
"Mom, things are pretty hectic and I've got to run.
But I'll call you in a few days—let you know when
you should drive down."

"All right, dear. We're really looking forward to
it. Your father won't admit it, but he's been a little
bored since he retired, and he's really interested in
seeing a movie being shot. And Lisa's just *dying* to
meet Garth Richards."

"I'll call as soon as I know what's what. 'Bye for
now.

"My mother," she told Nick as she hung up. "My
parents and sister want to come down for a few days
and see how movies are made."

"Your sister lives with them?"

"No, she's a year older than me and married. But
she's a big Garth Richards fan. And she's a teacher,
so she's free during the summer."

Wondering what her family was going to think
when they got a look at the man who was sharing the
house with her, she turned her attention back to
Crackers and told him to get into his cage. Instead,
he tucked his head under his wing, trying to make
himself invisible.

"I thought he hated being in there during the day," Nick said.

Carly shot him a warning glance. She was hardly happy about the way he'd been such a smart ass with Jay; she just hadn't had a chance to discuss it with him yet. And at the moment, she could certainly do without his taking the bird's side.

"He's got to learn he can't behave like that," she said. "And when Jay gets back here, I want him to see we're being cooperative. Crackers, move it," she added.

His head bowed, he shuffled along his perch and kicked a bar of the cage with one foot.

"In," she said firmly. "You can come back out at dinnertime if you promise to be good."

He gave the cage another kick, graced her with a bird's version of a dirty look, then eased inside.

"And the next time you get another birdbrained idea, remember this is what happens." She carefully latched the door, then turned to Nick. "As for you, were you *deliberately* trying to annoy Jay?"

"What? All I said was we weren't going to keep Crackers in his cage for an entire month."

"That's not what I was referring to. I meant your line about most of your experience being with cats. If you'd told him you meant the neighbor's pussycat, I'd have killed you. And when you asked if he'd like to see Crackers come swooping down at him again... What on earth were you thinking of?"

"Well, the guy's a schmuck and I—"

"That is *entirely* beside the point. The point is we want him to think Wild Action is terrific, remember? So when he goes back to L.A. he'll give his friends rave reviews about us."

"A guy like that can't have any friends. And stop talking to me as if I were twelve years old. You may own fifty-one percent of this operation, but don't try laying down rules about what I can and can't say to people."

"That's *not* what I was doing. I was merely offering a little constructive criticism—which you obviously can't take. Dammit, Nick, you're exactly like Gus."

"Oh? Now why does that sound like an insult? Yesterday, you told me Gus was the sweetest man in the world."

"Except when he was too stubborn to listen! Then he'd put a mule to shame."

Nick turned on his heel and started across the kitchen.

"Where are you going?" Carly demanded as he opened the back door.

"I've got a few mules to put to shame."

"We don't have any mules."

"Then I'll make do with the ponies."

Punctuating his exit line by letting the screen slam shut behind him, Nick headed around the side of the house—not wanting to admit to himself that Carly's criticism hadn't been completely off base. Put him face-to-face with a jerk like Jay Wall and he just couldn't resist saying the odd thing he shouldn't. It was a weakness that had gotten him into more trouble than he cared to think about.

Deciding to check out the camp while his temper cooled, he wandered down the drive to the field and surveyed the scene.

There were four generator trucks the size of large moving vans, as well as about fifteen equipment trucks and at least as many trailers and RVs. One of the outside trailers had a sign indicating it was the kitchen, and half a dozen tables with chairs had already been set up at one end.

The site was buzzing with people, all of whom looked busy, so he just walked around the perimeter of the ragged rows, sizing things up and trying to get his mind off Carly. But she was just too annoying to stop thinking about.

He really didn't like the way she'd talked to him like a damn drill sergeant, and he'd have had a lot more to say to her if her little lecture hadn't taken him by surprise. But now he was adding "control freak" to his list of her negative traits.

Glancing back at the house, he told himself he'd better not stay away too long. She'd *really* light into him if he wasn't there when Jay and Goodie arrived to see Attila. And hell, if he wanted any lunch he should probably head back right now.

He started up the drive and was about halfway along it when a woman materialized beside him. A redhead somewhere in her thirties, she was very good looking—in an overdone, L.A. sort of way.

"Hi," she said, giving him a smile that looked as if she practiced it in front of a mirror.

A Hollywood smile, he decided as he stopped walking and said, "Hi" in return.

"I saw you talking to Jay and Goodie when we first got here, so you must be...?"

"Nick Montgomery. The new partner in Wild Action."

"Oh? Last I heard, Gus Montgomery had died and Carly was in charge."

"Well, the partnership's a pretty recent development."

She nodded. "I'm Barbara Hunt, the set director. I just wanted to ask if it's okay to wander around a little. I'd hate to be the parrot's next victim."

"You're safe at the moment. He's locked up. And for the future, just don't wear anything orange."

"Oooh." She gave a little shudder. "Not my color at all. See you around, Nick," she added, heading off.

When he started toward the porch again, he saw Carly was standing on it—and not alone. She was talking with a lanky, bearded fellow who had *interest* written all over him.

That, Nick found annoying, although he couldn't figure out why. He'd known this was the wrong time and place for an entanglement even before Carly had started displaying her true nature. And since she had, he'd realized she was about as far from his ideal woman as she could be.

He headed up the steps, not sure if he should stop for an introduction or just leave her to whatever she was doing with this guy.

She made up his mind by saying, "Nick, this is Royce Chalmers. He's worked on a couple of the documentaries Gus and I were involved with, and he's Jay's number one cameraman for the film.

"Or at this point," she added to Royce, "should I be saying you're Jay's director of photography?"

When Royce laughed, the sound grated in Nick's ears.

"We've hardly done a full week's shooting, and Jay's already fired his director of photography," Royce explained. "A couple of reels of film got lost, and Screaming Jay blamed him."

"*Screaming* Jay?" Nick repeated.

"Yeah, that's what everyone calls him. Behind his back, of course. You'll see why. Or hear why, I should say."

"What?" Nick asked Carly when he noticed she was looking anxious.

"Nothing," she said quickly. "But Royce was telling me Jay's legendary for firing people. That he doesn't even bother hiring an assistant director anymore, because he always fires them after a couple of days."

"So this isn't the first time you've worked for him," Nick said to Royce.

"No, he's shot a couple of other pictures in Toronto, and he uses mostly local crews."

There was a moment's silence, then Carly glanced at Nick and asked, "Who was that redhead you were talking to?"

Before he could answer, Royce said, "Barbara Hunt, our set director."

He looked around like a street informer, worried that someone would overhear, then continued in a lowered voice. "Maybe I'd better fill you in about her so you don't say the wrong thing to anyone."

CHAPTER FOUR

A Walk in the Woods

"Barb is Brian Goodfellow's wife," Royce explained.

"Really?" Carly said. "He's a lot older than her, isn't he?"

"He's also a lot richer, which was probably *his* main attraction. At any rate, Jay never wanted her, but she got the job because Goodie's financing the movie. Then, about a week after she signed her contract, the story goes that they got into a hell of a row over something. The grapevine says they're both highly volatile and pretty unstable."

"She seemed normal enough to me," Nick said.

"Well, you can't believe everything you hear, but one version of the story is that she pulled a gun and threatened to shoot Goodie's balls off."

Nick felt a chill in his loins.

"Anyway," Royce went on, "whatever really happened, Goodie sent her packing. And now she's about to become ex-wife number four or five."

"Oh, Lord," Carly said. "And she went ahead with working on the movie? That must be awfully awkward."

"Yeah. When both the producer and director wish

you were anywhere else on earth, it can't be exactly comfortable.''

"Then why would she want to be here?" Carly asked.

"She says she wasn't going to throw away a job on a terrific film just because her presence would make Goodie uncomfortable. And it's obvious she figures he *deserves* to be uncomfortable. But I think the real reason she hung in is that she sees this movie as her big chance. She's worked on sets for years, but nobody's given her a shot at set director before—and you'll see why. She's in way over her head.''

"So if Jay's big on firing people, why not her?" Nick asked.

"Apparently he tried to, but she's not the type to take things lying down. She showed up at his office with a lawyer and threatened to sue both him and Goodie for breach of contract—and do whatever else she could to hold up production. That would have cost a fortune, so I guess they wanted the expense even less than they wanted her.

"But look, I've got to get going," Royce added. "I just thought I'd say hello before I headed back to Toronto. I was telling Carly," he explained to Nick, "that somehow all the camera filters got left behind. I've got to drive back and find them or we won't be filming tomorrow. But at least I came up in my own car, so I can just disappear for a few hours without telling Jay that somebody goofed.''

"But you'll miss lunch," Carly said. "I was about to make something anyway, so would you like to—"

Royce waved off the suggestion. "Thanks, but I'll be okay. I'm telling you, though, this is shaping up to be the worst-luck movie I've ever worked on.''

"You're the second person who's said something like that," Nick told him. "Goodie made a remark about thinking it was jinxed."

"Even Goodie's admitting it, eh? The big shots usually like to pretend everything's fine, but I guess there've been just too many problems to ignore."

As Royce headed off, Nick said, "You think this jinx thing makes the odds on Attila eating me higher than you were figuring?"

"Attila is *not* going to eat you," Carly said. "Movie people are simply like that. I mean, every so often they decide a shoot is jinxed. That doesn't mean it really is, though. It's just a silly belief—like believing bad luck comes in threes."

Nick forced a smile. But didn't she know bad luck often *did* come in threes? Hell, it had just happened to him.

And if she didn't realize that some superstitions had a basis in fact, she probably didn't know a damn thing about jinxes, either. He just hoped she didn't get a lesson about them when they took Jay and Goodie to see Attila.

"Nick?"

He looked at her.

"There's something I'd better tell you. Attila doesn't like people yelling. It really upsets him."

"And they call Jay, Screaming Jay," Nick said, an uneasy feeling settling in the pit of his stomach. "Well, we'll have to say something to him right away."

"Yes, but let *me* do it. You might say something that would...offend him."

"What? You mean something like, 'If you ever

raise your voice while I'm working with the bear, you'll be a dead man?' ''

"Well...yes."

"Fine, then you do the explaining. And if he forgets, I'll do the killing."

"HE'S NOT EXACTLY *huge,* is he Goodie," Jay said, disappointment dripping from his words.

Nick gave Carly a pained look. If Jay was standing on *their* side of the fence, in the field with Attila, he'd think the bear was downright enormous.

"You know, I should have gone with a grizzly. Or maybe a polar bear."

"That wouldn't have done much for the movie's integrity," Goodie said. "I mean, the kids are supposedly lost in upper New York State, and you'd hardly find a grizzly or a polar bear wandering around there."

"Oh. Yeah, I guess that's a good point. I just wish this one was bigger."

"He's actually *very* large for a black bear," Carly said. "And when he stands up... Show them, Nick."

"Attila, *two feet,*" he ordered—then tried not to let his relief show when the bear obediently raised up onto his back feet. He still hadn't shaken the fear that Attila was going to lash out at him one of these times instead of doing what he was told.

"Good boy. Now go and *say hello* to those men," he added, giving a hand signal.

Attila grunted, then took a couple of steps toward Jay and Goodie.

They almost fell over each other backing off.

"That fence *is* electrified, isn't it?" Goodie asked from several yards away.

"No, there's no reason for it to be," Carly told him.

"He doesn't have a problem with any colors or anything, does he?" Jay said nervously.

"No, as I explained, his only problem is he doesn't like people yelling."

"Want to come in here and feed him some chicken, Jay?" Nick pointed at the pail and pretended he didn't notice Carly giving him the evil eye.

He was still annoyed that she figured she had the right to lecture him, and he'd be damned if he was going to let her think he'd paid attention.

"Ahh...maybe I'll try feeding him another time," Jay said.

"You, Goodie?"

"Me? No, I have allergies. I'd better not get too close to him."

"Is there anything in particular you'd like to see him do?" Carly asked.

Nick shot her an uneasy glance, wishing she wouldn't push their luck.

"No," Jay said. "I mostly just wanted to see how big he was so we'll get the stand-in right."

"Stand-in?" Nick said.

Jay looked at him as if he were an idiot, while Carly explained. "It takes a minimum of two or three hours to light a set, so they use stand-ins for the actors while they're doing it."

Nick didn't know why they'd want to light an outdoors set, but he wasn't about to display his ignorance again. Deciding the answer must have to do with shadows or something, he tuned in on Carly once more.

"And for Attila's stand-in you'll use...what?" she was asking Jay. "A couple of big men?"

"Don't worry about it. We've got that all figured out. And as long as he can do everything the script calls for, I've seen what I need. But how about that pond?" Jay pointed across the field to it. "Does he like to swim?"

"Sure. Bears love to swim."

"Hmmm... Then maybe I should use some shots where—"

"Jay?" someone interrupted from a distance.

All four of them looked toward a man rushing down the hill.

"Must want something darned important to be running in this heat," Nick quietly said to Carly.

"I'm afraid there's more bad news," the man announced as he reached Jay and Goodie.

"What *is* it with this movie?" Goodie snapped.

"What's up now?" Jay asked the man.

"The lab just called, and they screwed up. All of yesterday's filming is a wipe."

"What?" Jay screamed. "You mean we'll have to reshoot an entire day?"

"Woof!" Attila said so loudly it almost made Nick's heart stop.

"It's okay, boy," Carly said gently as Jay whirled around. "Everyone really *does* have to remember the noise rule," she told him.

"You don't want him angry at you," Nick added for good measure.

"Yeah. Right," Jay mouthed. He eyed Attila for another second, then turned toward the man again. "What the hell went wrong?" he whispered fiercely.

"They don't know. But they're claiming it's not

their fault, that the film must have gotten exposed before it was shot.''

"Is that possible?" Goodie asked.

Jay shook his head. "Not unless someone intentionally did it. The lab people just want to make sure the blame lands on someone else."

"Is there anything I should do?" the man asked.

"You could go on a shooting spree in the lab," Jay muttered. "And I don't mean with a camera. But, no, what the hell is there to do?" he added, waving the man away and turning back toward Attila's field.

"Okay, just make sure he's ready to go in the morning. Hell, he looks like it'll take till then to get him brushed."

"Brushed?" Carly repeated.

Jay made one of his sweeping gestures. "All that scraggly fur hanging off him. He needs a good grooming before we shoot him."

"What about the movie's integrity?" Nick said. He'd liked that phrase when Goodie used it. "I mean, your movie's set in July. And as you can see, bears moult in July. If we brush him, he'll look less authentic." Besides which, Attila might not like being brushed, and he sure as hell wasn't going to try doing anything Attila didn't like.

"He wouldn't seem as fierce if they cleaned him up," Goodie said. "He'd look less wild."

"Well..." Jay took off his glasses, peered at Attila without them, then put them back on. "Okay. We'll shoot tomorrow with him like this and see how it comes across in the rushes. Assuming the lab doesn't screw up again and we *get* rushes." He glanced at Nick, adding, "Just so you're ready for it, I'm going to start with the scene where he's chasing the boys."

"Oh," Carly said.

Nick looked at her and felt a chill of apprehension. By now, he'd seen that anxious expression often enough to know something was wrong. So, despite what she'd told him, she must not be sure that Jay intended to shoot Attila running *separately* from the boys.

"What's the problem?" Jay demanded. "He can see Nick's hand signals from a distance, can't he?"

"Yes, of course. I only—"

"I've always heard bears are blind as bats," Goodie put in.

Nick didn't bother telling him that bats actually have some sight. He'd rather hear what the problem was.

"Half the experts say bears can't see well and the other half say they can," Carly said. "As for Attila, he seems to do just fine."

"Then what *is* the problem?" Jay asked again.

"Oh, there isn't one. Not really. I was just going to suggest that you leave the running scene until later and shoot some of the foreshadowing ones first. Ones where he's not really doing much. That would let him kind of warm up to the action."

Jay shook his head. "It's the action I want to be sure he's capable of."

"Jay," Nick said, "Attila is the Robert De Niro of bears. He's capable of anything."

Carly gave him a glance that said he was laying it on awfully thick—even though he'd only been trying to help. If she didn't want to do that scene first, then he didn't, either.

"Well, I still think we'll shoot the running scene tomorrow," Jay said. "Goodie and I are going to go check out the woods right now and decide exactly where we want to film it. Then the crew can start setting up at dawn.

"I'll let you know later where we'll be shooting and when you should get the bear there."

Carly nodded. "But wouldn't you like me to go with you now? If you don't know the forest, it's easy to get lost."

"I *never* get lost. Besides, when Gus and I were making arrangements, he drew me a map and marked some places he said sounded like what I wanted."

She nodded. "He mentioned that."

"Did he also mention that once I choose the sites we'll have to cut a road or two through the woods? To get the lights and equipment in? I paid dearly to have the contract allow for that."

"Yes, I've read the contract. I know the terms."

"Good." Jay gave them a curt farewell nod, then turned away with Goodie. "I guess," he said as they started off, "we've got to find your wife and—"

"Would you *please* stop referring to her as my wife?"

"I guess," Jay began again, "we've got to find *Barb* and take her with us. We're not going to come up with a location that won't need some set dressing."

"Maybe we could get *her* lost," Goodie muttered.

Nick waited until they were out of hearing range, then said, "Okay, what do we do if Jay expects Attila to actually chase the kids?"

"I can't imagine he will. But if he does, I'll just explain why it wouldn't be safe—and make sure the boys' mothers are there when I do."

"Then why did you look so worried when he said

he wanted to shoot that scene first? And why were you trying to convince him not to.''

She scuffed the toe of her sneaker against the ground. "I was just hoping you'd have more time to work with Attila before they got to that scene.''

"Because?''

"Because," she said with an unhappy shrug, "the most difficult thing to make him do is run on command.''

WHILE CARLY AND NICK were cleaning up after dinner she did her best to keep her eyes off him, but it was a losing battle. They were spending virtually every waking minute together, and that was fueling her attraction to him like oil-fueled flames.

He caught her watching him and grinned, sending a warm rush through her. She looked away, telling herself she'd better take her hormones in for a tune-up. They definitely weren't working in sync with her common sense. And they were making her so darned aware of him that she was having trouble concentrating, even though she *knew* she'd be out of her mind to get involved with him. If she did, she'd only be left hurting when he went back home.

Maybe some women could separate the emotional from the physical, but she wasn't one of them.

Besides, even if he was going to be around forever, he definitely wasn't the man for her. He could be just *too* aggravating.

Jay Wall had only been here since this afternoon. But already, every time Nick opened his mouth around the man she found herself praying he wouldn't say something to antagonize him.

"Carly?"

When she turned from the sink, he was standing far too close for comfort. Near enough that she could feel his body heat and see the warmth in his gray eyes.

That did funny things to her insides, so she casually edged away a few inches and tried to think of something innocuous to say.

"I'm really glad I found Dylan to help look after the animals" was the best she could come up with. "I don't know how we'd manage without him now that we're into the movie. And he's so reliable. Not all high school kids are."

"Uh-huh. From what I saw, he's doing a good job."

Nick seemed to be easing closer again, but before Carly had to retreat even farther along the counter, the Marx brothers began to bark and went racing to the front door—scattering the three cats in their wake.

"Company!" Crackers announced when somebody knocked.

Carly exhaled slowly, feeling a mixture of relief and something rather the opposite that she resisted putting a name to. "I wondered how long it would be until one of the movie people needed something," she said.

When she started for the front of the house, Nick tagged along, so she added, "Jay told me they'd be totally self-contained and that everyone would be instructed not to bother us, but I knew things wouldn't be entirely peaceful."

She told the dogs to sit, then opened the door and discovered Jay's number one cameraman standing in the twilight.

"You made it back from Toronto," she said.

Royce nodded. "A couple of hours ago. Some idiot stuck the filters in a storage room. That's how they got missed. But it didn't take me long to find them."

"Well, would you like to come in? Nick and I were just going to have coffee." She half hoped Royce would say yes, so she wouldn't be alone with Nick again for a while, and half hoped he'd say no, so she would.

"Thanks, but I only came to collect Jay. A lot of people need to talk to him—including me. I don't even know where we're shooting tomorrow."

"Jay's not here."

"What? Then where is he?"

"He must be somewhere in your camp," Nick offered.

Royce shook his head. "People have been looking for him for hours. And neither he nor Goodie showed up for dinner. That's what made me figure you'd invited them to eat here. Goodie *never* misses a meal."

"Well...maybe they went to a restaurant in Port Perry."

"Or maybe," Nick suggested, "they got lost in the woods."

"Oh, Lord," she murmured, instantly certain he was right. "Royce, was Barb Hunt at dinner?"

"Hell, I don't know. There are an awful lot of people in the camp."

"You'd better see if you can find her," Nick said. "Because she went off into the woods with the other two. So if she's not around, either..."

"She went off with Goodie? She's liable to be in a shallow grave by now."

Nick acknowledged the remark with a tight smile, then said, "Look, we'll go down to the camp with you. If none of them is there, we'll have to organize a search party and find them before they get eaten alive by mosquitoes.''

That, Carly thought, wasn't the only thing they might get eaten alive by. People were always spotting *wild* bears in the area.

She wasn't sure if she should mention that or not. If she did, they might end up with an awfully small search party. And as long as the searchers made a lot of noise, any bear that might be around would run the other way.

Just as she decided to keep quiet, at least until they got under way, Nick said, ''You know the woods pretty well?''

She nodded. ''And Gus told me which places he suggested to Jay—the ones he put on that map he drew. But they've been gone so long there's no telling where they'd be by now. We could take the Marx brothers, though. They'd be a help.''

Leaving the dogs in the house for the moment, Carly and Nick trekked down the drive with Royce and started asking people if they'd seen Barb Hunt recently.

No one had, and when she wasn't in her trailer, Royce began passing the word that Jay, Goodie and Barb were lost in the woods and that anyone willing to go searching for them should wear pants and a long-sleeved top.

''We're lucky there's a night search scene in the movie,'' he told Carly and Nick. ''We've got a whole carton full of flashlights.''

''Life imitating art,'' Carly said.

Royce laughed. ''Only if you consider a Jay Wall film art.''

By the time someone had located the flashlights and everyone who'd needed to change clothes had done so, it was completely dark beyond the perimeter of the camp.

"Okay, here's the drill," Nick told the assembled group. "When we get to the woods, everyone's going to fan out in a long line. And as you're walking, make sure you can always see the lights on either side of you."

Someone asked a question, and he was just answering it when Garth Richards swept through the crowd—trailed by his wife. He marched up to Nick and imperiously announced, "I'm Garth Richards. And you are...?"

"Nick Montgomery."

"Well, Mr. Montgomery, I'm not sure having anyone go out into the woods at night is a good idea. Someone could get hurt. Or more people might end up lost."

"It's okay, I know what I'm doing. I've organized searches before."

"Even so, I think the appropriate thing would be to call the police and let them handle it."

"It would be sometime tomorrow before they could provide as much manpower as we've got right here."

Garth's dark eyes flashed with annoyance. "Even so, I—"

"Mr. Richards, this is my property. Ms. Dumont's and mine," he added, nodding toward Carly. "And if people are lost on it, we're going to go looking for them. If you don't want to join us, fine. But those who do are coming with us right now."

While Carly was wondering whether her sister

would still be a Garth Richards fan if she'd seen that little performance, Nick turned and stalked off toward the house without a backward glance. Everyone with a flashlight started after him.

"Good Lord," she whispered, falling into step beside Royce. "That Garth's a real charmer. You'd think he *wanted* them to be lost all night."

"He probably does," Royce whispered back. "Jay, at least."

"Oh? Bad blood?"

"The worst. Jay had an affair with Sarina a year or so back. After he dumped her, she patched things up with Garth, and it's pretty obvious there's no love lost between them and Jay."

"Then why on earth are they making a movie with him? And why would he cast them?"

Royce shrugged. "We're talking Hollywood types. Who can explain half the stuff they do?"

When they reached the house, Carly quickly changed into jeans and a jersey, then sat down on the floor with the dogs and explained the situation.

"They can't really understand English, can they?" Nick asked when she was done. "I mean, beyond simple commands?"

"It's hard to know exactly how they get the message—it's partly the words and partly the tone. But they'll know I want them to look for people. They're really smart."

Once they went back outside, the search team started across the clearing—the Marx brothers bounding along in front.

"Royce," Nick said as they neared the tree line, "you anchor one end of the line and I'll take the other."

"Okay, everyone," he added more loudly, "Carly has some ideas about which way they might have gone, so she's going to walk a few yards ahead of the line."

"Oh, and everyone make a lot of noise," she put in. "So they'll hear us when we get close."

"And so the wild animals will hear us and get out of the way," one of the searchers called.

His remark was greeted with a round of laughter. Carly didn't join in.

"Keep an eye on Carly's light and watch your footing," Nick said. "We don't want any broken ankles."

Imagining how fast Garth Richards would say he'd told them so if there were any mishaps, she started into the woods with the dogs excitedly darting into the underbrush.

Not much moonlight made it through the trees, but between the little that did and the beams of the flashlights, she could more or less figure out where she was going. She headed for one of the areas Gus had recommended to Jay, and when that produced no results, she led the way to another. By the time they reached it, there'd been so many sounds of people slapping their skin that she knew the mosquitoes were tormenting everyone.

Then, ahead in the distance, Harpo began to bark. Within seconds, Chico, Groucho and Zeppo joined in.

"I think we've found them!" she called excitedly.

"Jay?" Nick hollered. "Goodie? Barb?"

Carly hurried in the direction of the barking, and sure enough, the dogs had done their job.

"Shee-it, am I glad to see you," Jay called when she was close enough that they could make out who she was.

"We thought the dogs were wolves before they started barking," Barb cried. "We thought we were goners."

As the other searchers converged on them, Goodie said, "It was the damn map that got us lost. We couldn't find a single site that was marked on it, and by the time we realized it was all wrong we didn't know where the hell we were."

"What?" Carly said. "That doesn't make any sense. Gus knew these woods like the back of his hand."

"I'm absolutely covered in bites," Jay complained.

"You think you're the only one?" Goodie snapped.

"I'm *so* glad I thought to slather on bug repellant before we started out," Barb said, causing both Jay and Goodie to glare at her.

"Could I see the map?" Carly asked.

Jay dug it out of his pocket and thrust it at her.

Shining her flashlight on it, she slowly turned it around, trying to make it bear some resemblance to reality.

"Jay?" she said at last. "What did you do with this after Gus gave it to you?"

He shrugged. "Stuck it in a folder, along with some other stuff I wouldn't need till we got up here. Why?"

"Just wondered. It *is* kind of inaccurate, so there's no sense in your trying to use it again," she said, putting it in her pocket. "I'll draw you a better one. And I'll also take the three of you out first thing in the morning and help you get your bearings. If we start about seven, we should be able to look at all the places Gus suggested by lunchtime."

"But it'll be too late to set up and start shooting,"

Goodie muttered. "Which means another wasted day."

Carly glanced around to locate Nick, then motioned him to step away from the others.

"What's up?" he asked.

"Nick, Gus didn't draw that map."

NICK, CARLY NOTED AS he paced across the kitchen again, was getting very adept at stepping over the dogs. But she still wished he'd come and sit down at the table with her.

For one thing, he was annoying Crackers. The cover was over his cage, but she could hear him rustling around instead of sleeping.

On top of that, something about the way Nick moved made it difficult not to follow him with her eyes—and she didn't want him to catch her watching him again.

If he decided she was attracted to him, she had absolutely no doubt what he'd do. She hadn't forgotten how he'd closed in on her by the sink earlier. And before that, she'd caught him watching *her* a few times.

She forced her gaze from him, thinking that all the fresh air she'd gotten in the woods had helped to clear her head, as well as strengthen her resolve. Even if the chemistry between them was sizzling, she'd be making *such* a big mistake if she—

"You're absolutely certain?" he asked once more.

She looked at him again. He was standing by the far wall, eyeing her.

"Nick, how many times do I have to tell you? Gus did *not* draw this map." She tapped it with her finger for emphasis. "The places marked on it are nowhere near where they actually are. And the printing isn't Gus's. It looks a lot like his, but it isn't. So someone must have taken his map out of Jay's folder and substituted this one.''

Nick paced across the room one more time, then finally sat down. "Well, if that's the case, then anyone who figures *Two for Trouble* is jinxed is way off base. This isn't bad luck, it's sabotage.''

"What?''

"We've got a saboteur on our hands. That's how *I'm* adding things up.''

The possibility struck Carly as far-fetched, but Nick *was* the detective here. "Okay,'' she said slowly. "Someone put a misleading map in Jay's folder so he'd get lost in the woods. But how would that sabotage the film? He certainly wasn't at risk of freezing to death in July.''

"No, but Goodie said it meant a wasted day. And he sounded as if that was darned significant.''

"Yes, of course. Except for the cast, everyone's paid by the hour. And, on location like this, there are all those rented vehicles and equipment and... Oh, a whole lot of things. Falling behind schedule can get really expensive.''

"And they *must* be falling behind schedule, right? I mean, given all the problems we've heard about?''

Carly nodded.

"And when you think about it, every single one of them could have been caused by someone in the cast or crew. Except for the lab screwing up. That would be getting us into some sort of conspiracy.''

"Not if the lab didn't actually screw up,'' Carly pointed out. "The people there claimed the film must have been exposed before it was shot, remember?''

"Right. Good thinking."

She managed not to smile, but his compliment pleased her far more than it should. Then she had a thought so horrible it drove the pleased feeling entirely away.

CHAPTER FIVE

Excitement in the Camp

NICK GAZED ACROSS the kitchen table, his uneasy feeling getting stronger by the second. Carly was wearing her there's-a-problem expression, and he could tell this one was something serious.

"Okay, what is it?" he said.

She didn't make him drag it out of her the way she usually did; she merely said, "Actually, there's more than *one* 'it.' But I just realized this saboteur could try something with the animals. I mean, he could easily toss poisoned meat into Attila's field. And everyone knows the Marx brothers are in the movie. The rabbits and the owls, too. So what if he figures he could cause a major delay by..."

When she looked as if she were about to burst into tears, Nick reached over and took her hand.

It was soft, despite all the outside work she did. Soft and warm. Trying not to wonder if she felt so good all over, he said, "I think the rabbits are okay. They'd be easy enough to replace that nobody would target them. And the aviary's locked up tight, isn't it?"

She nodded.

"And the dogs are safe with us, which just leaves

Attila. So how about arranging a twenty-four-hour watch for him?''

''You mean ask Jay if some of his crew would...'' She stopped midquestion when Nick shook his head.

''Uh-uh. With no idea who the saboteur is, we can't trust any of the crew. I was thinking of high school kids. Three shifts would do it, and Dylan can't be the only one who takes on odd jobs.''

''No, of course he's not. And I'll bet he'd be happy to line up some of his friends. Do you think it's too late to call him tonight?''

''A teenager? No, they never go to bed early.''

Slipping her hand from under his, Carly hurried over to the phone—then looked back across the room. ''Would you mind going and turning the pole lights on in Attila's field? Just in case?''

''Sure.''

The walk down the hill and back took several minutes, but when he returned, Carly was still on the phone. At his curious glance, she whispered, ''The line was busy.''

He sat down and watched her as she talked—her long hair silky smooth, her dark eyes full of concern—and he couldn't keep from thinking how darned sexy she was. That had to be why he'd kind of stopped reminding himself about her negative traits.

He'd also kind of pushed the idea of being careful around her to the back of his mind. But he could tell she was being careful around him.

He'd catch her gaze and she'd look away; he'd get too close and she'd step back.

Maybe he just didn't appeal to her. But that wasn't what the electricity between them was saying, so it was more likely she simply had no interest in a casual affair. And since she knew as well as he did that's all there could be between them, he'd bet she'd be pretty quick about putting him in his place if he got too friendly.

She said goodbye to Dylan and hung up, clearly relieved.

"He's going to get right on it," she said, heading back to the table. "And if he can't find anyone else to come over tonight, he'll be here in a while and take the first shift himself. Oh, Nick, that was such a good idea."

"Well, I'm not just another pretty face."

When she laughed, he felt an incredibly strong urge to reach for her hand. But not being crazy about rejection, he simply leaned back in his chair and reminded her she'd said there were a *couple* of problems.

"Right," she said, looking unhappy once more. "You know, I've been telling myself that maybe there wouldn't be any more trouble during the filming, but after that map... Well, now we know the problems aren't just going to magically stop. And if this shoot turns into a total horror show, word will get around. The cast and crew always put out the word."

"And?"

"And...do you figure Jay Wall would willingly take responsibility for a disaster? Or is he the type who'd relegate blame to everyone else involved—the cast, the crew and *us*."

"Ahh. You mean, so much for our reputation." And, as he'd been aware from the start, if Wild Action's reputation took a dive, his inheritance would be worthless.

That thought had barely formed in his mind before he realized it wasn't his major concern. Carly cared so much for the animals that he actually felt more worried about what would happen if she was forced to give them up.

He'd make out, one way or another—get a job on a different police force or start working as a private investigator for someone else's agency. Neither option was what he really wanted, but he'd simply be putting his dream on hold for a while longer. When it came to Carly, though... Hell, if she lost those animals, it would break her heart.

He gazed at her for another moment. Then, in his most reassuring cop tone, said, "Hey, let's not start assuming the worst just yet. Don't forget you've got a detective for a partner. And all we have to do is figure out who's behind the trouble and stop him— or her."

Carly eyed him uncertainly. "You really think we could?"

"You're doubting my abilities?"

She hesitated for a split second, then firmly shook her head. "Of course not. Oh, and if we *could,* Jay would be so grateful he'd say nothing but good about Wild Action for the rest of his life."

Knowing Jay, that was undoubtedly a vast over-statement, but Nick didn't dispute it.

"Okay, Mr. Detective, where do we start?"

"Well," he said slowly, "we start by not saying anything to anybody—which means it's a good thing you didn't tell Jay that map was a phony."

"I only kept quiet because there were so many other people around. But you really don't think we should say anything to him or Goodie?"

"No. They don't strike me as very circumspect. And... Oh, there are a lot of cop-type reasons that aren't worth getting into. But let's just play things close to the vest for the moment."

When she nodded, he went on. "You know a lot more about the movie business than I do, so give me the worst-case scenario. What happens if the filming falls further and further behind schedule and Goodie's looking at having to pump in more and more money?"

While she considered that, he watched her, knowing he shouldn't. Looking at her made him want to do more than look, and hadn't he told himself not five minutes ago that it was obvious she'd put him in his place if he tried anything?

"The worst-case scenario is that they'd stop production," she said at last. "But that almost never happens, because then *everybody* loses. So, either Goodie keeps pumping in more money or they begin cutting corners or both."

"Cutting corners how?"

"Well, first they'd start scrimping on the shooting. Jay would have to do fewer takes than he might like and print some scenes even though he's not entirely happy with them. Then they'd cut back on postproduction—put restraints on the editors and that sort of thing. Which means the picture would suffer and the odds on its being a flop would increase."

"And a flop would get us back to the problem of Jay trying to lay the blame on everyone else."

She nodded.

Before Nick could ask another question, the Marx brothers jolted awake and went into their guard-dog routine, barking furiously as they raced for the front door.

"Bad dog! Bad dog!" Crackers screeched from under the cage's cover.

"Gus and I said that too often when they were puppies," Carly explained, starting after the dogs.

Nick followed her down the hall, not *quite* able to keep his eyes off her cute little behind.

When she opened the door, the man standing on the porch was wearing an angry expression and a white cook's outfit with Chef Raffaello embroidered on the chest pocket.

If he'd come wanting to borrow a cup of sugar, Nick thought, he could at least have worn a smile instead of standing there looking like a character you'd see on "America's Most Wanted."

"Yes?" Carly asked.

"I need a gun," he said.

CARLY HURRIED DOWN the drive with Nick and the chef, her heart in her throat as she tried to see everywhere at once. If there was a bear cub in the camp's kitchen, mama probably wasn't far away.

"I didn't even get the light turned on before I saw it," the chef said. "But there was enough light from the camp to make out its fat, furry shape. And I just closed the door again so damn fast..."

Chef Raffaello apparently ran out of breath or words, so, after a moment, Carly said, "Nick?"

He looked at her.

"Bear-hunting season is in the spring. This late in the summer that cub's not likely an orphan. And a mama bear separated from her baby is one of the most ill-tempered animals on earth."

When Nick glanced at the rifle of Gus's he was carrying, she began desperately hoping there'd be no need for it. They certainly wouldn't have to shoot the cub. One way or another, she'd get it safely out of the trailer. But if mama came charging, there'd be no option but to shoot her.

That thought alone was enough to fill Carly's throat with tears. But there really *wouldn't* be an option. Not with all those people gathered around the kitchen trailer.

Jay was screaming at everyone to stay back, but nobody seemed to be listening.

"Dammit," Nick muttered as they plowed a path through the bystanders. "We could sure use better crowd control."

Jay spotted them and yelled, "We wouldn't have needed your help if this country didn't have such stupid gun laws! You know we couldn't bring a single gun across the border?"

Carly offered up a tiny prayer of thanks to Canada Customs, while Nick shouted to the crowd. "Listen, everybody, get the hell inside. If there's a mother bear around the camp, you don't want her to catch you in the open."

"You heard him!" Jay screamed. "Get moving."

Some people headed off. Others didn't, apparently more willing to risk a charging bear than miss the excitement.

Goodie, who was practically hopping up and down, closed in on Carly and said, "This means there are bears in those woods we were lost in, doesn't it?"

Nick turned to her, waving Goodie off as he did. "Okay, you open the door and stay behind it. I'll go in."

She made sure that nobody was *too* near, then whispered, "Are you forgetting you're not really a bear expert? *I'll* go in."

"Look, I've faced armed men and—"

"Fine, but I've faced unarmed bear cubs." Before he could argue further, she turned to the chef. "Where's the light switch in there?"

"Just to the right of the door."

She stepped over to the door and cracked it open. There wasn't a sound from inside.

Hoping against hope the cub wasn't directly under the switch, she slid her hand across the wall and found what she wanted. When she flicked on the light, there was still only silence inside the trailer.

Cautiously she pulled the door open further and peered in. And then she started to laugh with relief.

"What?" Nick demanded, so close behind her he was breathing down her neck.

"Look at our bear cub." She opened the door the rest of the way to reveal Rocky Raccoon sitting on a counter with one paw in a jar of jam and several shredded cookie bags beside him.

"He's a whiz at opening doors," she explained. Then she looked over at Rocky again and told him he was a bad boy. But she was so glad he wasn't a cub with a mean mama that she couldn't make herself sound angry.

"False alarm," Nick told the crowd. "It's just a tame coon."

"Your *trained* tame coon?" Jay demanded.

"Uh-huh."

"Well I sure as hell hope *Attila's* not trained to go into trailers."

SHORTLY AFTER CARLY and Nick retrieved Rocky from the camp's kitchen, one of Dylan's friends arrived to take the night shift with Attila.

By the time they got him settled in next to the field—with a deck chair, a couple of flashlights, a bottle of bug repellant and a thermos of coffee—it was past midnight.

"If you're taking people out scouting locations at seven in the morning, you'd better head straight to bed," Nick said as they walked back to the house.

Carly nodded wearily. It had been an awfully long day. Even so, she doubted she'd be able to fall asleep—not until she knew exactly how he figured they were going to ID their saboteur.

Once they were in the kitchen, she asked.

"You're not too tired to talk?" he said.

"I'm almost too tired to breathe, but I'll feel a lot better if I know."

She got a glass of iced tea for herself and a beer for him, and they took them out onto the front porch—the Marx brothers following, then scurrying down the steps to give the lawn a late-night check.

The cast and crew knew there'd be no early call in the morning, so a lot of them hadn't turned in yet. There were still lights on all over the camp, and the occasional murmur of voices and laughter drifted up the drive.

It made tonight entirely different from the norm. Usually, the only light came from the moon and stars, the only sounds from crickets and an owl or two. On nights like that, the porch often put her in mind of a perfect movie setting for a first kiss.

Stealing a glance at Nick's rugged profile, she told herself it was just as well the night seemed less romantic than usual. Then she tried to ignore the imaginary voice that asked if she was sure she meant that.

He pulled the other chair around to face hers, lowered himself into it and took a swig of beer.

She watched the cords of muscle in his neck, too tired to make herself look away. "So?" she said when he lowered the bottle.

"Okay. We can come at things from three different directions. One, we consider motivation. Two, we decide who our prime suspects are. And three, we keep our eyes and ears open and hope our saboteur makes a mistake. But let's start with motivation. *Why* would someone cause trouble? Who would have anything to gain from it?"

"Well, nobody has anything *obvious* to gain, because everybody working on a film wants it to be a box office smash. And everybody's stigmatized to one degree or another if it's a flop.

"I mean, its hardest on the director's reputation, but it's a black mark against the actors, too. And when word gets around about which crew members worked on a stinker, they sometimes don't get offered many jobs for a while."

"But Jay and Goodie have by far the most to lose."

Carly nodded. "Jay being Jay, I imagine he'd *really* hate to be associated with a turkey. And if that's what it turns out to be, Goodie's bound to lose a lot of money."

"Okay, then maybe we should be looking for a motive like revenge. I'll bet Jay's alienated a lot of people in the business."

"I'll bet he has, too. In fact..." She paused, her pulse skipping a beat as she remembered what Royce had said earlier. There'd been so much going on, she'd forgotten all about it.

"What?" Nick prompted.

"Royce told me something earlier. A year or so back, Jay had an affair with Sarina Westlake."

That was enough to make Nick lean forward in his chair. "Really?"

"Uh-huh. And Jay dumped *her*. At this point, neither she nor Garth has any use for him."

"Then why on earth are they doing this film with him?"

Carly smiled wearily. "I asked Royce the same question. He said we're dealing with Hollywood types, and nobody can explain half the stuff they do."

"You're sure Royce knows what he's talking about?"

"He usually does. As far as I know, any gossip he told me last time we worked together was on the money."

"Then I think we've just zoomed in on our prime suspects. Our saboteur could be Garth or Sarina or, most likely, the two of them working together."

"You really think so? Don't forget they'd be doing damage to their own reputations."

"Maybe they figure it's worth it. And it would explain why they agreed to star in the film in the first place."

"Yes…yes, it would, wouldn't it." Carly began to feel better. This detective stuff wasn't nearly as hard as she'd imagined.

"Unless Goodie's the target," Nick said. "And it's not Jay at all."

The "better" feeling rapidly dissolved.

"Who would hate Goodie?" Nick pressed. "Aside from his soon to be ex-wife?"

"I don't know of anyone else," Carly said slowly. "But what *about* Barb?"

"Well, she probably *would* love to get revenge, especially if Royce was right and she isn't Ms. Stability. But I don't have the impression she's Ms. Stupid, either, so I doubt she'd try to hit him in the wallet."

"No?"

"Uh-uh. If Goodie got into divorce court and proved he'd just lost a bundle on this movie, it would likely reduce her settlement."

"Oh, right. That makes sense. So we're back to Sarina and Garth?"

Nick nodded. "We'll start with them, but as I said, we'll keep our eyes and ears open."

"And by starting with them, you mean...?"

"Let's not get into that until tomorrow, okay? I can't give you the entire detective crash course in one session." With that, he rose, sticking his hands in the pockets of his jeans.

Carly called the Marx brothers, and they all headed into the house. It hadn't cooled down much, but the dogs raced directly upstairs—each to his favorite spot.

"You'd better lock up," Nick suggested. "We've got a lot of strangers around."

"I always lock up at night anyway, but I guess now we'd better remember to do it during the day, too. Especially when there are two little boys who might want to take Crackers outside again." The mere thought made her shudder.

Once the main-floor lights were turned off, she

trudged up the stairs ahead of Nick, the heat increasing with every step.

"You think we should splurge on a couple of air conditioners?" he asked.

"I think we'd better not splurge on *anything* until we see how the shooting goes." And when it was finished, of course, Nick would be leaving, so he'd no longer care about the house being hot.

"Well, good night," she said, stopping outside her bedroom door.

"'Night," Nick said quietly. "Carly?" he added as she turned away.

She turned back, her heartbeat accelerating.

But instead of making the move she'd expected, he said, "I was thinking maybe I'd go with you in the morning. Thinking that Jay, Goodie and Barb might be a pretty terrible trio to cope with on your own."

"Well..." It was sweet of him to offer, and she very much wanted to say yes. But her brain was warning her that taking some time away from him would be far wiser. She had to figure out what was going on between them and...

Oh, why was she trying to kid herself? She knew *exactly* what was going on. She just needed time to decide for sure what she was going to do about it. Her resolve to do absolutely nothing seemed to be evaporating at a very rapid rate.

"No," she said at last. "It's nice of you to offer, but one of us might as well get to sleep in."

He shrugged. "I'm not a great one for sleeping in. Besides, now that it's occurred to them that there are wild animals out there, they'll probably want to take Gus's rifle along. And I'd rather it was me carrying it than Jay or Goodie."

"I'd rather it was you, too," she said, doing her best to ignore the imaginary voice that was whispering in her ear again.

This time, it was asking why she didn't tell Nick that Gus had taught her how to shoot years ago? And that she could easily carry the gun herself?

"Then it's settled," he said, giving her a smile so warm it melted something inside her. "I'll see you for breakfast?"

She nodded, but neither of them turned toward their doors. Her heart began beating rapidly again.

"Carly?"

"Yes?"

"You're awfully worried, aren't you?"

Not as awfully as she'd have been if he weren't here to help. But she couldn't say something like that unless she was sure she wanted him to—

"Would a hug help? Or is it too hot?"

Of *course* it was too hot, but she suddenly wanted a hug more than anything in the world. "I think it *might* help," she murmured.

He gave her another smile, then stepped closer and folded her into his arms.

His body felt as hard and leanly muscled against hers as she'd imagined it would, and there was a slight scent of the outdoors about him that she loved.

She also loved the way he lightly rested his chin on her head and simply held her. If she'd had a fever of 112 degrees she couldn't have been any hotter, but she didn't want him to ever take his arms away.

When he finally did, he stepped backward and simply stood looking at her. The message in his eyes was clear. He was leaving the next move up to her.

Forcing her gaze from his, she stared at his cowboy

DAWN STEWARDSON   107

boots and mentally recited the reasons she'd be crazy to get involved with him. But the feeling that it was inevitable had been growing. And if it was, did it make sense to put off the inevitable?

From the long-ago past, she could hear her mother saying, "Never rush into anything with a boy, Carly."

Nick wasn't a boy, though. He was a man. A man she was inordinately attracted to. But also a man who'd be walking out of her life before the summer was over.

"And do you *really* want to be left hurting?" the imaginary voice asked.

Taking a long, slow, breath, she made her decision.

CHAPTER SIX

When Push Comes to Shove

NICK SHIFTED Gus's rifle to his other hand and glanced at his watch, wondering how many more sites they'd have to look at. It was getting close to noon, and this scouting expedition had turned out to be even worse than he'd anticipated.

Of course it didn't help that he hadn't slept all night. But it had been so damn hot in his bedroom....

The thought trailed off as he looked at Carly. The heat hadn't been the only thing that had kept him awake. He hadn't been able to stop their good-night scene from replaying over and over in his mind.

When he'd held her, her wonderful wildflower scent had been positively intoxicating. And she'd felt so soft and warm and womanly that he'd wanted to make love with her more than he could remember ever wanting anything.

But he'd *known* she didn't want to get involved with him. So why had it felt like someone punching him in the heart when she gave him a final, quiet, "Good night, Nick," and walked into her bedroom alone?

One thing was certain. He sure didn't want to feel like that again. And if he had any future thoughts about more than a business relationship with her, he was going to stop them in their tracks.

Forcing his eyes from her, he looked over at Barb Hunt. She was the only one of the terrible trio who hadn't been getting on his nerves all morning, and it was making him wonder just how exaggerated those stories Royce had heard about her were. At the very least, she could behave appropriately when she wanted to.

On this outing, she'd simply kept her mouth shut and made notes whenever Jay had talked about what set decorating would be necessary for the sites he liked.

Jay and Goodie, on the other hand, had been grade A pains. Goodie was making an obvious point of refusing to even look at his wife, and Jay had asked Carly about a hundred times if she was sure the map *she'd* drawn for him was accurate. And despite being slathered from head to toe with calamine lotion, both men were constantly scratching and complaining about their mosquito bites. To top it off, it was a wonder Goodie hadn't dislocated his neck looking for wild bears behind every tree. Nick was dizzy just from watching.

"Okay," Jay said with another glance around the clearing. "I think this'll do it." He looked at Nick and Carly, adding, "When we get back to base, I'll send some people out to cut a road through."

"You'll keep the cutting to a minimum," Nick said.

Jay frowned at him, but said, "Of course." Turning to Barb, he added, "And if you spend the rest of the day pulling together what we'll need for tomorrow, we should be ready to roll."

"Thank heavens," Goodie muttered.

With Carly leading the way, the five of them trudged off through the woods again. This time, they eventually emerged from the forest on the far side of Attila's field.

Jonathan, the gangly friend of Dylan's who was taking the day bear watch, waved to them, and Jay said, "Oh, I almost forgot. I want to see the bear swim."

"Not now," Goodie objected. "It's lunchtime."

"You think Raffaello's going to shut down the kitchen before we get there?" Jay demanded. "I *told* him we'd be back for lunch."

"I'd like to see the bear swim, too," Barb put in.

While the three of them started toward the field, Nick quickly closed the gap between himself and Carly, trying to ignore his panicky feeling. If there was a command to make Attila swim, he didn't know it.

"Carly?" he said, falling in beside her.

"I know," she whispered. "There was nothing in the script about swimming, so I didn't bother getting into it with you. I figured you had enough to learn."

"But Jay said something yesterday about maybe wanting some swimming shots. So we should have—"

"Don't worry. I'll look after it."

Nick nodded, mightily relieved.

"I just hope Attila listens to me," she added, putting the boots to his sense of relief.

When they reached the gate, she unlocked it and reached for the pail full of trout sitting beside it.

"Dylan already fed him a ton of vegetables and stuff," Jonathan told her. "But he said the fish was dessert and that you'd probably want to give it to him yourself.''

Nick's stomach turned over. The raw chicken was bad enough, now there was raw fish, too.

"Is fish his favorite food?" Barb asked.

"Uh-uh. Raw chicken," Jonathan said. "You oughta see him gobble it down."

Carly pushed the gate open, then glanced at the terrible trio. "Why don't you walk around to the other side where you'll be close to the pond?"

"Okay, but you come with us," Jay told her.

"No, I'm going to handle Attila this time. I haven't been working with him enough lately."

Jay looked at Nick. "You work with the birds?"

"No, just the bear."

"Then you show me the swim bit, because I want to talk to Carly about the owls."

"Oh, we can do that later," she protested. "We—"

"I have other things to do later. I need to talk to you about them *now*."

She glanced at Nick. He shrugged uneasily. He'd started feeling a *little* confident around Attila, but damned little. And if he didn't have a clue what he was doing...

"All right," Carly told Jay. "You start walking and I'll catch up in a minute. There's something I have to tell Nick, and I don't want to forget."

She waited until the other three had headed off, then put down the pail and said, "Okay. Here's the signal to go into the water, and the verbal command is 'water.'"

He watched closely while she repeated the hand signal a couple of times, then tried it himself.

"Good," she said. "And to make him swim, you just gesture which way you want him to go and say 'swim.'"

"Okay. Show me the hand signal one more time."

"Carly, are you coming?" Jay screamed.

Attila growled loudly.

Jay clapped his hand over his mouth and rapidly nodded in their direction, silently assuring them he'd remembered the noise rule.

"A little late, wasn't it," Nick muttered. "I swear, if he starts screaming while I'm in that field working, I really *will* kill him."

Carly glanced uneasily at Gus's rifle, then reached for it. "I'd better look after this while you're in with Attila. And good luck, but I'm sure you won't need it. He loves the water." With that, Carly started after Jay, Barb and Goodie.

Nick watched her walk away, wishing to hell he'd had time to practice the "water" signal in front of the mirror, the way he had all the others.

Reminding himself he was a quick study, he headed into the field and closed the gate.

"What are you going to do?" Jonathan asked.

"Give him a swim." *I hope.*

"If he wants to swim, doesn't he just go into the pond on his own?"

Nick picked up the pail and started away without answering. The last thing he needed was a kid asking annoyingly logical questions.

"Hey, Attila," he said, stopping as he neared the bear.

Attila eyed the pail and made a loud, snuffling noise.

"No, you know the drill. Work first, treats second.'' He walked on over to the fence and put the pail down near where Carly was standing with the others.

Goodie wrinkled his nose at the fish. Carly gave Nick a reassuring smile that didn't reassure him in the least. It only made him wish that she was doing this instead of him. But since she wasn't, he walked back to where the bear was standing.

''We're going to go over to the pond now, boy. Attila, *come*.'' Giving the hand gesture, he started off, telling himself ''So far so good'' when the bear lumbered after him.

He reached the water's edge, then turned to Attila again. Just as he was about to try to get him into the water, Jay said, ''Can he walk in standing up?''

Nick's anxiety level began climbing fast. He had no idea what the answer was, or what commands to use if it was yes.

''Sure he can,'' Carly said. ''We just give him the command to stand up, then follow it with the command to go into the water.''

Thanking his lucky stars his partner was quick on the uptake, he focused on the bear once more. ''Attila, *two feet*.''

The bear grunted and stood up.

''Good boy.'' He mentally reviewed the hand signal Carly had shown him, then gave it, along with a firm ''water'' command.

Attila started forward. He seemed to be walking straight *at* Nick, but he told himself it was only his nervousness making him think that. And then Attila stopped right in front of him.

Before he could decide what to do, the bear gave

him a hard shove with his front feet and sent him
sprawling backward into the pond.

Nick simply sat there, stunned, soaked and absolutely terrified, with six hundred pounds of bear glaring down at him.

Jay and Goodie began to laugh.

"Oh, Nick," Carly said, "this *isn't* the time to be
fooling around."

He looked at her in disbelief, saw how pale her
face was, and felt more terrified yet.

"Nick is such a joker," she told Jay. "I think he
inherited that from his uncle Gus. He gave Attila the
"shove" hand signal instead of the "water" one. But
Jay doesn't care about that one, Nick."

"Hey, maybe I do," Jay managed through his
laughter. "That was funny as hell, so maybe I'll get
him to push one of the kids into a stream or something. But let's see him swim now."

"Sure. Attila, you listen to me," Carly snapped in
such a no-nonsense tone that Nick suddenly found
himself sitting at attention.

"Water," she ordered, giving a signal.

He was sure the one he'd given looked exactly like
it, but Attila didn't go over and try to shove at her
through the fence. He merely grunted, then walked
obediently into the pond—stopping just before he
stepped on Nick.

"Good boy. Now *swim.*" Carly gestured to the left,
and Attila gleefully heaved himself into the water,
sending up a tidal wave that soaked Nick all over
again.

SINCE JAY AND GOODIE had walked up to the house
with them, Jay still asking Carly questions about what

the owls could do, Nick had been forced to keep quiet. And that had only made him more angry when he'd already been mad as hell—not to mention sopping wet.

He hated being made to look like a fool every bit as much as he hated being maneuvered or manipulated. And he sure didn't intend to give that bear any more chances to make him a laughingstock.

"Okay," Jay said, lingering on the porch even though Goodie was clearly dying for lunch. "We can't start lighting the set until the sun's fully up, so let's say you get the bear there about ten."

"Fine," Carly said. "We'll see you in the morning."

The instant she closed the door, Nick said, "Attila obeyed you."

"Thank heavens, huh?"

"So now you can go back to working with him."

"What?"

"I said—"

"I heard what you said. But why are you saying it?"

"Because I'm not crazy. Although I must have been temporarily insane when I agreed to work with Attila."

"You've been doing just fine with him."

"Fine? I gave him a wrong hand signal and almost drowned."

"Nick, you hardly almost drowned. You just got wet. And you're dripping on the floor, so why don't you go and change."

"I'll go and change after we finish this discussion. I don't know enough to be working with that bear.

What if I mistakenly gave him the hand signal that tells him to kill his trainer?''

''Now you're being ridiculous. You *know* there's no such signal.''

''*How* do I know? You didn't tell me about the ''shove'' signal. And you didn't mention the ''swim'' command until it was almost too late. How do I know what else you didn't bother telling me?''

Carly put her hands on her hips, looking annoyed. But he was the one who'd ended up in the damn pond, so where did she get off?

''I told you I didn't bother with those commands because there was nothing about swimming in the script,'' she said, enunciating precisely.

''Fine. You had your reasons. And I've got a reason to stop working with Attila. I don't like doing it. So now that he's listening to you again—''

''Nick, he listened to me *once*. When I was telling him to swim, which he loves doing. So the fact that he did one thing doesn't mean he's suddenly going to start obeying me all the time.''

''Maybe he will.''

''And maybe he won't.''

''Well, let's just see.'' Nick stomped over to the cupboard and took out a couple of big bags of marshmallows—which Carly had said Attila loved—then he headed for the door.

''Coming?'' he asked, opening it.

The Marx brothers eyed him eagerly. They were clearly getting tired of being kept in protective custody.

''Nick, you're soaking wet,'' Carly said.

''Yes, you already mentioned that. But I'm hardly going to catch pneumonia when it's hot as hell out there, so let's go back down to the field and see how Attila feels about doing a few other things you tell him."

"Do you have any idea how annoying you can be?"

"Yes. As annoying as Gus. Come on, guys," he added to the dogs. "You can come, too."

Without another word, Carly followed him out of the house and back down to Attila's field.

"You didn't change," Jonathan said.

"No," Nick replied. "I figured my clothes would fit better if I let them dry on my body."

"Oh, yeah, cool. My sister always does that with new jeans."

Carly unlocked the gate, asked Jonathan to keep an eye on the dogs, then went into the field with Nick. Attila spotted the marshmallows and came lumbering over.

"Here." Nick handed her one of the bags. "We don't want him to think I'm the only one who's got treats."

Carly muttered something under her breath. Nick ignored her.

"All right," she said. "I'm going to see if he'll run for me."

"But you told me that's the hardest thing to make him do."

"It is. It's also something he has to do in the scene they'll be shooting tomorrow."

"But—"

"What do you think, Nick?" she snapped. "That I'm going to cheat and give him the wrong command or something?"

"Of course not. I know what the signal to run looks

like. We were practicing it with him yesterday, remember?''

"Yes. And I also remember that he was running for you."

"Only now and then."

"Well, I'll bet now and then is better than he's going to do for me." She looked at the bear and firmly said, "Attila, *run.*"

Nick watched her hand carefully, and she *did* give the broad run signal she'd taught him.

Attila sat down and stared at the marshmallows she was holding.

"Bad bear. *Stand up.*"

Attila stood, but reluctantly.

"Good boy. Now I want you to *run,*" she said, giving him the signal again.

This time he yawned.

"All right, Nick," she said, stepping back. "You have a try."

"Attila," he said, waving his hand through the air, *"run."*

"Woof," Attila said.

"See? He didn't listen to me a damn bit better than he did to you."

"Maybe that's because you sounded so half-hearted. Besides, I had *two* shots at it."

Nick looked back at the bear. "You're a bad boy, Attila. Now let's try again. *Run.*"

Attila eyed the marshmallows for half a second, then broke into a loping run.

Carly smiled.

Nick swore to himself.

Attila kept loping along for a minute, then circled around and ran back for his treats.

THE GROCERIES HAD BEEN delivered while they were out scouting locations, and with Nick upstairs changing into dry clothes, Carly rapidly began making lunch.

Before calling in the order yesterday, she'd asked him what his favorite foods were and added some of them to her list. At the moment, she was glad she had.

When he'd started talking about not working with Attila anymore, she'd almost had a stroke on the spot. If he decided he'd had enough and packed his bag, she'd really be up the creek, so she was going to do anything she could to make him a happy camper.

Well, not quite *anything,* she mentally corrected herself. She'd been giving things a lot of thought, and her resolve was back to full strength. Even though walking away from him after that hug last night was one of the hardest things she'd ever done, she *had* done it. Which proved he wasn't completely irresistible. She just had to keep reminding herself of that and she'd be fine around him.

Lunch ready, she fed the cats and the Marx brothers. Just as she was filling the last dog-food bowl, she heard Nick's footsteps on the stairs. A moment later Crackers greeted him.

"Hi, Crackers," he said as she glanced over.

He'd changed into his cowboy boots, dry jeans and another of his cling-to-every-muscle T-shirts. This one was the same warm shade of gray as his eyes. She had trouble forcing her gaze from him, which warned her that maybe she wouldn't be exactly fine around him. But she *would* cope.

"Pastrami on rye," she said, gesturing toward the

sandwiches. "With a side of dill pickles and black olives."

When he smiled, she felt decidedly relieved. He'd apparently left his anger upstairs with his wet clothes.

"Add a beer to that and I'll love you forever."

His words made her heart skip a beat. Quickly, she turned to get a beer from the fridge, telling herself that words were all they were.

"Want to eat on the porch?" she suggested. It was somehow easier to ignore all those lean muscles when the two of them weren't in the confines of a room.

"Sure. The dogs would probably enjoy some more fresh air."

"No, I'll bet they'd rather stay here and finish their lunch. They know Crackers likes their kibble, and they hate finding feathers in it."

Following Nick out of the house, she decided that as soon as they were done with lunch she'd remind him he'd promised to give her the rest of his crash course in detecting. But just as she was taking the last bite of her sandwich, he said, "Looks like we've got company."

She glanced down the drive and saw Royce headed in the direction of the house, the two boys tagging along after him.

"Maybe I'd better go and put Crackers in his cage," she said anxiously.

"No, we won't let the kids out of our sight this time."

When she looked along the drive at Royce again, an idea popped into her head. "Nick?" She glanced back at him. "We're going to have to try talking to our prime suspects, right? I mean, that's a logical move, isn't it? To see if we can get any clues?"

He nodded. "It's a logical move, all right, but after that run-in I had with Garth Richards last night I'm hardly going to be his favorite person. Which probably means I'm not Sarina's, either."

"Well, *I* didn't put Garth in his place. So why don't I get Royce to introduce me to them? See where that gets us?"

"Ahh...yeah. Good thinking."

She wondered why, if it was good thinking, he didn't look very happy about it. But there wasn't much time to wonder before Royce and the boys reached the porch.

"The kids have been getting a little stir-crazy in the camp," he told them. "So they were wondering if they could ride the ponies. They said it's something they haven't done before."

"Except for, like, at birthday parties," Kyle said.

"I once did a commercial where I rode a pony," Brock told them. "But when I was just a kid. And I mostly just sat on it."

"Well..." Carly said.

"I wouldn't mind keeping an eye on them," Royce offered.

"Or *you* could," Kyle suggested, eyeing Nick's well-worn cowboy boots. "You could help us with the ponies 'cuz you're a real cowboy, aren't you?"

"No, he's not," Brock said. "He's a bear trainer."

"Well, actually, I *am* from out West," Nick said.

"See, I told you." Kyle rabbit-punched Brock's arm. "When we were in the house, I saw a cowboy hat hangin' in there."

"Nick?" Carly murmured, leaning closer so only he would hear. "You remember how to saddle a horse?"

"Of course."

"Then this is perfect," she whispered. "You watch the kids, and I'll get Royce to introduce me to Sarina and Garth."

Nick didn't look thrilled about baby-sitting, so before he could object, she turned to Royce and said, "Why don't we leave the cowboy in charge of Kyle and Brock while you give me a tour of the camp? I really haven't seen much of it."

"That all right with you boys?" Royce asked.

"Sure," they said in unison.

"Can you rope cows and stuff?" Kyle asked Nick.

"Well, we don't have any cows here, but if we did…"

"You could rope the bear," Brock was suggesting as Carly and Royce started down the drive.

"I'd better admit I want more than just a tour of the camp," she said as they walked.

"Oh?"

"Uh-huh. My sister's a huge Garth Richards fan. And she and my parents will be coming here for a few days while you're filming. So I thought it would be nice if I met Garth before they arrived and could introduce Lisa to him."

"Well, the way Garth is, I wouldn't want to go knocking on their trailer door. We could wander by the kitchen, though. He and Sarina were still having lunch when I left."

Carly nodded, wondering if Chef Raffaello had recovered from Rocky's visit. When she and Nick had left with the coon last night, Raffaello had been starting to clean up his kitchen and muttering something about raccoon stew.

He didn't look *quite* so surly today, she decided as

they reached the kitchen. He was standing behind the buffet table outside the trailer and actually gave her a curt nod.

"They've left," Royce told her, surveying the tables. "Raffaello?" he added. "Did you notice if Sarina and Garth went back to their trailer after lunch?"

"No, they went to feed the bear."

"What?" Carly said, her heart suddenly hammering.

"Yeah. Garth asked me for some meat and they took off with it. I just hope Goodie doesn't find out I gave away a roast or he'll kill me.

"But Garth's a method actor." The chef paused, rolling his eyes to give them his opinion of that. "And he said the only way he could get himself in tune with the bear's emotional makeup was to spend some time with it."

"Carly?" Royce said as she turned and started to run.

"What's wrong?" he called after her.

But she couldn't stop to explain. Not when their prime suspects might be in the process of poisoning Attila.

CHAPTER SEVEN

Ride 'em, Cowboys

HALFWAY DOWN THE HILL to Attila's field, Carly slowed to a fast walk and told herself everything was all right. Attila was puddling around at the edge of his pond, while Jonathan was talking to Sarina and Garth.

At least, Carly assumed the woman was Sarina—she was so covered up it was hard to be sure. Apparently she took the threat of UV rays very seriously, because she was wearing a huge floppy hat, big sunglasses and a flowing caftan.

"Carly, what on earth's going on?"

She hadn't realized Royce had come after her, but he was suddenly beside her. So what did she tell him?

Nick had said not to tell *anyone* there was a saboteur on the loose, but surely they could trust someone she'd known for years. And even though Royce was a bit of a gossip, she knew he could keep a secret if he wanted to.

"Are you just going to leave me in the dark?" he pressed.

Since she couldn't think of an even half-plausible lie, she said, "If I tell you, it absolutely, positively can't go any further."

"All right," he agreed slowly.

"This movie isn't jinxed. Somebody's deliberately trying to sabotage it."

"Get out."

"It's true. Nick and I have proof. And I've been worried that the saboteur might try to hurt one of the animals, so when Raffaello said that Garth was going to feed Attila…"

"You didn't really think Garth would… Oh, come on, there's no way Sarina would go along with hurting an animal. But you figure *they're* the ones trying to screw up the filming?"

They were getting too close to the field to continue the conversation, so she said, "I'll fill you in later, okay?"

When Jonathan glanced over and spotted her, she saw that he was managing to look starstruck, worried and relieved all at the same time.

"Carly?" he said. "Mr. Richards and Ms. Westlake wanted to give Attila a treat, but I told them I wasn't supposed to let anyone get within ten feet of the fence and that nobody who wasn't working for you was to feed him anything. Did I do right?"

"You did exactly what you were supposed to," she said, her words making the worry disappear from his face.

"We haven't *officially* met," she added, turning to Garth and Sarina and putting on her best smile.

Royce jumped in with, "This is Carly Dumont. She owns half of Wild Action."

Sarina took off her sunglasses and produced a smile of her own—one that Carly figured would make it into Jonathan's dreams tonight. "Yes, of course. We know who Carly is. And it's nice to *officially* meet you."

"*Very* nice," Garth said. "And you're obviously the lady who can help me. I want to study your bear for a bit—kind of get under his skin, figuratively speaking. And I just assumed giving him a treat would be all right."

"Well, I'm afraid we feed Attila a very strict diet," she said, even though it was an outrageous lie.

When Jonathan looked at her strangely, she gave a little shake of her head, warning him not to say anything.

"That means you should take the roast back to the chef, dear," Sarina said.

"Oh, yes, I suppose."

"Too bad you didn't bring raw chicken," Jonathan said. "Carly might have let you feed him that 'cuz it's his favorite treat."

She barely heard Jonathan's words. She was too busy mentally replaying the exchange between Garth and Sarina.

They were going to take the roast back to the chef. So if they *were* the saboteurs, at least it didn't look as if they'd be extending their efforts to include the animals.

Surely if they'd poisoned the meat, they'd never let it be served to people. But she still intended to keep a careful watch on the animals until she and Nick figured out for sure who was behind all the trouble.

Trying to force away the thought that they might not be able to, she glanced at Garth—and discovered he was looking expectantly at Royce. Then Royce said, "I'll take it back for you," and she realized Garth felt that returning the roast himself was beneath him.

"Why, thanks. That would be very nice of you."

He handed Royce the plastic bag he'd been holding, then focused on Carly. "What's that *thing* for?" he asked, pointing at the cave.

"For Attila to hibernate in."

"Really? He hibernates even though he's not living in the wild?"

"Well, when it's winter in the wild, it's winter in his field, too."

"And does he use it for anything else?" Sarina asked.

"Oh, he sometimes naps in it on hot days. It's relatively cool inside."

"Fascinating," Garth said. "This is so fascinating. Carly, could I possibly impose on you to stay here with Sarina and me for a while? So I can ask you more questions?"

"Sure. I'd be happy to help out." And, of course, it would give her a chance to ask a few questions of her own. She just wished she'd had time to talk to Nick about exactly what she should ask.

As Royce started back up the hill, she said, "I didn't realize either of you were actually in any scenes with the bear." They certainly hadn't been in *her* copy of the script.

"Oh, we're not," Garth said. "Only the children are. But I like to immerse myself in the whole gestalt of any movie I star in. It's the way I develop the character I'm playing."

"Yes, someone told me you were a method actor. It made me wonder why you'd want to work with a director like Jay. One who's into improvisation, I mean."

"This film was a chance for us to work together,"

Sarina said before Garth could reply. "It's never easy to find scripts with good roles for both of us."

"Ahh. And a director who improvises has no problem with method actors?"

"We all have to make compromises in this business," Sarina said. "Sometimes you even agree to work with people you detest because the part is right. And in this case, for Jay, it was worth compromising to get an actor of Garth's caliber."

When she smiled adoringly at her husband, Carly smiled, too. But she already had a sinking feeling that hanging around while Garth "developed his character" would prove nothing but a waste of time.

CARLY EVENTUALLY ESCAPED from Garth Richards's questioning and got back to the house—hot, depressed about her failure to learn anything from the stars and dying for a shower.

But when she neared the top of the stairs she could hear the shower was occupied. The water was running, and above its gurgle Nick was singing—a cowboy song, no less. Being put in charge of the pony rides had apparently taken him back to his childhood summers on that ranch.

She stood listening to him, her mood improving slightly. Attila wasn't the only one who responded to Nick's deep voice. And he even sang on key.

When he stopped and turned off the water, she hurried into her own room. If she looked the way she felt, she didn't want him seeing her. Oh, she knew she shouldn't give a darn about how she looked to her *business* partner. But she couldn't help the fact that she did.

After finding some clean underwear, shorts and a

top, she waited until he'd had time to get out of the bathroom. But she didn't wait *quite* long enough.

She opened her door when he was only halfway down the hall to his room—and only half dressed.

"Holy smokes!" he said, stopping in his tracks. "Don't you know better than to sneak up on people?"

"I wasn't sneaking up," she protested, trying not to stare at his bare chest. But those hard muscles were impossible to ignore. And he had the sexiest dark chest hair—not too much or too little, but just right.

She made herself look down, which turned out to be a bad move. He hadn't yet gotten around to zipping his jeans. When she forced her gaze all the way to the floor, she discovered that even his bare feet were sexy.

"You just get back from your afternoon with *Royce?*"

She met his gaze again, and it suddenly dawned on her that he was jealous. The realization started her blood racing. She had absolutely no romantic interest in Royce Chalmers, but Nick couldn't know that. And if he was jealous, it meant...

Oh, rats, it was too darn hot up here to think *what* it meant. Except that maybe she'd better wait until later to tell him she'd confided in Royce about the sabotage.

"You were gone for hours, you know."

"Yes, I know. But I wasn't with Royce much of the time. I...oh, I've got to tell you what happened, but can it wait until after I have a shower?"

Nick grinned. "Too bad you weren't ten minutes earlier. We could have saved on water."

"Very funny," she said, marching past him and

doing her best to look cool. But it was awfully hard to manage when the thought of showering with him had started her insides positively steaming.

As Carly closed the bathroom door, Nick mentally kicked himself. What the hell was the matter with him? The woman wasn't interested. At least, if she was, she was showing no intention of doing anything about it. So why the hell was he making juvenile insinuations?

He'd never acted like a lovesick adolescent around any other woman. At least, not since he'd actually *been* a lovesick adolescent. So why was he doing it with Carly? Maybe he *did* find her attractive, but...

"Hell," he muttered. "Find her attractive?" Her queen-of-understatement routine must have rubbed off on him. The truth was that, somewhere along the way, he'd developed an almost constant craving for her.

Regardless of that, he was damn well going to stop being an idiot around her. Tugging on a T-shirt, he headed downstairs—where there wouldn't be the sound of the shower to make him imagine her naked.

"Treat!" Crackers demanded the moment he walked into the kitchen.

He got some sunflower seeds from the cupboard and put them in a bowl. Then, since either Harpo or Groucho or Chico—Zeppo was the only one he had a positive ID on—was panting a mile a minute, he put down fresh water.

By the time he got around to getting the jug of iced tea and a beer out of the fridge, Carly had appeared.

Her hair was wet and hanging loose. It would have given her that innocent look she sometimes had except for the fact she was wearing another pair of shorts that would stop traffic and a sleeveless shirt he hoped she'd button a little higher if old Royce showed up again.

That was something else that never happened to him with other women. He wasn't the jealous type, but his blood boiled every time he saw the way Royce looked at her.

She smiled, and he erased all thoughts of the cameraman from his mind.

"I could use about a dozen ice cubes in that tea," she said.

He dug a couple out from the freezer, then followed her onto the porch. The Marx brothers immediately found shady spots on the lawn and got busy sleeping. Dogs, he'd discovered, were big sleepers.

"So?" he said after taking a swig of beer. "Did you meet Sarina and Garth?"

"Oh, Nick, I not only met them, I spent the entire afternoon with them. But it did us no good at all."

He listened as she proceeded to tell him the whole story.

"And after all that time," she concluded, "I have no more idea whether they're really our saboteurs than I did last night. It was like I got handed an opportunity on a platter and completely blew it."

"No, you didn't blow it. In fact, it sounds as if you did everything right. When you thought Attila might be in danger, you went straight to check on him. And when you had the chance to spend time with Garth and Sarina, you grabbed it."

"But I didn't learn anything."

"Well, you could hardly expect they'd say, 'You know, we hate Jay so much that we're trying to ruin this movie.'"

"No, of course not. But when I asked them leading questions, I couldn't tell whether their answers were the truth or lies."

"Hey, they're actors. They make their living by being convincing liars. So if it *is* them..."

"Yes?"

He shook his head. "It makes things a little tricky, that's all."

"So what do we do?"

"Wait and watch. And if there are any more incidents, we try to find out who was behind them."

"You think there might *not* be any more?"

"It's possible." He finished off his beer, then sat watching her while she mulled that over.

She didn't look convinced there was even a chance, which probably meant her detective instincts were pretty good. Unless their saboteur decided he was at risk of getting caught, why would he stop?

"There's something else I have to tell you," she said at last. "I told Royce that the 'jinx' was actually someone trying to sabotage the movie. And that Sarina and Garth are our prime suspects."

"I thought we weren't going to tell anyone," Nick said, trying to keep his annoyance from showing. He didn't like the fact that he was jealous of Royce, and he sure as hell didn't want Carly to realize he was.

"Well, when I got so upset about the roast, he knew something was up. And when he asked me what, I couldn't think of any way to avoid telling him.

"But what about *your* afternoon?" she added quickly. "What did you do after the boys had their pony ride?"

"Nothing. Just came back and had my shower."

"No, I mean, they couldn't have been riding for all that time, so..."

"Yeah, they were. They were having a ball, and I hadn't seen you come back to the house, so I just let them keep at it. We went down to the camp, and their mothers took pictures of them on the ponies. Then I let them ride along the perimeter of the woods."

He paused, noticing Carly's worried expression. "What? I didn't let them gallop the ponies or anything. Hell, they could hardly stay in the saddles, let alone go faster than a walk."

"No, I knew you'd make sure the ponies were fine. But what about Kyle and Brock? How did they seem when they dismounted?"

"Oh, a little weak in the knees, but that never lasts. I could tell they're really into the acting stuff, though. When they headed back to the camp, they were trying to outdo each other walking bowlegged."

"Nick, if you let them stay on those ponies the entire afternoon, there wasn't any *trying* involved. They'd practically never ridden before and... Oh, Lord, you know what's going to happen, don't you? Tomorrow, when Jay wants to shoot them running from Attila, they're going to be so stiff and sore they'll barely be able to walk."

"Oh, come on, don't you think you're exaggerating? More than a little? It's not as if Paint and Brush are big workhorses. They're just little ponies."

"Yes, but in case you didn't notice, Kyle and Brock are just little boys."

"DID YOU HEAR ALL the activity in the camp this morning?" Carly asked over breakfast. "I mean, how early people were up and around?"

"Yeah," Nick said between bites of toast.

"They were serious about starting to set up at dawn."

When he merely nodded, she poured herself more coffee, then topped up his mug without bothering to ask whether or not he wanted a refill. Crackers was being more talkative than Nick, and since her questions were barely getting grunts in reply, it didn't seem worth the effort of speaking.

She looked across the table and let her eyes linger on her business partner, certain there was no risk he'd catch her watching him this time. Not when he'd been avoiding eye contact since the moment he'd walked into the kitchen.

Yesterday, she'd never dreamed he'd still be upset with her this morning, but he obviously was. And she was certain he'd slept late solely to avoid her. The man really did not take well to criticism. And it had hardly even *been* criticism. She'd merely pointed out that he'd made an error in judgment by letting the boys ride for so long. It wasn't as if she'd accused him of being a deranged killer or something.

Nevertheless, it had been enough to make him decide he'd rather go for a walk than continue sitting on the porch with her. And when he'd come back to the house, it had only been to tell her that some crew member he'd been talking to had invited him to have dinner at the camp.

That was the last she'd seen of him. When he hadn't been back by midnight, she'd simply gone to bed.

Of course, she hadn't been able to fall asleep until she'd heard him come in. And after that, she'd still lain awake forever, unable to stop thinking about his jealousy of Royce. Finally she'd told herself that, given their situation, whatever his jealousy said about his feelings toward her was irrelevant. But even then, she'd found it hard to get to sleep.

From here on in, she was going to have to do a lot more sleeping and a lot less lying awake thinking about Nick Montgomery. If she didn't, she'd be a zombie long before he went back to Edmonton.

He glanced at his watch, then said, "Okay, let's get this show on the road. Otherwise, by the time we feed Attila, we'll be late."

"We don't have to feed him. I asked Dylan to come a bit early this morning and give him breakfast first thing. And I've already packed a cooler full of treats in case we need them to make him run. So all there's left to do is take him to the shoot site—just put him on his chain and go."

"Ahh. And once he's out of his field, if he wants to head in one direction and we want to go in another, who wins?"

She gave him a look that said she didn't find the question amusing. "He's a *trained* bear, remember? So he'd walk nicely even if he wasn't on a chain. But Gus felt that when we were on a job with him we should always use one—to make the cast and crew feel safer."

"Because nobody would ever realize that walking a six-hundred-pound bear on a chain is like walking a rottweiler on a piece of string?"

Carly pushed herself away from the table, thinking she'd rather Nick had stuck to his grunts than switched into his dry sense of humor mode. She was darned worried about whether or not Attila was going to perform well this morning, and what Nick considered witty was doing nothing to alleviate her anxiety.

"Bye-bye," Crackers said when she took Attila's collar and chain off the peg.

"Bye-bye, Crackers. You talk to the Marx brothers while we're gone."

Leaving the dogs sulking because they couldn't come along, she and Nick headed down to Attila's field, where Jonathan was just arriving to take over from the night-shift boy.

After chatting with them for a minute, she and Nick went into the field. When she put Attila's collar and chain on him, Nick was positively smirking. She didn't say a word about it, though, because at least his mood seemed to have improved. And the last thing she wanted to do was de-improve it again just before he had to work with Attila.

The road Jay's people had cut through the woods was wide enough that she and Nick could walk side by side. And as she'd predicted, Attila ambled along behind them like a perfect lamb. It was only when they were nearing the shoot site that he started to get a little frisky.

"Do we have a problem?" Nick asked anxiously.

"No, he always gets excited when he realizes he'll be working in front of a camera. He likes to be the center of attention."

One of the assistant cameramen wandered out of the clearing and nodded to them. "You're a little early. They're still lighting the bear's stand-in, but it shouldn't take much longer."

A few more steps and most of the site became visible through the trees. There were klieg lights set up all around the perimeter, portable generators to provide power, three cameras on large dollies and a small horde of crew members—most of whom were near Chef Raffaello's snack table, drinking coffee.

"Those people all get paid for standing around doing nothing?" Nick said.

"That's the way shoots work. It's always hurry up and wait."

Attila made a funny little snorting noise, stopped walking and raised up on his hind legs.

"Why's he doing that?" Nick asked.

"He just wants a better look."

"You're sure he's not thinking about misbehaving? I mean, what if he decides to take a run at someone or something?"

"Nick, he's never done anything like that. Besides, bears don't rear up when they're going to attack. They lower their heads and flatten their ears back."

"Well, even so, maybe you'd better give *me* the chain, just in case."

She handed it over, congratulating herself on keeping quiet again. But Nick's playing macho man was awfully silly. He knew as well as she did that, regardless of who was holding the chain, if Attila decided to take off, he'd be gone. Not that he ever would.

He dropped back down onto all fours, and before she realized anything was wrong he gave such a threatening snort that she jumped. Then, in a flash, he lowered his head, flattened his ears, and charged toward the clearing—yanking Nick completely off his feet and dragging him a few yards before he let go of the chain.

"Attila, *stop!*" she shouted, racing after him in utter horror.

By the time she reached the clearing, it was in pandemonium. Some of the crew were running for their lives, others were trying to climb trees. And Attila was attacking some sort of big furry monster at the far end of the clearing.

"Attila, *off!*" she shouted.

"Get him under control!" Jay was screaming. "Get him under control!"

Her heart in her throat, she slowly and cautiously crossed the clearing. Attila had totally flattened his victim, and when she realized it wasn't anything alive—only some bearskins and pieces of lumber— she offered up a prayer of thanks.

Now that all the pieces were lying motionless, Attila simply poked at the skins a few times with his snout, then turned and looked at her.

"Okay, boy," she murmured. "It's okay. *Come.*"

As gentle as a lamb again, he walked over to her. "Good boy." She stroked his nose. "Good boy. *Sit.*"

"What the hell was that about?" Nick whispered, materializing beside her.

"Oh, Lord, you're not hurt, are you?"

"No, but both Jay and Goodie look apoplectic. What the hell went wrong?"

"That was the problem." She waved her hand toward the things on the ground. "Those bearskins. It doesn't matter how well they're cured. There's always some scent of the bear left. So Attila smelled it and thought it was real."

"And instinctively attacked it."

She nodded. "When they were live bears, they must have been males."

"Dammit," Nick muttered. "All that worrying about him not running on command when what we *should* have been worrying about was him not stopping on command.''

He looked over to where Jay was cringing behind a tree and demanded, ''What the hell *was* this pile of rubble?''

''Our stand-in for Attila,'' the director said shakily.

''Well, why didn't you tell us you were planning on using bearskins? He thought they were a live bear. So, look, we're going to take him into the woods, where he can't see what's going on, and you have someone get those things the hell away from here.''

Nick reached down to where the end of the chain was lying and picked it up—which Carly realized would have struck her as funny under different circumstances. After all, everyone on the site had just seen how effective it was.

But as things stood, she felt a whole lot more like crying than laughing.

''You just wait a minute,'' Jay said from behind the cover of his tree. ''This is impossible. I'm not working with a killer bear.''

''He's *not* a killer,'' she protested, growing closer to tears by the second. ''If you hadn't used those stupid bearskins, he'd have been just fine.''

''I don't care. I'm not working with him.''

''You have to,'' Goodie said.

For a moment, Carly couldn't see him. Then she spotted his head sticking up from behind a rock.

''I *don't* have to,'' Jay snapped.

''Oh, yes, you do. In the first place, we've got a contract with these people. And in the second place, we can't waste time finding another bear and another place to shoot. Not unless you want to bankrupt me.''

''We'll use hot wires,'' Carly said.

"What?" Goodie demanded.

"Electric wires, like the ones they use around cattle pastures. We stretch them along stakes between Attila and the crew. Then you spray-paint them to blend in with the background. If Attila starts moving toward them, someone activates the current."

"If he moves as fast as he did last time, that some-one would have to have damn quick reactions," Jay muttered.

"Never mind about that," Goodie snapped. "Why the hell didn't you mention these wires before?" he asked Carly. "Why aren't they already in place?"

"Goodie, we only have them because some insur-ance policies require them. But they..." She'd been going to say they weren't really necessary, then thought better of it. At this point, everyone except her had to believe they were.

"Have you got green and brown spray paint on the set?" Jay asked Barb.

"Uh-huh. I had to spray some patches of grass and tree trunks."

"Well, how long will it take to get these wires set up?" Goodie asked. "How much more time are we going to waste?"

"It won't take long," Carly assured him. "Nick and I should stay with Attila and get him completely calmed down. But if you send somebody to find Dy-lan—the blond kid with the ponytail who works for us—he knows where they are. Once he brings them out here, we can get them in place pretty fast."

"Fast enough that we can start shooting after lunch?" Jay demanded.

She nodded. "Oh, and Dylan will need a hand, because he should bring a long length of heavier chain, too—twenty feet or so. I imagine people would feel safer if we chain Attila to a tree between takes.''

"Well..." Jay said.

"Do it," Goodie told him.

"Nick?" Carly said. "Let's get Attila out of here."

"Attila, *come*," he ordered, starting for the edge of the clearing.

She followed along, and they walked through the woods for a few minutes, finally stopping beside a narrow stream. After Attila had a drink, Nick looped the end of the chain around a huge log and sat down on its far end.

Carly joined him, still fighting back tears, while Attila happily began digging under the log for grubs.

"Great beginning, eh?" Nick said.

That did it. The tears started streaming down her face.

"Hey," he said quietly. "Hey, we'll redeem ourselves. We'll give Jay everything he wants and he'll forget all about this."

"But it would never have happened if Gus was here," she managed through her tears. "I should have thought to ask what they were using as a stand-in."

"You *did* ask. I remember. But Jay brushed the question aside."

"Well Gus wouldn't have let him. Gus would have made sure he knew exactly what was what. Nick, I'm not good enough to run Wild Action without him. Even if we get through this film, once you've gone back to Edmonton..." Her throat grew too full of tears to go on.

"Carly..." He edged nearer and tentatively put his arm around her. "It's going to be okay," he murmured. "We'll work things out, you'll see."

It would be so wonderful to believe him that she almost did. "You really think we can?" she whispered.

"Sure, we'll make it work." He shifted a little so he was looking into her eyes, then he put his other arm around her and drew her close.

She melted against him, breathing in his clean male scent. When a spark began to glow in her chest and a river of warmth flowed through her, she knew the way she was feeling was dangerous as all get out. But she didn't care. At the moment, she wanted Nick to hold her like this forever.

His chest was reassuringly solid, and his arms felt so strong around her that he made her feel he could protect her from all the evils of the world just by holding her tight.

"Know what?" he whispered against her ear.

The warmth of his breath fanned the growing ache of passion within her. "What?" she whispered back.

"From here on, things can only get better."

That actually made her smile. "Oh, Nick," she murmured. "Sometimes I really do like your sense of humor."

He drew back and looked at her. "Only sometimes?"

"Well..." The way he was gazing at her, with an ocean of warmth in his eyes, she doubted she could say another word. Not even if she could think of one.

Then he leaned closer and kissed her, rendering her unable to think at all. His kiss was warm and soft, but not too soft. And when he slowly traced her bottom lip with his tongue, it sent a hot rush of longing through her.

Pulling her closer still, he deepened the kiss. He

tasted of coffee and desire, and foolhardy as it would be, she desperately wanted to make love with him.

His body fit perfectly against hers. He kissed like the man of her dreams. And she'd fallen in love with him without even being aware it was happening.

When that last thought fully registered, she stiffened in his arms. As conscious as she'd been of her physical attraction to him, the realization that she'd fallen in love with him had come like a bolt from the blue.

"What?" he murmured against her lips. "What's wrong?"

"Everything!" an imaginary voice whispered fiercely.

Then Nick drew her lips to his again, and she closed her ears to the voice.

CHAPTER EIGHT

Between a Rock and a Hard Place

NICK WAS DOING HIS BEST to keep his mind on stringing the hot wire with Dylan, but his best wasn't nearly good enough.

Every two seconds his gaze strayed over to the edge of the clearing to where Carly was sitting with Attila. She'd said he'd be upset if someone didn't keep him company while he was on that chain, and there certainly hadn't been any volunteers among the crew.

He let himself watch her for a minute, thinking how incredible it had felt to kiss her. He'd never had such earth-shattering kisses in his entire life. They were just... Hell, there weren't words to describe the way she'd made him feel. Not any words he knew, at least. And he was positively aching to get back to the privacy of the house and take her in his arms again.

Then Jay walked into the picture and spoiled it—even though he was staying far enough away from Carly that he was beyond the reach of Attila's chain.

When the two of them started talking, Nick glanced at his watch. It had taken the fellow who'd gone looking for Dylan a hell of a long time to find him, which meant that these wires wouldn't be completely strung and painted until far later than Jay had been hoping.

But daylight lasted forever in July, so with any luck they'd still be able to shoot a fair bit of footage.

He forced his attention back to stringing the wire, hoping Jay wouldn't insist they work *too* late. The sooner the shooting was done, the sooner he'd be alone with Carly.

"Hey, Nick," a child said from behind him.

He glanced around to find Kyle and Brock eyeing him. They hadn't gotten to the site in time to see the earlier excitement with Attila—which was probably just as well. And after that, Jay had sent word that they should stay put in the camp until somebody came to get them.

"How are you guys today?" he asked, almost afraid to hear the answer.

They exchanged uneasy glances, then shrugged. "We're real stiff," Kyle whispered. "And Jay's gonna want us to run. And my mom said he's gonna freak out if we look stiff on camera."

"You figure you will?" Nick asked unhappily. If they did, there was absolutely no doubt whom Jay would blame.

"I ache all over," Brock said.

"Well, we're getting started so late that maybe Jay will only shoot Attila running today." If Attila co-operated, of course, which was a mighty big "if."

Kyle shook his head. "That's not the way it works. They shoot a sequence of us running, then a sequence of Attila running over the same ground."

"Or maybe they shoot Attila first," Brock put in.

"Maybe. But we all gotta do it at kinda the same time. So the light and shadows and all that stuff will be the same when they edit."

"The word's *continuity*," Brock added.

Nick muttered a few X-rated phrases beneath his breath. Carly had explained about the separate takes, but he hadn't realized they had to be done at virtually the same time. And since they did, there wasn't a chance of Jay's simply not getting to the boys today.

"Why don't you wander around for a bit," he suggested. "Maybe that'll loosen you up."

"We can't," Brock said. "We gotta go get our makeup done." When they started limping over to where their mothers were standing with the makeup woman, Nick glanced at Jay, hoping he wasn't watching them.

He wasn't. But it was only a matter of time before he noticed his ten-year-olds were walking like arthritic old men.

"That should about do it," Dylan said. "Just attach your end to that last stake and it's a wrap," he added, grinning at his movie terminology.

Nick secured the end of the wire, then looked around for Jay—who'd finished talking with Carly and was inspecting a big rock. Reluctantly, Nick called that they were ready for the paint.

While Barb and a couple of helpers hurried over with spray cans, Nick joined Carly and Attila, wishing his nerves weren't so on edge. But if Attila wouldn't run, or the boys couldn't...

"You'll do fine," Carly murmured, giving him such a warm smile that he wanted to kiss her on the spot.

Instead, he stood rubbing Attila behind the ear and hoping to hell she was right.

"Nick?" Jay said, coming toward them but stopping a few yards away and warily eyeing Attila. "Don't worry about trying to keep your verbal commands quiet. This film will need a lot of sound editing anyway.

"Now, I know I told you we'd be shooting Attila's running scene first, but before we get to it I want a scene of him wandering over to that big rock and pretending to dig around for something under it. I know it's not in the script, but Carly says he'll do it okay."

Nick nodded, wishing Jay weren't into improvisation. He knew the "dig" command, but they hadn't practiced it.

"It's a fake rock," Carly said. "Made of stucco. So don't let him smack it or anything."

He nodded again. But since, as far as he knew, there wasn't a "don't smack" command...

Dammit, he really wished Attila was working better for Carly. At least she had experience doing this sort of thing.

"Finished, Jay," Barb called.

"Finally," Goodie said, inspecting the virtually invisible wires. "*Now* can we get going?"

Jay walked out into the middle of the clearing, leaving only Nick and Carly on Attila's side of the hot wires, and in a voice just loud enough to be heard, said, "Can I have everyone's attention please? I've talked to Carly about the rules when the bear is on the set, and I want you to listen carefully.

"First, no yelling or sudden movements. Keep everything as quiet and calm as possible. Second, do not bring any food on to the set. And third, once I call 'Action,' no one off the set may move. Is everyone clear?"

Murmurs of "Yes" filled the air.

"Good. Then let's all be making the same movie, here." He looked over at Nick. "Cue the bear."

While Carly removed Attila's collar, Nick walked over to the fake rock. Royce and the other two cameramen were already behind their cameras, pointing them in Attila's direction.

"You're okay where you are for the moment, Nick," Jay said. "But when the cameras begin to roll, back up so you're not in the frame when Attila reaches the rock."

"Right," he said, trying to ignore the way his gut was clenching.

"Okay, no one move," Jay said. "Bells!"

Carly held her breath, hoping against hope they could do this first scene in one take. It would give Nick a world of confidence.

The crew was so quiet she could hear aspen leaves rustling in the breeze. Then Jay said, "Clear the eyeline...and roll it."

The soundman rolled his tape. "Speed," he said after a moment.

One of the production assistants lifted a slate in front of Royce's camera. "Scene eighty-two—Take one."

She slapped the hinged stick onto the slate. The clapping sound made Attila look toward it.

"It's all right, boy," Carly whispered.

Royce nodded to Jay.

"Action!" he said.

"Attila, *come*," Nick called, giving him the hand signal.

Without even the tiniest nudge from Carly, he started toward Nick and the fake rock.

Good boy, she said silently, breathing even more

easily when she saw that Nick remembered to take a few steps backward, away from the rock and out of camera range.

Just as Attila reached the rock, Nick held up his hand in the "stop" signal.

Attila stopped.

Nick pointed to the base of the rock and said, *"Dig."*

The bear wrinkled his nose, wiggled his behind, then fiercely butted the fake rock back a good three feet—leaving a mashed-in place where his head had hit.

"Oh, no! He ruined my rock!" Barb Hunt cried.

Carly's spirits sank all the way to her toes. So much for Nick's theory that things could only get better.

A second later, she realized Attila was scarfing down something that had been beneath the rock. Grubs was her first thought. But it was a fake rock, just put there for the filming. So how would grubs have gotten under it so fast?

"Cut!" Jay screamed.

When Attila stopped eating long enough to look angrily over at him, Nick grabbed whatever was still on the ground.

"What the hell is *wrong* with that bear?" Jay demanded.

"Nothing," Nick snapped. "Nothing except that somebody planted his favorite treat under the rock."

His words sent Carly into panic mode. Just because that roast hadn't been poisoned...

She took off at a dead run for the snack table. "Salt!" she told Raffaello. "I need salt!"

He handed her a salt shaker. She grabbed a second one, too, then raced over to Attila.

"Attila, *sit.*"

"Okay, boy," she murmured, unscrewing the tops of the shakers. "You're not going to like this, but trust me. Now, open up," she added, tickling him under the chin.

Expecting a treat, he happily opened his mouth. Feeling like a traitor, she upturned both shakers and poured.

By the time he realized it was no treat, she'd gotten most of the salt in. He shook his head furiously and tried to roar—which proved impossible with a mouth full of salt.

He spit out what he could but swallowed the rest. Enough that a few moments later he started to gag and throw up.

Carly's whole body went limp with relief. If he *had* eaten any poison, it was in that wet mess on the ground.

"BUT *WHY* WOULD ANYONE have planted that chicken?" Jay demanded.

Nick hesitated. By now, though, half the people on the set must have figured out that someone was into sabotage, so why not just come right out and tell Jay? "To disrupt the filming," he said.

"Why the hell would anyone want to do that?"

"I don't exactly know." He resisted the impulse to say that someone must be harboring a *major* grudge, but he wasn't going to pussyfoot around much longer.

While Jay muttered something to himself, Nick slowly surveyed the clearing. Carly was comforting Attila. Most of the crew were packing up equipment. Goodie, looking angry, was getting in people's way.

Clearly the fact that Attila was too upset to work any more today had both Goodie and Jay fit to be tied.

"But *why* would anyone do it?" Jay asked again.

"Well...could there be someone working on the film who might want to cause you grief? Someone who might have it in for you?"

"No."

"You're sure?"

"Of course."

Fleetingly Nick thought that he'd love to hear Sarina and Garth's comments on that.

"If I have problems with people," Jay continued, "I make certain they get worked out and everybody ends up happy."

"Ahh. Then I guess it was just because I'd heard about some of the other trouble you've been having that I couldn't help thinking..."

With Jay looking angrier by the second, Nick decided he'd better wrap this up fast. "At any rate, I just thought I'd raise the possibility, because that chicken didn't get under the rock by itself. Oh, and there's something else I should tell you. The map that got you lost the other day wasn't the one Gus drew. Somebody replaced his with an inaccurate one."

With that, Nick turned on his heel and went to have a good close look at the fake rock.

It was far too heavy for anyone to have lifted it up and stuck something beneath it. But given the uneven ground, sliding the chicken into one of the gaps between the base of the rock and the dirt wouldn't have been tough.

Once he was finished inspecting things, he headed over to where Carly and Attila were waiting. When they walked across the clearing, everyone gave them a wide berth, and he could practically hear a collective sigh of relief as they started off through the woods.

"Nick?" Carly said after they'd gone a few yards.

Before she had time to say anything more, Royce caught up with them. "Boy, you two were sure right about somebody trying to sabotage this film."

Nick tried to ignore the little stab of resentment he felt, but he was still annoyed that Carly had confided in Royce. Or maybe, he admitted silently, what was really bothering him was the way Royce always seemed to be hanging around her.

Whatever the reason, it didn't really matter that Royce knew. By this point, even Jay would have to admit that sabotage was the only explanation—as soon as he actually started thinking about it.

"But you were off base suspecting Garth and Sarina, eh?" Royce said.

"I'm not so sure about that," Carly told him. "Just yesterday, Jonathan mentioned to them that raw chicken is Attila's favorite treat."

"But they weren't on the set this morning, so they couldn't have planted it."

"They weren't there at all?" Nick asked.

"Uh-uh. They aren't in any of the scenes Jay was planning to shoot today."

Carly glanced at Nick again. "They could have gotten someone else to stash the chicken, couldn't they?"

"They could have, but it's not likely. It would have meant letting someone else know they'd been causing the problems."

"But... You mean you're thinking our prime suspects aren't guilty after all?"

"I'm not entirely ruling them out. I'm just saying they're not looking nearly as prime as they have been."

That obviously didn't make Carly happy, so he said to Royce, "You were on the set all morning? Sarina or Garth couldn't have come by without your knowing?"

Royce shook his head. "I was there from the crack of dawn. Jay and I were working out exactly what part of the clearing we wanted the running sequences in, then we had to supervise the lighting. Besides, the rock didn't get there much before you did. They didn't bring it onto the set until eight-thirty or nine."

"Who brought it?"

"Barb and a couple of technicians. They had it on a big dolly."

"And the three of them put it in place?"

"Well, the techs did the muscle work. And Jay did the supervising—made sure they got it at the angle he wanted and everything. Barb mostly just stood around reminding them to be careful. Telling them fake rocks are really hard to make. But you're figuring one of *them* put the chicken under it?"

"They'd be the obvious ones. You know any reason one of the techs might be into sabotage?"

Royce shrugged. "I haven't heard about anything. They're local guys. Toronto, I mean. So they're probably thrilled to be working on a Jay Wall movie. And with Barb hoping this film will lead to other set director jobs, I can't see it being her."

"No, Carly and I pretty well ruled her out long ago."

"Oh?"

"Uh-huh. Aside from the job thing, if Goodie looses his shirt on this movie and walks into divorce court crying poor…"

"Oh, yeah, I see what you mean."

"Okay, so if we eliminate those three, who else could have done it?"

"Hell, I guess it could have been almost anybody. Somebody's just wandering by, stops to have a look at the rock…"

Thinking back, Nick recalled how many people had been in that clearing. There'd been dozens of them.

"Let's try a different angle," he said. "We're assuming the point of all this is to screw Jay. So is there anyone aside from Sarina and Garth who'd have an obvious reason? Anyone who was on the set this morning?"

"Well, I guess there's… No, that would *really* be reaching."

"What would?"

"Oh, I was thinking about the chef, but that's crazy."

"Then what made you think of him? Did you notice him near the rock?"

"No, it's just that… Well, Jay and Raffaello have been at each other's throats since day one. Actually, according to the rumor mill, the problem started before Jay even laid eyes on Raffaello.

"See, Jay wanted to bring a chef with him from L.A. The one he usually uses when he's on location. But Goodie wouldn't go for it—said why should they fly this guy up, then pay him the princely wages he demands, when they could get somebody here a lot cheaper?

"In any event, Jay pulled one of his famous screaming routines at the very first meal Raffaello served in Toronto."

"Isn't that kind of unusual?" Carly asked. "Having a chef when you're shooting in a city with a zillion restaurants?"

"Well, you can play it either way. But having everyone eat together is the way Goodie likes it. I think he figures that if he lets people escape to restaurants, it wastes a lot more time. And Goodie's a real time-is-money guy."

"Yeah, we've noticed," Nick said.

They'd reached the edge of the woods, and since the camp and Attila's field lay in different directions, they paused where they were.

"Sit," Carly told Attila. "You have a little rest while we finish talking."

The bear obediently flopped down onto his haunches and Carly began stroking his neck.

"Let's get back to that screaming performance Jay put on," Nick said.

"Oh, it was a real scene," Royce told them. "He made it plain that he didn't like the cooking. And he told Raffaello it had better improve—fast. Then he said something about Italians not knowing how to cook anything but pasta and that they should have hired a French chef.

"Raffaello went ballistic at that, so Jay fired him on the spot. But Goodie intervened—I think mostly because he'd hired Raffaello personally, so he took Jay's criticism as an insult to him, too."

"What do you think?" Carly asked Nick. "Would public humiliation be enough to make Raffaello try to ruin the movie?"

"I guess it would depend on how hard he took being humiliated."

"He *does* have a hot Latin temperament," Royce put in.

"You know," Carly said slowly, "when Raffaello arrived on the porch the other night, when he thought there was a bear in his kitchen... Well, he didn't exactly scare me, but he certainly made me think he was a man I wouldn't want to cross."

Nick rubbed his jaw thoughtfully. The idea of a revenge-crazed chef struck him as decidedly off the wall, but you could never rule out anyone with motive, means and opportunity.

"Let's think this through," he said at last. "Raffaello certainly could have brought some raw chicken along this morning. Then all he'd have had to do was hide it."

"He'd have known about the rock scene," Royce said. "Once the rock was in place, Jay started going on about wanting the bear to dig under it."

"But you said you didn't actually notice Raffaello near it," Nick said.

"No. I wasn't paying much attention to what people were doing, though. When I wasn't behind my camera, framing shots, I was getting the grips to adjust the lighting.

"I mean, I'd have noticed if Garth or Sarina had shown up, because it would have been unusual. They're never around the set unless they're in a scene. But I wouldn't have noticed anything like a guy checking out the rock."

"Nick?" Carly said so anxiously that Attila gave a little snort.

"It's all right, boy." She patted him reassuringly,

then looked at Nick again. "I was just thinking, Garth got the roast he was going to feed Attila from Raffaello. So if it *was* poisoned, Raffaello could have done it as easily as Garth."

"Probably more easily," Nick muttered. "Hell, I've had some pretty strange suspects in my time, but a chef with an attitude...?"

"You've had some pretty strange suspects in your time?" Royce said.

Nick swore under his breath. It wasn't like him to think out loud.

"It's okay," Carly told him. "Royce can keep a secret."

"Yeah...well..."

"In real life, Nick's a police detective," she explained to Royce. "In Edmonton. He's only helping me here for a few weeks because Wild Action was suddenly half his and we had this movie lined up. And with Gus gone, I desperately needed help."

"You're serious." A grin spread across Royce's face. "But if you're not really a bear trainer," he said to Nick, "how did you get him to work for you?"

"You call the way he behaved this morning working for me? But listen, keep the detective bit quiet, okay? I don't want Jay thinking we've been trying to pass me off as a bear expert when I'm not." Even though that was exactly what they'd been doing.

"Sure, no problem. I won't say a word." Royce glanced in the direction of the camp. "Well, I guess I'll head back to base. After spending the morning in the sun, I could do with about a gallon of ice water. See you later," he added, turning to go.

"And Royce?" Nick called after him. "If you hear

about anyone else having a serious grudge against Jay, let me know, eh?"

"Sure thing."

Nick, Carly and Attila started in the direction of his field, Nick's conscience nagging him loud and clear. It had been easy, at first, to simply avoid mentioning that he was no longer a detective. But with each passing day, he was feeling more uncomfortable about lying to Carly.

What could he do, though? Tell her the truth at this late date? By now, he knew her well enough to be certain she wouldn't take it well. She'd somehow twist things around in her mind and decide he'd been playing her for a fool. But if he *didn't* tell her...

He mentally shook his head. For the last little while, the thought that he'd probably never see her again once this movie was made had been bothering the devil out of him. But he just couldn't see any hope of working out something permanent between them. There were too many obstacles.

Still, given the way he felt, he shouldn't be lying to her.

Before he could decide whether he should just bite the bullet and come clean, they'd reached Attila's field, and she said, "You think he'll be safe enough with only the boys watching him? This last episode has me wondering if I shouldn't bring a sleeping bag down here and stay with him twenty-four hours a day."

"I think he'll be just fine with the boys. They've been doing a good job so far."

"I guess," she said slowly.

They got the bear into his field, and after she'd

reminded Jonathan no one was to get anywhere near the fence, they started for the house.

By that point, Nick had put the idea of coming clean onto the back burner, because a growing suspicion had begun worming its way into his mind. He told himself he was way off base, but once he smelled a rat he always wanted to pursue it right away.

At last he said, "How well do you know Royce?"

Carly gave him a curious glance. "I thought I told you. He worked on a couple of documentaries that Gus and I were involved with."

"No, I mean do you know him *really* well or do you just run into him on jobs now and then."

"Why are you asking?"

"Carly, just give me an answer, okay?"

She shrugged. "If you're asking has there ever been anything between us, the answer is no."

Nick smiled to himself. That *wasn't* what he'd been asking, but he sure liked the answer. "Well, regardless of that, you obviously trust him, but..."

"But what?"

"Something's bothering me. It was Royce who told you about Sarina having an affair with Jay."

"Uh-huh."

"Has anyone else said anything about it?"

"No. But I haven't talked to many of the movie people."

"And what about the blowup between Jay and Raffaello? Everybody must know about that, but nobody except Royce has referred to it."

"Well, as I said, we haven't really been talking to that many people, so—"

"I have. Last night, when I had dinner in the camp, I was talking to a whole lot of people."

"Nick, what are you getting at?"

"The possibility that Royce has been feeding us red herrings. That Sarina and Jay never had an affair and that there was never any big scene between Jay and Raffaello. That maybe Royce has just been blowing smoke so we wouldn't realize *he's* our saboteur."

CHAPTER NINE

Everybody's Talkin' 'Bout It

CARLY STOPPED DEAD and stood staring at Nick. He had to be joking, but his expression said he wasn't.

"Royce?" she said at last. "You think it's *Royce?*"

"I'm saying it could be."

"Why? Just because he happened to mention both the affair and Jay's scene with Raffaello?"

"No. That's only part of it. I've been thinking back over all the incidents we've heard about.

"Jay fired someone because a couple of reels of film went missing. And the lab claimed they didn't screw up that processing, remember? They said the film must have been exposed before it was shot.

"Both those problems were related to film, and Royce is the number one cameraman. And then there were those camera filters that mysteriously got left behind in Toronto."

"Nick, it was *Royce* who had to drive all the way back and find them."

"Sure. But maybe he wasn't the one who noticed they weren't here. And maybe he was hoping nobody *would* notice until they needed them. And, today, he could have slipped that chicken under the rock as easily as anyone else."

"But what about the roast? I don't see how he could have had anything to do with that."

"No, so maybe the story there was exactly what you were told. Maybe Garth just asked Raffaello for something to feed Attila, and the roast was what Raffaello gave him."

Carly had to admit that everything Nick was saying added up to Royce being a suspect, but she just couldn't buy the idea that he was their man. "What about motive?" she asked.

"Good. You've been paying attention in detective class," Nick said.

Then he smiled. And even though sex had been the last thing on her mind, his smile suddenly made her hot all over.

Lord, everything about the man was sexy, from the tips of his toes to his gorgeous eyes. Even his hair, which she'd initially thought was far too short, was starting to look so good that she'd been running her fingers through it in her dreams last night.

Forcing her brain back into gear, she said, "Why on earth would Royce want to cause trouble? If this movie's a hit, it'll be great for his reputation."

Nick shrugged. "Maybe there's something more important to him."

"Like what?"

"Well, this isn't the first time he's worked for Jay, so somewhere along the way *he* could have developed a major grudge against the guy. Or maybe somebody's *paying* him to cause trouble. Money's a great motivator."

"I just don't think it could be him."

"Well, we can easily find out whether those stories

of his are true. And he drops way down on the suspect list if they are.''

''If they are, I don't see why you'd leave him on the list at all.''

''Because so many of those incidents were film related. At any rate, I'm going to wander down to the camp and check out the stories—catch someone to talk to before dinner.''

''Just you?''

He nodded. ''I think I should handle this on my own.''

''Why?''

''Oh...people talk more freely to one person than to two. And it'll just seem less obvious.''

She felt a stab of annoyance. ''You mean you think I might be too obvious.''

''Well, you aren't quite detective, first grade material yet.''

That line would have annoyed her, as well, except that Nick delivered it with another smile. If he could bottle the effect of his smile, he could retire and stay here with her forever.

The thought lingered in her mind, making her ask herself how she'd feel about his doing exactly that. Then she forced the question away unanswered, because it didn't matter how she'd feel. He'd be leaving in no time at all.

She took a couple of backward steps toward the house, not quite able to force her eyes from his. ''I guess it's just as well if you go on your own. The Marx brothers will be wanting their dinner.''

''Crackers, too.'' Nick held her gaze, sending another rush of heat through her.

''Crackers, too,'' she agreed.

"And the cats."

"Of course. I wasn't forgetting about them." But she had been. And about Crackers.

That made her feel awfully uneasy. If just gazing into Nick Montgomery's eyes could make her forget about the animals, she was in even deeper than she'd realized.

"I'll see you in a little while, then," he said, turning to leave.

"Oh, wait a sec. With everything that's been going on, I forgot to mention I'll be out tonight."

"Out?"

"I have a painting class. And I'm meeting a friend for dinner before we go."

"I didn't know you painted."

"I guess there's a lot we don't know about each other. We've never had time to talk about anything except Attila and the movie."

"Yeah, I guess that's true."

He simply gazed at her for a minute, and the look in his eyes tempted her to cancel her plans for the evening. But she knew she needed time alone—to think. Because she'd developed the terrible sense that no matter what she did, it might be a mistake.

If she got further involved with him, she'd only feel worse when he left. On the other hand, now that she'd kissed him, now that she knew how wonderful it had made her feel, she suspected that if she didn't make love with him, she'd regret it for the rest of her life.

So what was she going to do?

Telling herself she wasn't going to do *anything* until she could make a decision that felt right, she checked her watch. "Actually, I've got to get going pretty soon. So if you're not there when I'm ready to leave, you've got your key?''

He nodded.

''Good. Well, there's lots of food in the fridge. Or maybe you could have dinner at the camp again.'' With that, she forced herself to turn away.

NICK MIGHT HAVE BEEN dying to be alone with Carly tonight, but as he headed for the camp he did his best to convince himself it was a good thing she was going out.

If she wasn't, he was pretty certain they'd have ended up in bed. When you added the way she made him feel to the way she'd kissed him earlier, there was little doubt where a few hours alone would have led. And he'd have wanted things to lead there so badly that he'd have had no trouble ignoring his conscience.

But right now it was telling him, in no uncertain terms, that he couldn't make love with her until he'd told her exactly how things stood. After all, he *was* a man of principles, even if he *had* glossed over a few details recently. So he was going to have to admit that he hadn't been quite straight with her.

He'd have to explain how he'd quit his job, then tell her about his plans to start up his own investigation agency back in Edmonton—just as soon as he could get enough equity out of Wild Action.

He wasn't going to try to snow her into thinking there was a chance he might stay on here, that there was a chance for a long-term relationship. It just wouldn't be right.

But if he could live with the reality that there

wasn't, maybe she could, too. Especially if he told her how he felt about her.

After he did that...

Well, what happened then would depend on her. But before he came clean, he had to figure out the best way of explaining that he hadn't exactly been lying to her—that he'd merely failed to correct her false assumptions.

When he reached the camp, it looked as if pretty well everyone who'd been on the set was back. He spotted Jay talking to the makeup woman, and Goodie was lurking around the kitchen trailer—even though Raffaello couldn't possibly have had time to get dinner ready yet.

As he wandered between a row of trailers looking for someone he knew to try a few questions on, a female voice called, "Hi there, Nick."

Glancing to his left, he saw Barb Hunt, and decided she'd be as good as anyone.

"Hey, just the lady I was looking for."

"Oh?" She flashed one of her Hollywood smiles and wandered over.

"Yeah, I wanted to apologize for the way Attila wrecked your rock. I don't imagine it'll be the easiest thing to fix."

"No, but I'm not really blaming him. I mean, with that chicken there and all... What did you make of that?"

"Well, it struck me that somebody was trying to interrupt the filming."

Barb nodded. "From what people are saying, that's what everybody figures."

"And who do they figure it was?"

"Who knows?" She glanced around, clearly making sure there was no one nearby. Then, her voice lowered, she said, "Most of us would have put our money on the stars, but they weren't on the set."

"Oh?" Nick said. He often learned a lot more by playing dumb than by filling in the gaps.

"Uh-huh. I don't normally tell tales, but since you and Carly are probably the only ones working on the picture who don't know... Well, to be blunt, Garth and Sarina hate Jay's guts."

"Really? Why?"

"Because Sarina had an affair with Jay a while back." Barb paused and wrinkled her nose. Obviously she found the idea of getting it on with Jay disgusting. "And it came to a very messy end."

"Really?" Nick said again. So Royce *hadn't* fabricated that. "Then why are they doing this movie with him?" He'd been curious about that from the first minute he'd heard the story.

"Because Goodie twisted their arms. He's got the movie rights to an absolutely fabulous bestseller, and he dangled the staring roles in front of their noses. But he said that if they wanted those, they had to commit to *Two for Trouble*."

"So they're here but they're not happy about it."

Barb laughed. "I think you could safely use a stronger term than *not happy*."

"Still...they weren't on the set this morning."

"No. Which kind of lets them off the hook, doesn't it? Unless they got someone else to do it."

"I guess they could have. But, you know, until you told me about them, I was figuring it might have been Raffaello."

"Oh, you heard about that set-to, did you? Jay can

be *so* rotten to people. It's a wonder someone hasn't murdered him by now.''

Nick smiled, but he was hardly happy. Since Royce hadn't made up either story, he was no longer looking guilty as sin. Which had to put Raffaello at the top of the list, even though it seemed darned improbable that he was their man.

But maybe there were other likely suspects he didn't know about—and Barb might.

"Since that chicken was obviously planted," he said, "are people starting to figure some of the other problems were caused deliberately?"

"For sure. You can practically see everyone looking at everyone else, wondering if *they're* the troublemaker. I mean, you've seen the way Jay acts, so who knows? There could be dozens of people in this camp who'd just love to see him fall on his face."

Terrific. Nick had gone from having a couple of really strong suspects to what was sounding like an almost endless list of possibilities.

Hell, this was reminding him of a Peter Sellers's line from one of the old Pink Panther movies: "I suspect everyone, and I suspect no one."

"So there are dozens of people who might have it in for Jay," he said, focusing his attention on Barb again. "But there aren't any obvious suspects?"

"Well, as I said, Sarina and Garth seemed to be until today. But even if they'd been on the set..."

"What?"

Barb shook her head. "Everyone working on a movie wants it to be good. It's our names up on the big screen when the credits roll. I mean, even the lowliest production assistant gets her few seconds of glory. So when you really start thinking about it, the idea that anyone in the cast or crew would want to screw things up..." She paused and looked toward the kitchen trailer.

"You know," she said, turning back toward Nick, "what you said about Raffaello's got me thinking. He's one of the few people who has nothing to lose if the movie flops. And when Jay was screaming at him that day, you could tell he was absolutely furious."

Nick could feel his adrenaline starting to pump. Sometimes an improbable suspect *did* turn out to be the perp. "But would Raffaello have had the opportunity to cause any of those other problems?"

"Oh, sure. When you've got a chef on the set, he's always wandering around everywhere—making sure the snack table's looking okay and all kinds of things. After a few days, he becomes the invisible man."

While Barb looked in the direction of the kitchen again, Nick wondered if a chef became invisible enough to pick up a couple of reels of film and stash them under his uniform.

"You think we should say anything to Jay?" Barb asked. "I mean, I'd *really* like these problems to stop. This film could do a lot for my career, but only if it does good box office."

"Well...I'm not sure talking to Jay's a good idea. Not right now, at least. I raised the issue of sabotage before I left the set, and he wasn't buying it. So we should probably just let him think on it awhile—until he's ready to accept the obvious."

"Oh, yeah, I guess. It's never smart to try telling Jay something he doesn't want to hear.

"So," she went on, flashing another of her smiles, "I saw you having dinner down here last night. You want to hang around until the kitchen's open and do a repeat?''

He was just deciding that was a good idea, that he might pick up something of interest, when she added, ''I don't know if anyone's told you what my situation is, but if you heard Goodie and I are married, you heard stale news. We're splitsville, so he could care less if you and I ate together.

''Oh, unless you and Carly are...more than business partners?''

''No, no, that's all we are.'' But he was sure as hell hoping that would change.

NICK WAS ALL CARLY could think about as she drove home from Port Perry, which was hardly surprising when he'd been on her mind the entire evening.

They'd had a nude male model at their class, and the whole time she'd been trying to paint him, she'd been imagining *Nick* nude. She seemed to have become positively obsessed with the man.

Not that it was *only* physical attraction involved, although she strongly suspected she'd be better off if it was. But she'd fallen for him for a lot of different reasons.

Initially, of course, she'd just been so darn grateful that he'd given up his vacation time to stay and help her. But the better she'd gotten to know him...

Oh, she'd come to love his dry sense of humor, the way he just dug in and did whatever had to be done, how good he was with the animals and... She shook her head. She could list a hundred different things, but it all came down to the fact that she'd fallen in love with the man. That she wanted to make love with him.

Do you want to be left hurting when he goes? she asked herself again. But the question had lost its power—defeated by her desire.

Maybe, in the long run, she'd regret that. But in the short run, she wanted Nick too much to resist.

She turned down the Sixth Line, her heart beating faster with every click of the odometer. By the time she reached the gravel drive, her heart was racing a mile a minute.

The camp, she absently noted on her way past, was showing no signs of settling down for the night. Of course, it had still been twilight when she'd left Port Perry, so it wasn't all that late.

Ahead, the house stood in darkness, and disappointment rippled through her. Nick must be in the camp.

She parked and went inside, where the Marx brothers treated her to their usual frantic greeting. After they retreated and gave the cats a chance to say hello, she talked to Crackers for a minute, then took the dogs out for a brief walk—down the hill far enough toward Attila's field to see that Craig, the kid on this watch, was awake and alert.

When she got back to the house, the phone was ringing and Crackers was crying, "Phone. Phone."

"Hi, Carly," her mother's voice greeted her.

"Oh, hi, Mom," she said, feeling a stab of guilt. She'd promised to phone back and let them know when it would be a good time to come, but with all that had been happening she hadn't gotten around to it.

"How's the movie going?"

Fleetingly, she pictured Attila destroying the stand-in bear. Then a replay of the chicken-and-rock fiasco flashed through her mind. "Fine," she said. "It's going just fine."

"Oh, good. Then it would be all right if we came down *soon?* We were thinking about the day after tomorrow. John's company is sending him to some training course in Chicago, and you know how your sister hates being in that big old house alone."

"Ahh..." Carly thought rapidly. Surely tomorrow they'd get Attila's running scene shot. And once that was a wrap, it would be relatively clear sailing.

"Dear? Would that be all right?"

"Sure. The day after tomorrow's great."

"Good. We thought we'd leave right after breakfast."

Which meant they might be here before she and Nick had even *had* breakfast. The drive from Kingston was only a couple of hours, and her parents were *very* early risers.

"Well, I don't know what the shooting schedule will be yet. But if I'm not in the house when you arrive, just make yourselves at home.

"No, wait, I've been keeping the house locked because there are so many strangers around. But there'll be a kid watching Attila's field, so I'll leave a key with him."

"You have someone watching Attila's field?"

"Uh-huh. With all those people... I just don't want any of them bothering him."

"Oh, of course. Well, we'll see you the day after tomorrow, then."

"Right. Say hi to Dad for me."

Once she'd hung up, she poured a glass of iced tea and sat out on the dark porch to wait for Nick.

Rocky ambled across the lawn and kept her company for a while, and when he went off to do coon things she simply sat gazing out into the moonlight, listening to the crickets chirp and thinking what a romantic night it was. And that Nick would soon be here to share it with her.

But when she eventually spotted him coming up the drive, her stomach gave a sick lurch. Not only was Barb Hunt with him, they were walking arm in arm.

Carly's face began to burn and she felt positively ill. Only this morning, Nick had been kissing her as if he were madly in love with her. And his long, lingering glances had been telling her that, too. But apparently he liked to spread his love around.

Angrily telling herself it was just as well she'd discovered that before he'd spread much her way, she pushed herself out of the chair and started across the porch, hoping she was hidden by the darkness.

She hadn't quite made it to the door when Nick called, "Carly? Where're you going?"

Silently swearing, she turned in time to see him disentangling his arm from Barb's. "I assumed you two would like some privacy," she said icily.

"Privacy?"

"Oh, it's not what you think," Barb said. "Nick didn't seem *entirely* stable on his feet when he was leaving, so I just thought I'd walk him home."

Looking at him again, Carly wondered how she could have missed the fact that he was tipsy—if not downright inebriated.

That probably meant she'd jumped to the wrong conclusion about him and Barb. But it also dashed any thoughts of romance.

"I figured if our bear trainer fell and broke his leg,

Jay would be positively suicidal,'' Barb added. "At any rate, I'll see you both tomorrow." She gave a little wave, then started back down the drive.

While Nick cautiously negotiated the porch steps, Carly said, "You're drunk."

"I certainly am not. I just had a couple of beers."

"Some *couple*." She turned and marched into the house.

"Maybe it was three," he said, trailing her inside.

"Maybe you missed counting a few," she muttered, locking the door and heading for the stairs.

He followed her, and when they reached the upstairs hall, said, "I don't know why you're making a federal offence out of this. I really don't drink much. Especially not for a cop. But I figured I'd better keep up tonight. You know, be one of the boys. Because Barb and I were sitting with these other people at dinner and—"

"You had dinner with Barb?" she said, wishing that didn't annoy the hell out of her. But if he'd had dinner with Barb, and he'd still been with her at ten o'clock...

"Well, I didn't have *you* to eat with, did I? You went off to paint your...whatever it is you paint."

"Tonight it was a nude man." She liked the way that information made Nick's jaw drop.

Then he recovered and grinned at her. "Naaah, you're joking."

"No, I'm serious. We quite often have live models, and tonight's was a very well-built nude man."

Nick's grin was abruptly replaced by a frown. "Well, anyway," he said after a minute, "as I was saying, there were all these other people at dinner, so

I hung around talking to some of them—fishing for clues."

"Did you catch any?"

"Any what?"

"Clues. The ones you were fishing for."

"Ahh. That time you *were* joking, right?"

"Nick, if you can't even tell whether I'm joking or not, it's time to call it a night."

"Oh," he said, looking distinctly disappointed.

"And maybe you should have a hot shower before you go to bed. If you don't, in the morning you'll wish you had." She walked into her room and closed the door as he muttered something.

She wasn't positive, but she thought it was, "Maybe I should take a *cold* shower."

AT BREAKFAST, NICK WAS feeling a little fuzzy around the edges. The headache pills he'd taken hadn't kicked in yet, so there was a dull thudding in his temples.

His stomach wasn't doing too well, either. He was certain Carly had cooked the bacon and eggs with extra grease, intentionally trying to punish him.

"This is a short day for us, isn't it?" he said, hoping he was right. The way he was feeling, it was going to be tough getting through even a couple of hours.

She nodded. "After they shoot Attila's running scene, Jay's going to concentrate on the boys—shoot their running sequence, then some earlier scenes. I think he's planning on the ones where they break their compass and realize they're lost.

"So what should we do while that's happening?" she added. "Hang around the set and see if there are any new 'problems' or spend our time asking questions in the camp?"

"Well, maybe neither. The more I've been thinking about things, the more hopeful I'm getting that our troublemaker might have decided to back off."

"Really?"

"Uh-huh. After that incident with the rock, *everybody's* realized that someone's intentionally been causing trouble. And Barb mentioned that you can practically see everyone watching everyone else, which is going to make it pretty hard to set up more incidents without getting caught. So if this guy has a brain, he'll quit while he's ahead."

"Oh, Nick, I sure hope you're right."

He forced down another piece of bacon. Then, when Carly got up to get something from the fridge, he lowered his plate onto his lap.

Zeppo helped him out by greedily wolfing down the leftovers, but Crackers blew the whistle on them, crying, "Oh-oh! Bad dog! Bad dog!"

"Damn feathered rat fink," Nick muttered under his breath, trying to get the plate back onto the table.

He wasn't quite fast enough to keep Carly from looking his way and catching him. "Feeling a little green around the gills?" she said.

"Just watching the cholesterol."

"Oh. Good. Because if Attila balks at running, I'd hate you to have to work at persuading him when you were hung over."

"Well, I'm not, so let's get going." Pushing back from the table, he grabbed the cooler she'd filled with bear treats.

They said goodbye to the dogs and Crackers, then

collected Attila from his field and took him to the shoot site.

The morning was incredibly muggy, which wasn't good. Attila might decide it was too humid for running. But as they walked, Nick tried to think only positive thoughts.

They'd left the hot wires in place yesterday so there wouldn't be much work to do before they could get going—which meant they'd get a good, early start on the shooting.

And Kyle and Brock should be feeling back to normal, in which case Jay wouldn't nail him to the wall for letting them ride the ponies. All in all, by the time they reached the set, Nick had decided this might be a pretty good morning. And later...

He glanced at Carly, not at all certain what would happen later. But it could hardly be any worse than what had happened last night, when he'd gone to bed aching with wanting her.

The buzz on the set died as people noticed Attila had arrived. He was obviously still making them nervous.

Then Jay looked over and called, "Oh, good. Perfect timing. We're just ready for you."

Nick nodded, telling himself that positive thinking worked. He only wished he could positively think his headache away. It was hanging on with annoying tenacity.

"Barb's not finished repairing the rock," Jay added. It had been moved to the "safe" side of the hot wires, and he gestured to where she was working. "So we're going to begin with Attila's running scene."

Nick nodded again, and he and Carly walked Attila

around to the far side of the wires. He put the cooler down behind a real rock, where it would be out of sight from the cameras, then they led Attila to the end of the clearing and into the surrounding woods. The scene required him to charge out of it and across the clearing.

When they reached the markers that indicated his starting point, Carly removed his collar and chain, then gave him a hug. "You work nicely for Nick and there'll be serious treats," she murmured.

Nick could have done with a hug himself, but all he rated was a quick "Good luck."

"Okay," Jay said. "Everyone remember the rules. Quiet as you can be, and nobody off the set moves while we're shooting. Cue the bear, Nick."

"Let's do it, fellow," he said to Attila, backing away into the clearing. He checked where the cameras were and kept moving until he figured he had to be out of even a wide shot.

"Okay," Jay said again. "Bells! Clear the eyeline... Dammit, Carly, move farther away from the bear! Right...and roll it."

There was a few moments' hush, then the soundman quietly called, "Speed."

The production assistant said, "Scene 121—Take one." She clicked the hinged stick onto the slate with barely any noise.

"Action!" Jay said.

Nick stared through the trees to where he could make out Attila's big shape and called, "Attila, *run*." He made the hand signal even broader than usual because of the distance, but the bear didn't move.

He tried again—with the same nonresult.

"Cut!" Jay said, giving him an evil look. "You want to go have a talk with him?"

Nick unhappily headed back across the clearing and into the woods. "Can't you prod him or something?" he asked Carly.

"Not without being in the frame."

"Then what do we do?"

"You'll have to entice him."

"And how do I do that?"

"Get some of the raw chicken out of the cooler, then come back and show him you've got it."

With his hangover, the thought of handling raw chicken was enough to start Nick's stomach churning. "Can't I use something else?"

"There's a bag of marshmallows. You could try them if you'd rather."

While he walked all the way to the cooler, then back to the woods again, he could feel Jay fuming.

Stopping a few yards from Attila, he dangled the bag as temptingly as he could and said, "Look what I've got, boy."

The bear gave an interested growl.

"They'd really hit the spot, eh? So you just come running when I call, and they're all yours."

"Well?" Jay said as Nick headed back out into the clearing once more. "Is he going to cooperate?"

"There's only one way to find out."

This time, when they got to the part where the P.A. said, "Scene 121—Take two," Nick was praying.

It didn't help. Attila stayed right where he was.

"Cut!" Jay snapped.

Before he could say anything else, Carly appeared at the edge of the clearing and called, "Jay?"

"What?"

"If Nick ran ahead of Attila with some treats, kind of made a game of getting Attila to chase him, how close could he be to the bear without getting in the frame?"

Nick froze on the spot. *Get Attila to chase him? Did Carly figure he'd developed a death wish?*

"Royce? How far?" Jay asked.

"Oh, as long as he gave us a good ten feet of separation, we could probably handle it."

Nick looked from Royce to Jay, then at Carly. They were all serious about this. But there was no way, not in a million years, that they were going to convince him to do it.

CHAPTER TEN

Birds Do It, Bees Do It

NICK STOOD WITH Carly on the edge of the clearing, pretending not to notice that she was glaring at him. But it was tough to ignore a woman shooting daggers with her eyes.

"Well?" she finally demanded. "You're *sure* you won't change your mind."

"No. I am *not* having a bear chase me."

"Fine. Then I'll do it, even if Jay *is* going to think it's strange that we're trading places. Give me the marshmallows."

When she reached for the bag, he tucked it behind his back. He suspected he'd feel even more frightened watching her do it than doing it himself—which was saying an awful lot.

"Give them to me."

"No. Attila's not listening to you any better than he was when I first got here."

"Well, maybe he'll surprise us."

"Or maybe he won't, and Jay will have a fit."

"Nick, what would make Jay have a fit would be not getting his scene, so give me the damn marshmallows."

"No. I can run faster than you." He wasn't sure that was true, but he probably could.

The issue, though, was whether or not he could outrun Attila, and that was a very different kettle of fish. Or bag of marshmallows, as the case may be.

"Then you *will* do it?"

"Dammit, Carly, neither of us should be doing it."

"But it's the only solution. You run, Attila chases you, Jay gets the footage he wants and everybody's happy."

"Not *this* everybody. You think I've forgotten what you told me way back? How I shouldn't run when I'm around Attila? How it would excite his predatory instinct?"

"That was before he got to know you. He'd never hurt you now that you're his buddy."

"You're damn right he won't, because I'm not going to tempt him."

"You wouldn't be tempting him. You'd only be playing a game with him. Come on, Nick. He's never so much as scratched you."

"No, but I've never acted like prey around him, have I?"

"Oh...dammit, we can't stand here arguing all day. Give me the freaking marshmallows."

"Hey!" Jay called impatiently. "Can we get a move on here?"

When Nick still didn't give her the bag, Carly said, "Look, Attila really wouldn't hurt you. I promise. And remember what's at stake, what's going to happen if Jay *doesn't* get what he wants."

Reluctantly, Nick looked into the woods to where Attila was waiting. He really *was* a gentle bear. And they *had* become buddies—of sorts. And if it was the only way to make him run...

Telling himself he must be out of his mind, he said,

"All right. But if he kills me, I hope your conscience bothers you for the rest of your life."

"Oh, Nick, I love you for this!"

He exhaled slowly, imagining how he'd feel if she actually *did* love him, while she looked in Jay's direction and called, "It would help if I gave Attila a little prod. I know that would make you lose the first few seconds of filming, but I'd get out of the frame as fast as I could."

Jay gave a weary shrug. "Just get the damn bear running. Whatever you have to do."

Carly turned back to Nick. "Okay. We'll show him the marshmallows again. Then, once you've backed out into the clearing and Jay calls 'Action,' give Attila the 'run' command and start running yourself. As soon as you make it across the clearing, you can stop behind one of the trees on the other side and give him his treats."

Sweating far more than the temperature called for, Nick followed Carly through the trees toward Attila. "Okay, boy," he said, dangling the bag of marshmallows once more, "we're going to try this another way. This time, I'm going to run, too."

"Woof." The bear eyed the bag and twitched his nose.

"I'm just going to take a bit of a head start." Nick slowly backed away, waving the bag in front of him.

Attila didn't take his eyes off it.

"I think this is going to work," Carly whispered.

"Okay," Jay said as Nick emerged from the woods. "Clear the eyeline...and roll it."

The soundman got up to speed. The P.A. said, "Scene 121—Take three." Jay said, "Action!"

"Attila, *run,*" Nick called, giving the signal with

one hand and waving the marshmallows with the other.

A second later, Attila was crashing through the trees.

Nick wheeled around and began to run—more out of sheer terror than because it was the plan. He hadn't realized *quite* how petrifying it would be to have six hundred pounds of bear charging after him, even if it *was* his buddy.

"Faster, Nick," Jay shouted. "Faster! He's gaining on you! Hurry or you'll be in the frame!"

Attila was *gaining* on him? If he had afterburners, he'd turn them on, but he was already running flat-out.

He could hear people laughing, so he must look damn funny. But if *they* were being chased by a bear, they sure as hell wouldn't be laughing. They'd be as petrified as he was.

The far end of the clearing was getting closer, but so was Attila. The pounding of his feet was growing louder by the second, and Nick could practically feel bear breath on the back of his neck.

He raced on and was just about to the trees when disaster struck. He tripped and went sprawling onto the ground, the bag of marshmallows flying through the air. An instant later every ounce of breath suddenly whooshed out of him and the world went black.

For a horrified moment, Carly stood rooted to the spot. Then Jay yelled, "Cut! And print! Thank heavens, that was a terrific take!"

His voice set her in motion, and she yelled, "Attila! *Off! Stand!*" She raced across the clearing, frantically telling herself that he'd actually fallen over Nick more than he'd landed on top of him.

Attila obediently stood up and hurried to get the marshmallows.

"Oh, Nick," Carly murmured, dropping to her knees beside him. "Oh, Nick, please don't be badly hurt."

She felt for his pulse and found it, so at least he was alive. But he wasn't conscious, which filled her throat with tears and her heart with dread.

"Is he okay?" Jay called.

"Don't try to move him!" Goodie said. "I'll call for an ambulance on my cellular."

She was vaguely aware of a chorus of other anxious voices, but nobody ventured to Attila's side of the hot wires. It didn't matter, though, because there was nothing any of them could do. And nothing *she* could do, no matter how desperately she wanted to.

Her tears began to spill over, but just as they did, Nick moaned.

"Oh, Nick, are you all right?"

When he grunted in reply, it sounded enough like a "yes" that her heart soared.

"Ambulance is on its way," Goodie called. "Someone better go meet them at the house and bring them out here."

"Damn good thing that was the only bear scene we had scheduled for today," Jay muttered to someone loudly enough for Carly to overhear.

She felt like killing him but didn't even look his way. She simply asked Nick if he could move.

Groggily, he pushed himself into a sitting position. His T-shirt was ripped, and he was covered in dirt, but he didn't wince as he felt along his arms and legs.

After he checked his ribs, he said, "Nothing seems

to be broken. I guess he just knocked the wind out of me."

"Thank heavens," she murmured, feeling weak with relief. "He did *try* to avoid you, but he was too close to miss you altogether."

"Oh? You mean only three or four hundred pounds of him landed on me?"

She smiled. "It might even have been just one or two. But you *do* feel all right?"

He gave her a wry look. "Carly, I feel as if I just went ten rounds with Mike Tyson."

CARLY WANTED NICK TO wait in the clearing until the ambulance arrived and the paramedics checked him over. But much to her dismay, he insisted on heading back to the house.

By the time she got Attila on his lead and the three of them started off—Nick limping badly—Jay was already setting up to shoot Kyle and Brock running.

"I'll bet neither of *them* trips," Nick muttered, glancing back.

"Nick, it doesn't matter that you tripped. You did a terrific job. I mean, it's awful that you got hurt, but you didn't fall until after Jay had all the footage he needed. And you should have heard how happy he was that he got his take. He was downright ecstatic."

"You mean I was lying there unconscious, under a bear, and all Jay was worrying about was his damn take?"

"Well, if it makes you feel any better, all I was worrying about was *you*."

"Yeah?" He flashed one of his turn-her-to-jelly smiles.

It made her recall how she'd come home from her

art class last night wanting to make love with him. And if he hadn't had too much to drink...

"*Why* were you worrying about me?"

"Oh, mostly because I didn't know if you had any insurance." She smiled to say she was teasing, then left it at that—even though she was tempted to tell him the truth. Tell him that when he'd been lying there motionless all she'd been able to think of was how much she loved him.

But this wouldn't be a good time or place to instigate that discussion, so she said, "Getting back to Jay, the important thing is that you gave him what he wanted."

"Yeah, but that was *one* scene."

"I know, but it was Attila's only real tough one. The rest are just the foreshadowing ones, and for most of them it's simply a matter of posing him or getting him to walk a little."

"Unless Jay comes up with more improvisations."

Carly frowned, not wanting to think about that possibility. "I'm sure we'll be fine from here on in," she said at last. "The scenes with the rabbits and the Marx brothers will be relatively easy. And Jay doesn't need much from the owls."

As they reached the edge of the woods, she added, "I'll take Attila to his field while you go and wait for the paramedics. And make sure you let them check you over *thoroughly*."

"Anyone ever tell you you're bossy?"

"I'm not bossy. I just don't want you keeling over dead on me."

She and Attila only made it about halfway to their destination before an ambulance turned off the Sixth Line into the driveway. Hurrying the rest of the way, she hustled Attila into the field, barely saying two words to Jonathan, who was on watch duty.

Even so, by the time she got to the house, the paramedics were standing on the front porch with Nick, ready to leave.

"Is he all right?" she asked.

"He's going to be pretty stiff and sore for a few days," one of them said. "But he looks basically okay."

"A long hot bath would be a good idea," the other one suggested. "With Epsom salts if you've got any."

She nodded. Gus had been a great believer in Epsom salts.

Once the two men climbed back into their ambulance and started down the drive, she turned to Nick. "Come on. You'd better get into the tub."

"No, I think I'll pass on that idea. Who wants a long hot bath when it's ninety degrees out? All I need is a quick shower to wash off the dirt."

"Well, at the risk of seeming bossy, I'm going to get some Epsom salts and run the bath."

WHILE NICK WAS IN the tub, Carly walked the Marx brothers, fed the animals, then made lunch for herself and Nick.

When there was no sign of him by that point, she began to worry. What if he'd been hurt worse than the paramedics had realized? What if he'd suffered a concussion? And what if it had made him pass out and he'd drowned in the bathtub?

That frightening possibility in mind, she raced up the stairs, breathing a sigh of relief when she reached the hallway and saw that the bathroom door was standing open and the room was empty.

"Nick?" she said.

There was a mumbled response from his room.

She walked a few steps along the hall and looked through his open doorway. He was lying on the bed with a towel wrapped around his waist.

Seeing him almost naked started a sweet ache inside her. Trying to ignore it, she said, "Lunch is ready."

"Mmmm. Mind if I just lie here for another ten minutes? You ran that bath so hot, I think it took as much out of me as Attila did."

"Sure. I stuck the sandwiches in the fridge, so they're safe from the animals."

Deciding that a shower would really hit the spot, she headed into her own room and grabbed an elastic to keep her hair dry.

The shower turned out to be a quick one, because there wasn't much hot water left, but it made her feel far more alert.

After giving her neck a little spritz of perfume and freeing her hair from the elastic, she pulled on her robe, tied the sash, then started back to her room.

"Carly?" Nick called as she reached her doorway.

She crossed to his side of the hall. He was sitting on the edge of his bed, wearing jeans now but still bare-chested. And looking at his dark chest hair made her fingers itch.

"I have to talk to you about something," he said, his expression anxious.

It made her very uneasy. What if he'd decided that the latest incident was the last straw? What if he was leaving right here and now?

She glanced over to his closet and saw that he hadn't started packing. Not yet, at least.

"All right," she said, leaning lightly against the door frame. "What are we talking about?"

"Well...it's a little difficult to explain, but... Could you maybe come in and sit down for a minute?"

"Sure," she said slowly, suddenly very aware that all she had on was her robe.

He was a toss-everything-on-the-chair kind of man, so the only place to sit was on the edge of the bed. She perched there beside him, her heart racing and that sweet ache beginning inside her once more. He smelled of soap and summer. And when he looked at her, his eyes were so warm she could feel their heat in her heart.

Nick gazed at Carly, trying to make the right words form in his mind. But yesterday, when he'd convinced himself he had to come clean, she hadn't been sitting beside him, smelling like desire and wearing only a thin robe. And he hadn't been hard with wanting her.

"Nick? Is something wrong?"

"No...not exactly. It's just that..." He tried to force the rest of the words out, but he simply couldn't.

What on earth had made him think he could make her understand? How was he even going to start? By saying, "Carly, I haven't been quite straight with you, but just let me explain?"

Hell, she wouldn't hear beyond the "I haven't been quite straight with you," and she *wouldn't* understand. She'd think he'd taken her for a fool. But maybe if he told her how he felt about her first, then got around to explaining things...

"It's just what, Nick?"

He cleared his throat. "Carly, I didn't expect this

to happen, but I guess we don't have much control over...over who we fall in love with.''

She smiled. Tentatively at first, then it reached all the way to her eyes. "Oh, Nick," she murmured. "Oh, Nick."

She wrapped her arms around his neck and kissed him so enticingly that every single thought in his head was of her.

Burying his hands in the rich silk of her hair, he breathed in her wonderful scent. Her kisses were the most delicious things he'd ever tasted, and he wanted her so desperately he'd die if he couldn't have her.

He deepened their kiss, easing them both down onto the bed, then undoing her sash and sliding his hands beneath either side of her robe. As it fell open, leaving her all but naked, she reached for his zipper.

Quickly getting rid of his jeans and her robe, he snuggled close to her, kissing her throat, smoothing his hands across her baby-smooth skin, caressing her breasts—first with his hands and then with his mouth.

"Oh, Nick," she whispered, raking her fingers through his hair. "You're not too stiff and sore for this?"

He stopped and grinned at her. "You know, sometimes you say the darnedest things."

"Sorry. And I didn't mean to interrupt what you were doing, either."

At that instant, he knew he was going to love her forever.

"NICK?" CARLY MURMURED, cuddling her sweat-slicked body even closer to his.

He kissed her shoulder. "Mmmm?"

"We've been here for hours. Do you think I should go down and get those sandwiches?"

"Do you want to move?"

That was a truly silly question. She wanted to stay right here with him for the next hundred years. "No, but I figured you might be hungry."

"Well...yeah, now that you mention it. But I'll go."

"You're not too stiff and sore?"

That made him laugh. "You know, for the rest of my life, every time I hear that phrase I'm going to remember today."

"Really?" she said, a little cloud of unhappiness drifting through her mind. *Remember?*

But she'd known all along he was going to leave. Had known when she'd chosen to get this involved with him. Which meant that worrying about it now was foolish. She'd be better off just enjoying the time they had together and not thinking about the future.

She disentangled herself from the sheets and Nick, then grabbed her robe off the floor. "There's no iced tea made, so I'll go get things. Yc   just stay where you are. And you'd like a beer?"

"Uh-uh. After last night, I think I'll go with tea."

He watched Carly until she'd disappeared down the hall, then stretched and grinned to himself.

He'd fallen in love with the most fantastic woman in the entire world. And even though he wasn't sure how they were going to handle the logistics, he *was* sure they were going to turn this relationship into a permanent one.

Maybe that hadn't been his thinking earlier, but things were far clearer in his mind now. It was obvious he'd be insane to do anything but spend the rest of his life with Carly.

He propped himself up against the headboard, then fantasized about their future together until she came back upstairs. When she did, she looked as if she'd seen a ghost.

"What's wrong?"

"I...nothing, I don't think." She put the tray of sandwiches and tea on the bedside table and sat down on the edge of the bed.

Now that the food was in front of him, he realized he was starving. But he left the sandwiches alone and waited to hear about whatever she didn't *think* was wrong.

"It's just...Nick, Dylan brought the mail up from the box this morning and left it in the kitchen. I had a boo at it while I was downstairs, and there's a letter for you."

She drew it out of the pocket of her robe, hesitated, then added, "From Gus."

It took him a second to get up to speed. "You mean from *our* Gus?" he asked. "Our *deceased* Gus?"

She nodded. "It's his handwriting."

A funny little shiver ran up Nick's spine. He'd never gotten a letter from a dead man before, and it was a weird feeling.

Carly sat down on the edge of the bed and held the envelope out to him. "It's postmarked Port Perry. It was mailed to you in Edmonton, then somebody forwarded it here."

"My neighbor. She said she'd send on anything that looked interesting." Nick took the envelope, ripped it open and unfolded the pages. The letter was dated about a year ago, and began:

Dear Nick,

I left this with a friend, and instructed him to mail it a couple of weeks after my death.

By now, you're aware that I bequeathed you a share of my estate, and I sincerely hope you intend to make a trip east to see about the property and business firsthand—for several reasons, which I'll get to shortly.

I suspect learning about your inheritance raised a lot of questions in your mind, and I'm writing this letter with a view to answering some of them.

First, you must wonder how I even know you exist, let alone where you live. Well, that's an easy one.

I still have a friend in Edmonton who over the years has kept me up to date on our family—not that there's much family left now. I know you have some relatives on your mother's side, but with me gone you're the last of the Montgomerys.

Nick glanced at Carly, saw how curiously she was eyeing the letter, and handed her the first page. Then he read on.

This brings me to one of the reasons for the bequest. My friend tells me that, as far as he's been able to establish, you're an intelligent, personable man who's interested in the opposite sex. (I couldn't help wondering about that when you never married, but I have to assume my friend's information is accurate.)

At any rate, I've always thought it would be

a shame if our branch of the family tree died, but the older I got, the less I wanted the responsibility of a wife and children.

So, Nick, at this point you are it. The Montgomerys' only potential procreator, we might say. And since you apparently haven't found the right woman on your own, I thought I might be able to help you out.

Which gets us back to my hope that you'll be making a trip east, and thereby meet Carly Dumont, because she's a truly wonderful woman. After living in the same house with her for many years, I can attest to that. But for some reason, she hasn't found the right man.

"Why, the old devil," Nick said. Leaning forward, he cupped Carly's chin with his hand and kissed her.

"That was nice," she said when he finished. "But why was Gus an old devil?"

"He's playing matchmaker from the grave. He's a little late, though, isn't he?"

"What do you mean?"

Grinning, Nick handed her page two and turned his attention to the next one.

I imagine you're curious about why I divided the inheritance the way I did. Well, at one point, I intended to leave everything to you—out of guilt. I'm sure you're only too well aware what I mean by that.

He nodded to himself. Carly had said that Gus got into the animal actor business when he won a share of Wild Action in a poker game. Most likely, though, the money he'd used to buy out his partner, as well as to purchase this property, was money he'd stolen from the family business.

"Nick?" Carly said. "What Gus says here—about the fact that you've never married. Why haven't you?"

"Never met the right woman."

She eyed him for a moment, then said, "In a city the size of Edmonton, you've met thousands of women. And some of them must have been pretty close to right."

"Well...then maybe it's partly because I've always known what bad husband material cops are. You run into so much garbage that it gets hard to relate to normal people. Then there's the shift work, and... Oh, a lot of different things. But the bottom line is that the divorce rate on the job is awfully high. And I always found it hard to believe I'd be an exception."

"Then you're *never* going to get married?"

He swallowed uneasily, but this wasn't the moment to come clean. If he did, they'd get into a big discussion and it would be tomorrow before he got to finish reading this letter.

"Not as long as I'm a cop," he finally said. Then he looked back down at the page before she could say anything more and picked up where he'd left off.

But the longer Carly worked for me, the more I felt that she deserved a share of things, since I never paid her half of what she was worth. And the longer I thought about it, the more it seemed right to give her a controlling interest.

Wild Action means so very much to her that I didn't want you in a position where you could

force her to sell it. (I hope you're not the sort of
man who would do something like that, but I
couldn't be sure when I only had my friend's
information to go on.)

At any rate, I imagine that by now I've answered most of your questions except for one.
Why did I do what I did, way back when?

Quickly, Nick turned to the next page, curious to
see if Gus would admit the truth.

"Don't I get that one?" Carly said.

She was expectantly eyeing the page he'd just finished, so he handed it to her.

By the way, if you do go east and meet Carly,
I'd appreciate your not telling her I stole the
money. She always thought more highly of me
than I deserved, and I'd hate her illusions to be
shattered after I'm gone.

But, that aside, the question is, why did I em-
bezzle the money? Well, as you know, your
mother grew up in the house next door to your
father and me. Beyond that, I don't know what
they told you, but your mother and I dated for a
while.

Nick paused. His parents had never told him that,
but it *could* be true.

I was madly in love with her. At least I
thought I was at the time. But her feelings for
me weren't nearly as strong. So, being a little
crazy in my younger years, I decided I had to do
something stupendous to win her. And the most

stupendous idea I could come up with was to get my hands on so much money that I'd be able to buy her anything in the world.

When Nick turned to the next page, Carly reached for the one he'd just finished, saying, "Come on, I'm dying to see *what* he did, way back when."

"Ahh...he's gotten into some personal, family stuff. I...just let me finish the whole thing, okay?"

"Okay," she said, clearly disappointed.

But she'd be a lot more disappointed if she learned that Gus had practically plunged his family into bankruptcy. And since Gus didn't want her illusions shattered, so be it.

Pretending he couldn't feel her eyes on him, Nick continued reading.

If I just had enough money, my naive reasoning went, she wouldn't be able to resist me. And that's what made me steal from the family business. There's no excuse for having done it, except that I was an idiot, but at least now you know the reason.

In any event, I told your mother I'd acquired this fortune and asked her to run away with me—said we'd get married in some romantic place like Paris. Needless to say, the running-away part was important. I knew it wouldn't take long for my father and brother to discover what I'd done.

But instead of being swept off her feet, your practical mother's first question was where had the money come from? I couldn't tell her the truth, of course, so I said I'd won it at the race track. Unfortunately, I said it before I realized it wasn't racing season. Your mother picked up on that in a second, though, and decided I must have done something illegal to get it. And she told me in no uncertain terms that she'd never marry a criminal.

So there I was with my big plan blown up in my face. There was no way of simply putting the money back without anyone ever knowing, and I just couldn't face my father and admit what I'd done. (I expect you are aware that your grandfather was a most unforgiving man.)

Under the circumstances, I couldn't see any alternative but to take off, and so I did. After that, your mother began dating your father. And the rest, as they say, is history.

Well, Nick, I can't think of anything more to say—except to tell you that I know the odds on you and Carly falling in love are pretty remote, but I've always been a man to buck the odds.

Oh, and if you ever do have children, I've always hoped there'd someday be another Augustus Montgomery—even if I didn't want to take on the responsibility of being a father.

So maybe after you have a Nick Junior and another son to name after your father, you might consider a "Gus."

If I'm watching from somewhere, that would really tickle me.

Love,
Your black sheep uncle, Gus.

Nick folded the last couple of pages, then held out his hand for the others.

''You're not going to let me read the rest?'' Carly asked.

''Maybe later. But the only other thing he said about you was that he hopes we get married and name a son after him.''

Nick expected her to laugh at that, but she didn't. She simply said, ''Name a poor defenseless little baby Gus? Oh, I don't think so. Although I might be able to live with naming a girl August.''

Nick gazed at her, his heart hammering. Was she saying that the idea of marrying him and having children…?

Hell, he didn't know whether she was or not. At the moment, he wasn't sure he'd know black from white. His thoughts had begun to spin so fast, his head felt dizzy.

Until a few hours ago, he'd been thinking that all he and Carly could have was a short-term thing. Now, suddenly, he was thinking in terms of the rest of their lives.

He liked that, and yet it scared the hell out of him. But right this second just *had* to be the time to explain how things really stood with his job and all.

Then Carly eased closer and wrapped her arms around his neck, and that thought got lost in the spin cycle.

CHAPTER ELEVEN

The Moment of Truth

IT WAS ALMOST eight o'clock, but the sun was nowhere near setting, so after Nick lit the candles on the kitchen table he closed the shutters. Then he let his mind drift back a few hours.

He still wasn't sure which had surprised him more—Gus's off-the-wall suggestion that he and Carly should get married or the fact that she hadn't said the idea was ridiculous.

Of course, she really hadn't said *anything*—except that she wouldn't name a baby Gus. And then, after they'd made love again, the issue hadn't resurfaced. But they had to talk about what was going on between them. About where, if anywhere, it might be leading.

Before they did, though, he just *had* to tell her the truth. He couldn't put it off any longer, no matter how angry it made her.

He glanced at the table one more time. The candles, a white cloth, the good cutlery and dishes, salad and wine on the table, and his specialty—pepper steaks—under the broiler.

It was the best he could do. He only hoped it was enough to put her in the right frame of mind to see the humor in the situation.

"Now, no smart remarks from you," he warned

Crackers. "And no begging at the table," he told the Marx brothers. "I want this dinner to be perfect."

He considered telling the cats to behave themselves, too, but since they never listened to him, he didn't bother—simply gave the table a final once-over, then headed for the front porch, where Carly was sitting with a glass of iced tea.

"Okay, dinner's ready," he said, opening the screen door.

She followed him to the kitchen and stopped in the doorway. "Oh, Nick, this looks so...romantic."

"Hey, I'm a romantic kind of guy." He held her chair, then got the steaks out of the oven and the vegetables from the microwave.

Sitting down across from her, he poured the wine and raised his glass. "To Gus. For bringing us together."

She smiled one of her fabulous smiles. "I'm awfully glad he did. If you hadn't been here the last little while, I don't know how I'd have survived."

"Well...helping out is as much to my benefit as yours."

"No, Nick, it isn't *nearly* as much. We both know that."

He told himself this was the moment to bite the bullet, but he'd just put a piece of steak in his mouth.

Then Carly started talking about something, and before he knew it, they'd finished eating. They'd drunk most of the wine, too, which was probably a good thing. If she was a little mellow, she might be more receptive to his explanation.

He cleared his throat, then made himself begin. "Carly, there's something I have to tell you."

Halfway through his sentence, the phone started to ring.

"Oh, Lord," she said. "That reminds me, there's something I have to tell you, too. My mother called last night to say that she and my dad and sister are arriving in the morning. With everything else that's been going on, I forgot to mention it."

Nick watched her hurry to the phone, thinking it was a damn good thing he'd decided to get this straightened out tonight. He could hardly have had her introducing him to her family as an Edmonton police detective—then have to explain why she hadn't known the truth.

After she'd listened to her caller for a minute, she said, "No, there's no problem, Dylan. And thanks for letting me know."

"What's up?" he asked as she headed back to the table.

"Nothing, really. He just thought he should tell me that Craig and Jonathan are switching shifts tomorrow. But where were we? You were saying you had something to tell me."

"Right. And you're going to think it's pretty funny." He really hoped there was at least a chance of that, although he knew the odds weren't good.

She smiled encouragingly.

"You see, way back when we met, that day in Bill Brown's office, I—"

This time, it was the Marx brothers who interrupted him—taking off on red alert.

"Company!" Crackers announced over their barking. "Company!"

Muttering to himself, Nick trailed Carly to the front

door. She opened it to reveal Jay standing on the porch.

"Look at this," he said, making a sweeping gesture through the air.

"Look at this sunset. I've got to use it. I want an owl sitting on a branch, silhouetted against the orange. Then we'll shoot him in twilight. And, finally, in total darkness. Royce is getting the cameras set up, so come on. There's no time to waste."

"HOOT, OLLIE," Carly tried again.

But Ollie the owl was *not* in a hooting mood. Jay had found a dead tree only a few feet into the woods that they had Ollie perched on. And to make him visible in the darkness, Royce was using an enormous arc light—which he called "the brute" and said gave off the equivalent of 12,000 watts.

Ollie had never been in such a bright spotlight before, and he apparently didn't like it any more than Carly did.

The night was warm, and sitting in the heat from the brute she was downright hot, but somebody had to hold the end of Ollie's invisible lead.

She glanced over at Nick, who gave her a weary smile. He looked, she thought guiltily, dead on his feet.

Stiff and sore as he'd been, they probably shouldn't have spent the entire afternoon making love. At the very least, she should have convinced him to take a nap.

But just the thought of making love with him made her long to get back to the house. She wanted to be in his arms again, and she wanted to hear what he'd been going to tell her before Jay had interrupted. Of course, she was pretty sure she knew what it was, but hearing him say it would make it official.

She smiled to herself, silently laughing at the way her heartbeat accelerated every time she pictured Nick taking her hands in his. Now that they'd fallen in love, he'd say, they were somehow going to have to solve the problem of the thousands of miles between their worlds.

At any rate, that was what she was praying he'd say, because she wanted it more than she'd ever even imagined wanting anything.

"Jay?" Goodie said, breaking the silence on the set. "Why don't we call it a night and dub a hoot in editing."

"Shhh," Jay hissed.

"Don't 'shhh' me. Do you realize how much film you're wasting?"

Carly glanced at her watch, hating to imagine the answer to that. They'd been out here for hours, shooting Ollie against the sunset, then in the dusk, and now with—supposedly—only the moon and stars for light.

Jay had decided that intercutting various shots of Ollie, with ones of the lost boys, would effectively show the passing hours. That struck her as a nice artistic touch, but when it came to the hoot, she thought he was getting carried away. Nobody would know if the sound was dubbed.

Just as she was thinking that, they lucked out. Something rustled in the leaves, Ollie's gaze snapped toward the sound and he produced a long, reedy "Hoooot."

"Cut. And print." Jay called. "That's a wrap, folks. And they're forecasting a cloudy day tomorrow, which would wreak havoc with our continuity, so we're going to do some of the night shooting instead of day scenes. Which means you can all sleep late. We won't start getting organized until the afternoon.''

While Carly was pushing herself up off the ground, Jay turned to her and added, ''We'll need the dogs tomorrow night.''

''You mean the German shepherds I'm bringing in for the search party scenes or—''

''No, no.'' He impatiently waved her words away. ''Just your wolf dogs. We'll do some howling scenes, and the one where the kids spot them and are scared half to death. Oh, and I'm adding a scene where they chase a deer, then tear it apart. That might be effective in the moonlight.''

''Chase a deer and tear it apart?'' she said uneasily. ''Jay, this is a *family* movie.''

''Well they won't *really* be doing that. We'll shoot the dogs running and a deer running, and edit. Just like with the boys and Attila.''

''But the kids in the audience won't know that's what you did. They'll think the Marx brothers killed Bambi.''

''She's right,'' Goodie said.

''Then we'll run a notice across the screen with the opening credits, saying that scenes depicting injury to animals have been simulated.''

''How may kids do you think read the credits?'' Goodie demanded.

Jay glared at him but said, ''Okay. Forget the chasing part. I still want a scene of the wolves tearing something apart, though. It'll illustrate what they could do to the boys. Barb can put something together that'll look like a dead animal.''

''At any rate,'' he added, glancing at Carly again,

"I won't need the dogs until about eight at night, so you and Nick can have the day off."

As she nodded, someone turned off the brute. The heat from it immediately began to dissipate, and her eyes gradually adjusted to the moonlight.

By the time they had, Nick was at her side. "Let's get out of here before Jay thinks up any more scenes to add," he whispered. "But I trust you noticed there were no problems on the set tonight. And I hear the afternoon shoot with the boys went fine—which means we've gone the entire day without our saboteur doing anything."

"So maybe he *has* decided to quit before he gets caught."

"With any luck."

Carly coaxed Ollie onto her shoulder, hoping with all her heart that the problems really *had* ended for good. Especially with her parents and Lisa arriving tomorrow. She'd have to spend as much time as she could with them, so playing detective would be almost impossible.

She was just about to say that to Nick when a woman called his name.

As they turned, Barb Hunt caught up with them and said, "Okay if I walk along with you for a minute?"

"Sure," Nick said. "What's up?"

"Well, what we were talking about yesterday..." She hesitated, glancing toward Carly. "About the things..."

"You mean the things that have been happening," Nick said.

When she glanced at Carly again, he added, "She's as concerned as I am. There's no reason to hedge."

Barb nodded. "Okay, then you're probably going to figure this is crazy, but I've been thinking there's someone else who might be causing the trouble."

"Who?"

"Well…"

When Barb looked around, Carly did too, but there was no reason anybody would be near them. They were walking toward the house while everyone else was heading for the camp.

"Okay." Barb took a visibly deep breath. "It could be Goodie."

"What?" Carly said, her tone so surprised it made Ollie do a little shuffling step on her shoulder.

But the idea of Goodie causing the problems made about as much sense as Jay's doing it. Which meant Barb must simply be trying to cause her husband grief. What sort of grief did she figure Nick would give him, though? Unless she had evidence.

"Wait a minute," Nick was saying. "Every time something goes wrong, Goodie's complaining about how much money the delays are costing him."

"I know," Barb said. "But he's a sneaky bastard. And the more I think about it, the more I'm wondering if he has a master plan."

"To do what?"

"Gain control of Get Real Productions."

"I thought it was already his company."

"No, not his alone. He has a couple of silent partners. They initially put up a lot of working capital, and between them they've got a controlling interest. Goodie doesn't like that, but when he decided he wanted to start Get Real he didn't have enough money of his own."

"I'm missing something here," Nick said. "How would losing money on this movie help him?"

"Well, none of the films he's made so far have done great box office. And his partners are getting tired of waiting for a good return on their investment, so if Goodie suggested buying them out, they might go for it."

"Has he got the money to do that?" Carly asked. "I mean, if he didn't have enough in the beginning..."

Barb shrugged. "Goodie never talked to me about his finances, not even before our marriage hit the skids. But I was thinking, if *Two for Trouble* bombs, his partners might even be willing to sell out at a loss.

"And that would give Goodie control before he started work on his next movie. That's the one I told you about, Nick. The one based on a blockbuster novel. He figures it's sure to be a smash."

"Goodie trying to ruin his own movie," Nick said. "Would he really do that?"

"Well, he hasn't been speaking to me lately, let alone confiding in me. But yeah, I think he might."

"It just sounds so crazy," Carly said.

Barb shrugged again. "There's a saying in L.A. that goes, 'All directors are crazy, and producers are downright certifiable.'"

"SO YOU REALLY DON'T think it could be Goodie?" Carly asked as she locked the kitchen door.

"My instinct tells me it's not," Nick said wearily. "But my instinct isn't infallible, so I guess we'd better try to keep an eye on him."

"Along with continuing to try to keep an eye on the chef, Sarina and Garth?"

Nick nodded. "We're liable to end up cross-eyed by the time the movie's finished."

Carly gave him a wry smile. "But hopefully whoever it is has stopped."

"Yeah. Hopefully." He leaned against the kitchen counter, watching her give the Marx brothers fresh water and thinking that he was totally exhausted. Not to mention stiff and sore, to use the phrase of the day.

Even so, he knew he still had to deal with the little matter of telling her the truth. If she hadn't been so keen on discussing the possibility of Goodie as suspect while they'd walked the dogs, he might even have had it over and done with by now.

But he doubted it. He was still trying to work up his courage again.

As they started for the stairs, she wrapped her arm around his waist. It made him decide that bed would be the best place to tell her.

At the top of the stairs, she smiled again—an inviting one this time—and said, "Your place or mine?" Then she glanced into his room, at the tangle of sheets they'd left behind earlier, and decided on hers.

She flicked off the hall light but didn't bother switching on the bedroom one. And when he followed her into the room, she turned toward him in the moonlight and snuggled her body against his.

He breathed in the meadow-fresh scent of her hair, thinking that there was nothing he'd rather be doing than holding her like this. Then she began playing with the buttons on his shirt, and he felt a strong stirring of arousal.

"Carly...we have to talk," he said reluctantly.

"I know. You want to tell me something. I haven't

forgotten. But I just can't seem to be alone with you and not touch you. Actually, I can hardly keep my hands off you when we're *not* alone."

He swallowed hard. Since he felt exactly the same way, maybe the talking could wait for just a few more minutes.

Even with only the moonlight, Carly could see the desire in Nick's eyes, and it sent a frisson of excitement through her. They made fast work of their clothes, then virtually fell onto the bed.

"Have I told you lately that I love you?" he whispered, trailing hot kisses down her neck.

"Not lately enough," she managed to say. "You could tell me every minute and I'd never get tired of hearing it."

Nick didn't tell her again, but she didn't really mind. Not when he kissed her instead. A long, sweet, endless kiss that made the dull throbbing of desire inside her grow stronger and stronger.

His tongue, hungry in her mouth, sent heat racing through her, and when he cupped her breasts and began to graze her nipples, electric currents of need rushed excited messages to every single nerve ending in her body.

She felt sharp slivers of delight everywhere he touched her, and as she reached down and encircled his hardness with her fingers, she heard his heartbeat thud with his need.

When she began caressing him, he groaned and slid his hand down her belly to the dampness of her arousal, his touch making her gasp with need. Instinct made her move against him, loving what he was doing.

Gradually, the sensations became almost too much,

filling her so she could scarcely catch her breath. She desperately wanted him inside her, and as he finally thrust into her, she felt a sweet surge of heat.

Each thrust carried her closer to the edge, making her more and more frantic until she couldn't breathe at all. Then, for one soul-shattering space in time, a shock wave of liquid fire seared her. She half cried, half sighed his name, clinging tightly to him while he came, then clinging still as her shudders slowly began to subside.

At last, they faded entirely, and she was breathing normally once more.

"You okay?" Nick murmured.

"Oh, Nick," she whispered against his shoulder. "I'm an entire universe beyond 'okay.'"

He smiled, then shifted to his side, stretching his body out along hers and cradling her tightly to him.

A whisper of a breeze drifted in through the window over their moist bodies. It was deliciously cool, but as hot as the room was, she'd far rather have the heat of Nick's strong male body pressed against her than a cool breeze.

Being with him like this felt so right she couldn't keep from smiling. If she could spend every night of her life in the same bed as Nick Montgomery, she'd die a happy woman.

"What are you thinking?" he asked.

"Can't tell," she teased. "Your ego's big enough already."

That made *him* smile, which made her want to start all over again. But before she could lift a finger, the phone began to ring.

Nick tensed at the sound. In his line of work he'd had a lot of late-night calls, and they were never good news. "Who'd be phoning at this hour?" he asked as Carly switched on the bedside light.

"It must be my mother. Maybe they're not coming tomorrow after all."

He let his gaze wander over her naked body while she lifted the phone from the bedside table to the bed, thinking it was the most gorgeous body in the world.

Then he looked at her mouth as she picked up the receiver. It was the most gorgeous mouth, as well. And it kissed to perfection.

After she said hello, he heard nothing for a second. Then a voice he recognized came booming over the line so loudly that Carly jerked the receiver away from her ear.

"Oh, I hope I don't have the wrong number this late," his ex-partner said. "But is Nick Montgomery there?"

"Yes, just a moment." Carly handed him the receiver.

"Ben," he said. He desperately wanted to tell him to speak quietly for a change, but before he could get another word out, Ben launched into boom mode again.

"This is what happens when a guy quits the job?" he demanded.

Nick felt something freeze inside him, and there was suddenly a taste like ashes in his mouth.

"I wanted to let you know I've got the guys lined up to move your stuff," Ben went on. "I know it's late there, but I've been calling all night. And, hell, now that I finally get you, you're with a sexy-voiced woman. Man, I can hardly wait to retire, although I guess Ida's going to cramp my style some."

"Ben, listen. This is bad timing, okay? I'll call you back."

He put down the receiver, his gaze locked with Carly's. There was confusion in her eyes.

"You quit your job," she said.

He nodded.

"You mean, you called long distance and just quit? But when? And why didn't you tell me?"

"I... No. That's not..." He shook his head. He'd mentally rehearsed this a hundred times, but now that he'd been thrown a curve, he could feel panic growing inside him.

When he looked at her again she was smiling. He didn't know why, and that really worried him. She sure as hell hadn't been smiling whenever he'd imagined this scene.

"Oh, Nick," she murmured. "Oh, Nick, you're the sweetest man on earth. And I love you so much." She draped her arms around his neck and gazed at him adoringly.

It made him feel like a drowning man going under for the third time. He wasn't sure exactly what she was thinking, but if he didn't straighten her out right now, he knew she'd end up killing him.

He took a deep breath, then said, "Carly, listen to me. I've been trying to tell you this almost from day one, but the timing just never seemed right. I quit the force before I left Edmonton. The very day I got Bill Brown's letter. The day before I flew to Toronto.

"In hindsight, I know it was a really dumb thing to do, but the letter said that Gus had left the entire estate to me. And when I phoned to ask about it, I got told that Wild Action was making pots of money. And I'd had it up to my eyeballs with the job, so..."

He stopped talking. Carly had undraped her arms from around his neck and was trying to tug the sheet over her nakedness—all the while glaring at him.

"You quit your job before we even met. You never had a job to go back to at all," she added, giving the sheet another hard tug.

When that knocked the receiver off the phone, she grabbed both parts and heaved them through the air. As they crashed onto the floor, she succeeded in getting the sheet tucked around herself.

"Carly, just listen," he said, trying to ignore the fact that she was now covered up while he was still buck naked.

"You quit your job and lied about it. So what else have you been lying about? And what the hell game did you think you were playing?"

"I haven't been playing *any* game."

The coldness of her expression sent a shiver down his spine, but he pressed on. "And I didn't exactly *lie*. I just didn't mention I'd quit."

"Oh, puh-leese!"

"That's all it was!"

"That's all it was? You mean I hallucinated the part where you pretended to call your boss and asked for time off? So you'd make me think that your only motive was to play white knight and help a damsel in distress?"

"Carly, I didn't *try* to make you think that. I didn't intentionally set out to make you think I was being some kind of Sir Galahad. But by the time I realized that's the way you were reading things... Look, I know I should have explained. I've known it all along."

"Then why not explain right now," she said icily. "I can hardly wait to hear."

"All right," he said, scrambling to get his thoughts organized. "Brown had barely said that Gus had actually only left me forty-nine percent of Wild Action before you started talking about how it was just earning enough to scrape by and that if you screwed up with this damn movie, it would probably bankrupt us. So, not surprisingly, I felt like a bit of an idiot for having rashly quit my job. And I didn't see any reason to admit my idiocy to three strangers."

"Strangers? You're calling me a stranger?" Looking absolutely furious, she waved her hand at his nakedness.

"Well you were a stranger then!"

"I don't believe you, Nick Montgomery. I simply *do not* believe you."

"But it's the truth. I—"

"That is *not* what I mean! Dammit, the truth is that you only volunteered to help because you could see your inheritance going down the toilet. And if I'd known that from the onset, I wouldn't have cared much. But to put on an act about having to take time off work, to make me think you were rearranging your life to do me a favor..."

"I told you! I didn't intentionally try to make you think that."

"Well, intentional or not, it just makes me so mad! And to let me go on believing your lies all the way into bed is unforgivable!"

"All right. I made a mistake. But I didn't lie about loving you."

"Oh, and I'm supposed to believe that just because you say so? The way I believed you had a good job and that you were trying to help save Wild Action mostly for me? Dammit, what you were *really* trying to save was your own ass! Which I'd like you to get out of my bed. Right this second!''

"Carly, I know I said this before, but I honestly did mean to explain."

"Sure you did."

"I did."

"Then what stopped you?"

"I...well...it was..."

"Dammit, Nick, just get out of my bed!" With that, she burst into tears.

"Carly, I—"

"Get out!" She fiercely wiped her eyes. "I don't know how I could have thought you were wonderful when you're positively despicable. You know what I assumed when that man said you'd quit?"

He shook his head, feeling more miserable than he'd ever felt.

"I thought you'd phoned Edmonton and quit because you'd decided you wanted to stay here with me." Fresh tears began to flow, but she kept going. "How could I have been such a moron, when all the time you were laughing at me behind my back?"

"Dammit, Carly, I wasn't—"

"Dammit, yourself! I want you gone in the morning."

"Look, just calm down a little, okay? We're a long way from home free with Jay, so you still need my help."

"I don't need *anything* from you. I... Oh, rats, I wish to hell I didn't! But the minute this shoot's finished, I want you out of here. We'll have to get the

lawyers to figure out some way to divide the estate,
because once this movie's done I never want to see
you again.''

CHAPTER TWELVE

Long Day's Journey into Fright

THE MORNING WAS WARM, but gray with threatening rain. It matched Carly's mood to perfection.

She didn't bother making anything for breakfast because she knew she'd never be able to eat. After she'd spent half the night crying, her throat was aching, still tight with tears.

But at least she didn't have to face Nick quite yet. There was no sign of either him or the Marx brothers, so he must have taken them for a walk—undoubtedly to avoid her.

They could only avoid each other for so long, though. And she didn't know how she was going to cope with having him around until the shooting was finished when she was so...

Heartbroken might sound melodramatic, but it was the right word. She'd fallen in love with him thinking he was someone special, a man she could trust, and learning that he'd been lying to her from the very beginning had been devastating.

Since her stomach wasn't up to coffee, she simply poured herself a glass of orange juice, then went into the solarium and morosely sat down beside Crackers.

The parrot didn't utter a sound, which told her she was giving off really bad vibes. And she could feel them getting even worse when she spotted Nick coming across the clearing with the dogs.

Merely seeing him made her want to run and hide. But she could hardly spend the day locked in her room when her parents and Lisa would be arriving any minute.

She only hoped she was up to putting on a good act for them so they wouldn't realize something was wrong.

The kitchen door opened, and the Marx brothers bounded in to greet her. Ignoring Nick, who followed them inside, she gave hard hugs all around.

The dogs weren't wolves in sheep's clothing like some people she could name.

"Carly, could we please talk about last night?" Nick said quietly.

She looked in his direction without meeting his gaze, telling herself to keep a tight rein on her emotions. "I think we've already said everything there is to say," she managed evenly. "So let's just go back to being strictly business partners and give Jay the rest of the scenes he wants. In the meantime, my parents and sister will be here any time, and I've still got some things to do."

Standing up, she added, "Maybe you should work with Attila a couple of times today. We'd better keep him sharp until Jay's finished shooting his scenes." With that, she walked out of the room.

Nick watched her go, pain twisting up through his chest.

"Trouble," Crackers said. "Trouble."

"Tell me about it," he muttered.

All four dogs trailed after Carly without a backward glance—as if wanting to ensure that he knew where *their* sympathies lay—and it took every bit of his willpower to keep from following right along with them. He wanted to make Carly listen to him.

On the other hand, he wasn't a total fool when it came to women, even if he *was* having trouble believing that right now. So, as much as he wanted to fix things between them, he knew it would be smarter to give her some time, to let her calm down enough that he'd be able to make her understand.

But what if he couldn't? What if, by the time the movie was finished, she was still convinced she wanted him out of her life? What if he'd lost her through his damn stupidity?

That thought scared the hell out of him. He might not be sure how they'd work out the logistics of a life together, but he knew he'd still want her when he was old and gray. And he sure didn't want to spend the rest of his life pining for a lost love.

Running his fingers through his hair, he told himself to try thinking only positive thoughts again. All he needed was a plan. Or maybe he'd better make that a dozen of them. As angry as she was, he doubted one would be enough.

Grabbing Gus's cowboy hat from its peg, he headed back outside. She'd asked him to work with Attila, so he'd make doing what she wanted Plan A.

And when her family got here, he'd do his darnedest to charm them. If they liked him, it certainly wouldn't hurt. Then, for Plan C...

He started down the hill, not able to come up with a Plan C. He would, though. He'd win her back if he had to work his way through the entire alphabet.

"AND THIS IS MY sister, Lisa," Carly said, looking at her sandals rather than at Nick, because every time she looked at him she could feel someone turning a knife in her stomach.

But she just couldn't seem to keep her eyes off him, and when she glanced up he was giving Lisa a killer smile.

"It's a real pleasure meeting all of you," he said, extending the smile to include her parents.

Carly cringed inside, thinking how she'd been so thoroughly taken in by those open and honest-looking smiles.

When she forced her gaze away from him again, her mother caught her eye and gave her a look that said, "Doesn't *this* seem like an interesting man." Lord, if Mother only knew. They hadn't even made it into the house yet, and Nick was already winning them over. Apparently, the rest of her family were no more perceptive than she was.

"It's too bad your husband couldn't come," he was saying to Lisa.

"Oh, he's away—gone off to a training course in Chicago for two weeks. But since he's not a Garth Richards fan, he doesn't figure he's missing much."

Just as Carly was about to suggest they go inside, Lisa whispered, "Oh, look, it's *him*."

She glanced down the driveway and saw Garth— accompanied by Sarina.

"Did you *ask* them to drop by and meet us?" Lisa said.

Carly shook her head, wondering what the stars wanted.

She didn't have to wait long to find out. She'd barely introduced them before Garth said, "We came to ask a favor. We've been feeling positively stifled out here in the middle of nowhere, and when we woke up and saw this dreary morning... Well, we decided the only way to cheer ourselves up was to go to Toronto for a first-class lunch.''

"Oh, you don't have to go that far," she told him. "There are a couple of really good restaurants in Port Perry. My favorite is called—"

"We have our hearts set on a *big city* restaurant," Garth interrupted. "But Jay says he can't spare a vehicle and driver. And when we called the limo service we used coming here, they were completely booked for today. So..."

"So you'd like to borrow my van?" Carly concluded.

"Well, it's very kind of you to offer," Sarina said. "But I'm afraid we'd need a driver, too. You see, I don't drive, and Garth's license is...temporarily suspended."

"Some states have ridiculous drinking-and-driving laws," he muttered.

"So our original thought," Sarina went on, "was that it would be fun to treat you and Nick to lunch."

Before he had a chance to open his mouth, Carly said, "I'm afraid Nick's got a hundred things to do today." There was no way in the world she was going anywhere with him, let alone all the way to Toronto and back.

"Oh. Well, as I said, that was our *original* thought. But now that we know your family's here, why don't the four of you come? There's room in your van for six, isn't there?"

While Sarina was speaking, Lisa gave Carly a surreptitious but sharp poke in the ribs—her way of voting for going.

Then their father said, "Well, thanks. It's nice of you to invite us, but I've had enough traveling for today. And the Toronto traffic does terrible things to my wife's nerves.

"But what about you two?" he added, glancing at his daughters. "You look tired, Carly. A little break and a nice lunch would probably do you good."

"Yes, you don't look your usual self," Mother chimed in. "So why don't you and Lisa get changed? Your father and I can settle ourselves in after you've gone."

"And once you're settled," Nick said, "I'll take you down to the camp and introduce you to some of the other movie people. We could probably even have lunch there."

Mother shot Carly a second look, this one saying Nick was positively charming.

"You're sure you don't mind taking a perfect stranger to lunch?" Lisa was asking Sarina and Garth.

"We'd be delighted to have you," Garth told her.

"Then we'd be delighted to go. We'll only be a few minutes." Lisa took Carly's arm and propelled her into the house.

"Lisa, this is ridiculous," Carly complained the instant they were out of hearing range. "I don't want to go for lunch with those two."

"Oh, don't be a party pooper. You know I've seen every Garth Richards movie ten times. And spending a few hours with him will be fantastic!"

That's what you think, Carly said silently.

"Besides, you don't like Mildred Walker any more than I do."

Carly had no idea what the relevance of that remark was, but it was true. Mildred Walker had been their principal in high school, and now Lisa was teaching under her—which she claimed was the worst aspect of her job.

"Come on, Carly. Just imagine the next time Mildred starts in on her Marlon Brando story. You know, the one about how she met him at a cocktail party centuries ago. Picture her face when I tell her that Garth Richards took me to lunch."

THE RESTAURANT AT THE TOP of Toronto's CN Tower was floor-to-ceiling windows and slowly revolved to afford a hawk's eye view of both the sprawling city and the choppy gray water of Lake Ontario.

Even under a gloomy sky, it was a lovely spot. And Carly knew that if she hadn't been feeling so miserable, she'd have enjoyed lunch. Even if Garth *had* talked about himself practically nonstop.

But the way things stood, the panoramic views that Lisa and Sarina were still oohing and ahhing about left her cold. And she hadn't even tasted the food, which the others said was excellent.

When the waiter arrived with the bill, Garth didn't even glance at it, simply handed over his gold card. Then he looked around once more, as if he just couldn't believe nobody in the place had recognized him.

Carly finally took pity on him and said, "I don't know if you've noticed, but most Canadians are pretty reserved. In a classy restaurant like this, it would be unusual for anyone to bother you and Sarina for autographs."

"Really?"

Given his expression, he was thinking that Canadians didn't know what they were missing.

"Well...dear..." Sarina murmured to him.

"Oh, yes." He looked across the table once more. "You know, Sarina and I were thinking. We're not in any of the scenes Jay's shooting tonight, so it would be fun to stay in town. We can pick up some theater tickets and have a nice dinner, then hire a limo to drive us back tomorrow."

An uneasy feeling began curling around in Carly's stomach—mingling with the sick one that had been lodged there since last night. She'd bet the bank that Jay would have twenty fits if she arrived back without his stars.

"What about tomorrow?" she said. "Are you sure Jay isn't planning on shooting any of your scenes in the morning?"

Sarina lifted her shoulders in a graceful shrug that said, "Who cares?"

It made Carly feel like reaching across the table and shaking her. Sarina and Garth weren't the ones Jay would try to murder if he wanted them and they weren't there.

"Well...maybe we should at least phone him and make sure he won't be needing you," she suggested.

"Oh, he still has days of shooting that don't involve us," Sarina said blithely. "And if he *was* intending to do any of our scenes in the morning, he can always improvise."

The waiter had returned, so Garth dealt with the charge slip. Then he graced Carly and Lisa with his famous Latin-lover smile. "When we get back to ground level, Sarina and I will just grab a cab."

Carly's blood was simmering, but what could she do? She could hardly hog-tie them and take them back kicking and screaming. Although, if she had any rope in the van, she'd be tempted to try.

"Want to sneak in a little shopping before we start back?" Lisa asked as they headed for the elevator.

"No, I take after Mom when it comes to Toronto traffic, so I don't want to end up driving in rush hour."

Lisa didn't say another word aside from her good-byes to Sarina and Garth, but after they'd climbed into their taxi, she said, "What on earth is wrong with you today?"

"With me? Nothing. So what did you think of the real-life Garth?"

"Let's just say I won't be seeing any more of his pictures ten times. But that's not what we were talking about. What's with *you?*"

"Well…it's just that I'm worried about how Jay's going to react to this—to Sarina and Garth staying here. He's not going to like it, and I'm the one he'll blame."

Lisa shook her head. "There's something else. You looked like death warmed over when we arrived this morning, and you've been about as talkative as a clam."

When Carly didn't reply, Lisa was silent the rest of the way to the parking lot. Once they'd climbed into the van, she automatically dug into the glove compartment for Carly's map of Toronto. She knew, from experience, that her sister needed a navigator.

"Is the movie not going well?" she asked as Carly started the engine.

She pulled out of her parking space before answering. "We had a few rough days," she said at last, "but things seem to be all right now."

"Then what's the problem?"

"Okay, Lisa, there *is* a problem, but I can't talk about it and drive in the traffic at the same time."

That bought a silence that lasted, with only a few random comments from Lisa, until they'd made it all the way up to the highway.

"There's not much traffic now," Lisa said then. "So can you please let me in on what's wrong?"

Carly shot her a miserable glance, told herself she was *not* going to cry, and said, "It's Nick."

"Ahh. Nick of the warm gray eyes. He should have been my first guess."

By the time they'd traveled another twenty miles, Carly had recounted pretty much the entire story. And she had managed not to cry, even though she'd come close.

Lisa gazed silently out at the ever-darkening day for a minute, then said, "But you *are* in love with him."

"I thought I was, but... Lisa, I feel as if he suddenly pulled the rug out from under me. No, not just the rug, the whole darn floor. And I'm still sitting on I don't know what—absolutely stunned.

"I mean, I was going merrily along thinking what a darling he was for helping me out. So to discover that he was mostly concerned with taking care of his *own* interests... And he was probably laughing at me the whole time because I'd been so gullible.

"And if that friend of his hadn't phoned, I'd *never* have known the truth. I mean, Nick sure wasn't going to volunteer it."

"I thought he told you he was just waiting for the right moment."

"Oh, sure. You know how long he's been here.

Can you really believe there was no right moment in all that time? It just makes me... Oh, I don't know whether I feel more stupid, hurt or angry."

That said, Carly focused her full attention on the road, because a whole horde of bikers on serious motorcycles were roaring past. Despite the hot mugginess of the afternoon, they were wearing jackets—some denim, some black leather, all with Devil's Dice emblazoned across the back.

"So," Lisa said once the sound of their engines was fading. "After Nick's friend phoned and the two of you were having your big fight, did he come up with some reason for lying?"

Carly shrugged. "It was a darned lame one. He said... Well, as I told you, until he walked into Bill Brown's office, he thought Gus had left the entire estate to him. And when he discovered that wasn't true, he realized he'd been pretty dumb to just march in and quit his job. So his excuse for not telling us was that he didn't want us to think he was an idiot."

"Well, it *was* a pretty dumb move, so I can understand that."

"Maybe at first it made a little sense," Carly admitted grudgingly. "But as soon as he suggested staying on to help out and I asked him if he'd be able to take the time away from work... Well, that's when he *definitely* should have admitted the truth, right? Instead of making that stupid fake call and pretending his boss had told him he could stay for a while."

"Yeah, that *was* pretty dumb."

"And since he's been at the house, there must have been a zillion times he could have explained things to me. But he just didn't."

"Well, I guess the longer he kept quiet..."

"Are you trying to make excuses for him?" Carly demanded.

"No," Lisa said quickly. "I was just thinking about that line, 'Oh what a tangled web we weave...' I mean, you sound as if you're certain he made a conscious decision to deceive you, but—"

"You *are* trying to make excuses!"

"No, I'm just wondering if maybe... He seems like such a nice guy, Carly. It's hard to believe he's deep-down rotten."

"I thought he was a nice guy, too. Until last night."

"Well, maybe after the first lie or two, he just figured he'd already dug himself in too deep to tell you the truth without looking like a *major* idiot."

"If that's the case, then he *is* a major idiot." As she said that, Carly caught something in her peripheral vision and glanced to her left.

Her heart leapt to her throat. Two burly Devil's Dice members were riding alongside the van, and they were both motioning her to pull over onto the shoulder.

"Gun it," Lisa said nervously.

Before Carly's brain relayed the message to her foot, one of the bikers swerved in front of them. A second later, his brake light went on.

"Oh, no," Lisa said as Carly hit her own brakes.

The biker in front slowed to a crawl, while the one still riding along beside them motioned toward the shoulder again.

"What do I do?" Carly said, half wishing Nick was with them, and half wishing she didn't want his help.

"Can you pull out and pass?"

"Not without driving into the one beside us."

"Then pull over. Otherwise, someone's bound to rear-end us."

Trying to control her panic, Carly pulled off onto the shoulder and stopped—now *desperately* wishing Nick was there.

Despite how angry and upset she'd been last night, despite thinking she never wanted to see him again, he'd demonstrated he was a good man to have around when there were problems.

The motorcycle in front of the van had stopped when she did. The other one had pulled up tightly behind it. And within seconds, both bikers were standing beside her door—one of them holding a sports bag. The other one motioned Carly to roll down the window.

"Don't do it," Lisa whispered.

"Let's cooperate, lady," the man said, producing a gun. He held it close to his chest, so nobody driving by could see it, and motioned again for Carly to roll down the window.

Her hand shaking, she did.

"Okay," the one with the sports bag said. "There's a problem up ahead and I wanna put this bag in your van. Stick it on the floor in back."

He passed it through the window. Carly put it in the back. It was heavy, and she was afraid to even think about what might be in it.

"After you get a couple of miles past the trouble," the man continued, "pull over and wait for us."

While he was speaking, a cell phone began to ring. The other biker took it out of his pocket and answered.

"Yeah, yeah, we already heard," he muttered. "We got it under control."

As he stuck the phone back in his pocket, he said, "Don't even think about ditchin' the bag, eh? Or about not waitin' for us. 'Cuz it'd take about two minutes to get the address that goes with your plates, an' if we hadda waste time comin' after you, we'd be damn mad. Hear what I'm sayin'?"

"Yes," Carly told him, her heart pounding. "Yes, loud and clear. But what's this trouble?"

"You'll know it when you see it."

Without another word, the two men got back on their bikes and took off.

Carly looked at Lisa, seeing her own fear reflected in her sister's pale face. "Now what do we do?"

Lisa shrugged nervously. "Do *you* want them coming after us?"

"Of course not!"

"Then we'd better do as they said."

Shoving the transmission back into Drive, Carly checked the rearview mirror and pulled out onto the highway—telling herself there was no other real option. Metal guardrails divided the eastbound lanes from the westbound ones, so she couldn't turn around. And even if she could, she certainly didn't want those two coming after them.

"What do you think's in that bag?" Lisa asked, her voice cracking a little.

"I don't know. Other guns maybe. Or drugs."

Lisa gave her a "Yikes!" look and didn't say another word.

A couple of miles down the highway, the traffic slowed abruptly. Up ahead, Carly could see what the "trouble" was. It made her throat go dry and her palms grow wet.

"Oh, no," Lisa whispered. "It's a takedown."

Carly swallowed hard. There was a line of motorcycles parked on the shoulder, and there had to be at least two dozen cops wearing bulletproof vests. They were armed with semiautomatic rifles that they had trained on the Devil's Dice members.

Some of the bikers were simply standing on the shoulder. Others were being searched by yet more cops. And, up ahead, three other officers were stopping each passing car and exchanging words with the drivers.

"Oh, Lord," Carly murmured. "What do we say when they stop us?"

"I don't know. Yes I do. You've *got* to tell the police what happened."

Carly knew Lisa was right, but it didn't stop the fear that was nibbling away at her insides. What would happen after she told the police? Her palms sweating, she slowly drove on until it was her turn to stop.

"Afternoon, ladies," the officer said when she rolled down her window. "You don't happen to know any of those gentlemen on the shoulder, do you?"

She could feel the sides of her lips twitching, but no sound was coming out.

The cop eyed her suspiciously for a moment, then peered into the back and spotted the sports bag.

"Mind letting me have a look at that?" It wasn't a question.

Lisa made a strangled little sound, then said, "It's not ours, Officer." She gave a tiny nod toward the side of the road and added, "It belongs to one of them."

"All right," the cop said. "I want you to both keep your hands where I can see them. And I want you to get out of the van slowly. Then you just stand facing it and place your hands on the roof."

CHAPTER THIRTEEN

Just When You Think You're Out of the Woods...

NICK HEADED UP THE hill from his afternoon session with Attila, dying for a cold drink. It was hot as hell and so humid he couldn't believe it wasn't raining yet.

But when he reached the house the phone was ringing, so he grabbed it instead of a beer.

"Oh, Nick," Carly said before he'd even finished his hello. "Thank heavens you're there."

She sounded so frightened his heart lurched.

"What's wrong?" he demanded, visions of traffic accidents dancing before his eyes. "Are you hurt?"

"No, I'm just scared half to death. Lisa and I got arrested. The police think we're bikers' chicks."

"They think you're *what*?" He couldn't have heard right.

"Bikers' chicks."

He *had* heard right, and under different circumstances he'd have had a hard time not laughing. Whatever was going on, no cop in his right mind would take either Lisa or Carly for bikers' chicks—especially not when they were dressed for lunch in the city.

"There was a takedown on the 401," she was explaining. "And two guys from the Devil's Dice stashed a bag of cocaine in the van. Then the police were stopping all the cars, and when they stopped us the cop asked about the bag and we said it belonged to one of the gang members. And now Lisa's terrified, because if a teacher ends up with a drug conviction she loses her job, and—''

''Carly, try to calm down and listen. This is just a misunderstanding. Everything's going to be all right. Neither of you is going to end up with a drug conviction. You're probably not even going to be charged. They *haven't* charged you with anything, have they?''

''Oh, Nick, I don't even know. They said we had to come with them to the detachment, and when we got here—''

''Which one? Where is it?''

''At Whitby.''

''Fine. I'll be there just as fast as I can. And if they want to question you, tell them your lawyer's on his way and you've been instructed not to answer any questions until he arrives.''

''But you're not a lawyer,'' she whispered.

''If you need one, I'll get you one. But I should be able to straighten this out myself. Now, you're going to be all right until I get there?''

There was a momentary pause, then she said, ''Yes. Yes, of course. I feel better already just knowing you're coming.''

He couldn't help smiling at that. It was the nicest thing she'd said to him since last night. Hell, it was the *only* nice thing.

''Oh, and don't breathe a word to my parents. My dad had a heart attack a couple of years ago, and if you told him we'd been arrested, he might have another one.''

''Don't worry, they're not around. They were just watching me work with Attila, and when I finished they said they wanted to take a walk in the woods before it starts to rain.'' Which meant, he realized, he couldn't ask her father for his car. But he'd borrow one from somebody else.

With a quick goodbye, he hung up, then strode rapidly down to the camp, where he spotted Jay talking to Royce.

When Jay saw him, his expression turned as black as the day had grown. Earlier, Nick had introduced Carly's parents to the director, and they'd told him about the lunch excursion to Toronto.

Jay had *not* been pleased to learn his stars had flown the coop, and…

It suddenly struck Nick that Carly hadn't said a word about Sarina and Garth. So what was the skinny on them? Had they been arrested, too? Hell, if they had, Garth would have thrown a tantrum the size of Alberta.

''You look like a man in a hurry,'' Royce said.

''Only because I am. Carly had a little trouble on the highway. I need to borrow some wheels to go help her out.''

''You can take mine.''

''You mean Sarina and Garth are stranded in a broken-down van in this heat?'' Jay demanded. ''What if one of them gets heat stroke or something? It could throw my schedule off.''

Nick was tempted to tell him that if they got tossed into jail for possession it could *really* throw his schedule off. Instead, he said, ''I'm sure Sarina and Garth are fine. The place Carly called from was probably air-conditioned.''

THE ONTARIO PROVINCIAL Police detachment at Whitby looked like a dozen different cop shops Nick had been in, and when he walked through the front door he felt right at home.

It would have been nice to still have his detective's ID to flash, but at least he knew the ropes. Within minutes, he was talking to Paul Robson, the sergeant on duty, who turned out to know a couple of fellows on the Edmonton police force.

"Biker chicks?" Paul grinned. "Did she really say we thought that?"

Nick nodded. "I didn't *figure* any of your guys would seriously think they were, but when she said they'd been arrested..."

"Oh, hell, they're not under arrest. The guys just brought them in for questioning. You know how it is. They had a healthy stash of coke in their van, so even though it wasn't theirs, we couldn't just let them drive on."

"But there won't be any charges."

Paul shook his head. "All we'll do is take their statements and have them look at a lineup. We figure we know which bikers had the stuff, but we want a positive ID."

"Then it's okay if I see Carly and Lisa?"

"Well...yeah. But, for the record, I'd better go along. Come on," he added, starting off. "They're in an interview room."

"What about the other two?" Nick asked, falling into step.

"What other two?"

"Weren't there two other people in the van? A couple of movie stars?"

"Movie stars? Not that I heard about. And if there had been, our guys would have brought them in, too. Along with the bikers' chicks," he added with a grin.

Nick forced a grin of his own, but what the hell had happened to Sarina and Garth? If Carly'd lost them, Jay would go ballistic.

When the door of the interview room opened and Nick walked in, relief swept through Carly. She'd never been so happy to see anyone in her life, and before she even knew what she was doing, she was wrapping her arms around him.

"Hey," he whispered. "Does this mean I'm forgiven?"

"It means I'm really, really, glad you're here," she whispered back. "We'll talk about the rest of it later."

"You okay?" he said, glancing at Lisa.

"Yes, but I could use one of those hugs, too."

Nick laughed, then went over and pulled her up into his arms.

Watching them, Carly realized she already knew how that "later" talk was going to go. Sitting in this little room, she'd been staving off thoughts of a drug conviction by thinking about Nick.

And now that she'd taken time to consider everything, she could kind of see how maybe his first innocent omission had started a chain reaction until he'd gotten in so deep that he'd dreaded the prospect of 'fessing up.

And if, as he'd kept insisting, he hadn't intentionally set out to deceive her... After all, it wasn't as if he'd been concealing the fact that he was a serial killer or something.

He finished hugging Lisa, then looked over at Carly.

She gave him a little smile, and the warm one he gave her in return made her glad she had. She wasn't entirely over her anger, but she was so in love with him that the thought of never forgiving him had been getting very difficult to contemplate.

"Okay," he said. "Sergeant Robson and I discussed things, and it turns out you're not actually under arrest. All you have to do is give statements and identify the bikers who put the coke in the van."

"You mean from behind a one-way mirror?" Carly asked hopefully. She'd far rather not have to face them again.

"Sure, we can do it that way," Robson said. "And I'll have a couple of officers take your statements right away." Glancing at Nick, he added, "You can wait in my office if you'd like."

"Thanks. I just want to ask them a quick question first." He looked at Carly. "What happened to our stars?"

"They're staying in Toronto overnight. I gathered that was their plan all along. They just didn't bother mentioning it until after lunch."

"Terrific. And *we're* the ones who get to tell Jay."

She merely shrugged. In comparison to the past couple of hours, delivering a little bad news to Jay would be a piece of cake.

BY THE TIME THE police were finished with Carly and Lisa, the rain that had been threatening was coming down in buckets.

They raced to the van while Nick ran for Royce's car, and Carly got the engine started as fast as she could.

She was just about to say she'd never been so glad to get out of a place in her entire life when Lisa beat her to it.

"Until Nick got there, I was scared stiff," she added.

Carly nodded. Nick was definitely a good man to have around—for a whole lot of reasons.

"You're going to be okay with him now, aren't you?"

"I...yes."

"Good. Because I was thinking, since he doesn't have a job to go back to..."

That made Carly smile. Lisa and she had *always* thought alike. And the possibility that Nick might decide to stay on made her feel warm inside.

The feeling lasted through all the chitchat on the way home, but a chill set in when she pulled up to the house. Through the front window, she could see her parents were sitting in the living room—with Jay.

Nick pulled up beside the van, then the three of them dashed through the rain and onto the porch.

"Wait," she whispered when Nick reached for the door handle. "Jay's in there."

"Yeah? He must be waiting for us. Or, more likely, for Sarina and Garth."

"Well, regardless of what he wants, I have to ask you something before we go in. Did you tell *anybody* that we got mixed up in that takedown?"

"No, I just said you'd had some trouble on the highway."

"Good, because on the way home, Lisa and I decided it would be better not to tell Mom and Dad about it. Even after the fact, they'd get upset.''

Nick gave her a slow, wicked smile. "You're not asking me to lie...are you?"

She felt her face growing warm but did her best to look cool. "No, I'm not asking you to lie. I'm merely asking you not to mention something."

"Really," he said, drawing the word out. "Look where it got me the last time I didn't mention something."

"Very funny. But, just for this once, it'll be okay."

"Well...if you say so." He opened the door and gestured for Lisa and Carly to go in.

"You first," she murmured nervously.

"Oh, good, you're back," Jay said as the Marx brothers greeted them at the door.

"You boys go and lie down," Carly ordered after they'd gotten their pats.

"Is everything all right?" her mother asked. "You fixed whatever was wrong with the van, Nick?"

"He's a regular mechanic," Lisa said.

Jay peered around the three of them toward the door. "You dropped Sarina and Garth off at their trailer?"

"Well..." Carly said.

"Good. Now, the reason I've been waiting for you is to ask if you can get those German shepherds for tonight's shoot."

"I don't think this rain's going to let up," Nick said.

"I know, but I've decided to use it. We'll leave the wolf scenes for another night. Having them wandering around in the rain wouldn't produce the feeling I want. But I got to thinking that the search party slogging through a rainy night would be really effective. We can intercut shots of the searchers with ones of the lost boys—soaking wet and chilled to the bone.''

''Ahh.'' Carly said, realizing that telling Jay wasn't going to be a piece of cake after all. ''The boys' parents are part of the search party, aren't they?''

''Of course. You know that. You've read the script.''

Lisa shot Carly a glance that said she'd just clued in. ''Sarina and Garth are playing the boys' parents, right?''

''Uh-huh.'' Carly unhappily looked at Jay again. ''Jay, Sarina—''

''Oh, I know what you're going to say. Sarina won't like the idea of getting soaked. But she's never happy unless she's got something to complain about, so can you get those shepherds on short notice or not?''

''Probably. Their owner doesn't live far from here. But there's a different problem.''

''What?''

''Sarina and Garth stayed in Toronto.'' Nick said.

''*What!*'' Jay screamed.

The Marx brothers' heads shot up off the floor. From the solarium, Crackers called, ''Trouble! Trouble!''

''You!'' Jay shouted, pointing his finger at Carly. ''How could you let that happen?''

''Dammit, Jay,'' Nick snapped. ''Don't yell at *her* about it. Garth and Sarina don't take their orders from Carly. So when they said they were going to stay over and come back tomorrow, what was she supposed to do?''

"She was supposed to bring them back, that's what!"

"She tried to make them come," Lisa put in. "But they were determined to stay."

"They *know* I sometimes change the shooting schedule at the last minute. But they take off anyway, and now we're going to waste *more* time. Dammit, there are so many jerks in this business I don't know what I'm doing in it."

Carly glanced at Nick and knew they were sharing the same thought. Who could possibly fit in with a bunch of jerks better than Jay Wall?

SINCE JAY COULDN'T SHOOT his search party scenes without Sarina and Garth, everyone had the night off. And when Carly's father decided he wanted to take his family and Nick into Port Perry for dinner, they ended up at Carly's favorite restaurant.

The Russell House was a charming turn-of-the-century brick structure, with several separate little areas to dine in, and the owner led them to the closed-in porch—where Carly's mother not very subtly orchestrated the seating so that Carly and Nick were side by side.

"So," her mother said over predinner drinks. "Nick was telling us a little about himself while you were gone today."

Carly shot him a swift glance, wondering exactly what he'd told them.

"It'll be exciting, won't it? To start up his own business, I mean."

"Yes. Very." Carly glanced at him again, finding it more than a little unsettling that her parents knew more about his plans for the future than she did.

"Oh?" Lisa said. "Carly didn't tell me you were starting a business, Nick. What sort?" she added, giving Carly a sidelong look.

"Well, I'd like to start my own private investigation agency."

"I guess a lot of ex-police detectives end up in that line of work," her father said.

Nick nodded. "It's what we know."

Carly uneasily sipped her wine. It might be what he knew, but she couldn't imagine there'd be much call for a private investigation agency around Port Perry. So where did that leave *them?*

She could hardly ask. In fact, she could hardly ask anything at the moment. Her parents would think it was awfully strange if they realized Nick had never told her about this. But if they'd just magically vanish for a couple of minutes...

Telling herself that wasn't going to happen, she caught Lisa's eye and silently asked for more help.

They hadn't played this game in years, but Lisa hadn't lost her touch. "Where are you thinking about starting up?" she asked.

Nick looked at Carly, his expression so uncomfortable she felt a chill around her heart.

"In Toronto?" her mother asked.

Nick's gaze lingered on Carly for another second, then he looked at her mother. "No, it would have to be in Edmonton. That's were all my contacts are."

The chill turned to ice. Even though they'd never talked about a future together, the way Carly felt about him... The way she'd been certain he felt about her...

"Yes, I guess contacts are essential in that sort of game," her father said.

"Especially when you're just getting going," Nick agreed.

There was a taste like burnt toast in Carly's mouth, and she found herself wishing *she* could magically vanish.

"Carly?" her mother said. "Is something wrong? You look awfully pale."

"I just feel a little... I think maybe I should get a breath of fresh air. I'll only be a minute." She pushed back her chair and fled to the front door.

It was still raining, but there was a sheltering overhang above the front steps and a wooden railing that she rested her hands on for support. She couldn't recall ever feeling weak-kneed before, but she'd been on such an emotional roller coaster for the past while that it had to be physically catching up with her.

For a moment, she simply stood in the pale glow from the light over the entrance, staring out through the rain. Then, behind her, the door opened and Nick said, "Let's talk, okay?"

Turning, she gazed at him, thinking that if hearts could cry, that's what hers was doing right now. He was the only man she'd ever really loved, and she couldn't have him.

He reached out and took her hands in his. "Carly, nothing I said last night was a lie. Especially not that I love you."

She swallowed hard and bit her lower lip. The man she loved, loved her. That should make her incredibly happy. Instead, she was filled with a feeling so bittersweet it was making her ache.

If he was going back to Edmonton, it didn't matter whether he loved her or not. Because even if he asked her to go with him, she couldn't. Trying to set up what she had here, halfway across the country, would take a million dollars and a million years. And she had neither.

"Last night," he went on, "I intended to finally make myself tell you the truth. That's why I made a nice dinner—because I wanted all the help I could get. But then Jay interrupted, and...

"At any rate, when we got back to the house I was still determined to explain things to you. Then Ben phoned and beat me to the punch.

"But the point is, I knew I *had* to tell you, because I wanted us to talk about the future, and you had to know the truth before we could do that."

"Word is," she murmured, "*your* future is a private investigation agency in Edmonton."

"I...look, I'm really sorry that came as a surprise. I'd assumed I'd have a chance to fill you in, and I didn't. But your mother started asking questions while you were gone, so I told her my plans. I mean, the plans I've had for a long time. But now...with you..."

"Yes?" she whispered, almost afraid to hope that falling in love with her had changed those plans.

"Carly, I love you. I don't want to live the rest of my life without you."

"Oh, Nick." She moved into the warm circle of his arms, resting her cheek against his chest. But simply standing there, listening to the reassuring beat of his heart and breathing in his scent brought tears to her eyes.

He was saying all the right things, yet there were no certainties. *Two for Trouble* had the potential either to make or break Wild Action. And if it was the latter, if the agency didn't get much work in the near future, she'd be scrambling simply to keep it going, while Nick would have to search for a job. And if all his contacts were in Edmonton...

"I can't pack up and move Wild Action out west," she finally said.

"I know. I haven't forgotten. We're mortgaged to the hilt. And if things don't work out with this movie..."

"Don't even say it."

"You're right. We shouldn't be talking at all."

With that, he tilted her face toward his and kissed her, a long, loving kiss that promised her the world.

But she'd happily settle for only a tiny corner of it, as long as she could share it with him.

CARLY STOOD ON THE front porch with her mother, watching her father, Lisa and Nick load the car and absently thinking back over the past week.

Once it had started raining, it hadn't stopped for days—which had given Jay the opportunity to shoot all the wet-and-miserable-type scenes he'd wanted. And he'd shot so many takes of the search party slogging through the rain that she just *knew* he'd done it to get back at the film's stars for their little escape to Toronto.

Surprisingly, he hadn't thrown one of his screaming fits when they'd shown up the next day. But given Sarina and Garth's grumbling, the water torture had been far more effective punishment. At any rate, the sun had finally reappeared, everyone had breathed a collective sigh of relief and they'd gotten down to shooting the remaining scenes.

Best of all, from Carly's point of view, there hadn't been a single incident since the chicken under the rock. And with the shooting here virtually finished, she'd almost stopped worrying.

There were only a couple of scenes left. Jay wanted some shots of the Marx brothers traveling through the woods at twilight. And he wanted to reshoot the one of them tearing apart prey. He hadn't liked the rushes of the nighttime version, so they'd reshoot the scene this afternoon. Then, in the morning, the cast and crew would be moving on to Camp Run-a-Muck.

"Carly, you look lost in thought," her mother said.

She smiled. "Yes, I guess I was. Just thinking that everyone will be gone tomorrow."

"Well, we'll be gone far sooner." Her mother glanced toward the car, then looked back at her. "We didn't overstay our welcome, did we?"

"No, of course not." They *had* stayed longer than they'd originally intended, though, so fascinated by the magic of making movies that they hadn't wanted to leave.

"That's everything," her father said, closing the trunk.

Lisa headed over to Carly and her mother, while her father shook hands with Nick. "Good luck with the last day of shooting," he said.

"And good luck with Nick," Lisa whispered to Carly. "Although, from the looks of things, you don't need it. The man's positively mad about you."

Carly couldn't help smiling, because she knew Lisa was right. Of course, she was positively mad about him, too, which made things ideal.

Her mother gave Nick a hug and invited him—for about the hundredth time—to come and visit them in Kingston.

Then Lisa hugged him, saying, "Thanks again for helping us out on the highway."

Finally, the three of them climbed into the car and headed down the drive.

"Alone at last," Nick said.

"Except for that camp full of cast and crew," she teased, but she knew exactly how he felt. For the past little while, they might as well have been living in a goldfish bowl.

Things had been so hectic that they'd had no time alone together to talk. And making love had been out of the question.

Her parents had adored Nick, but she'd known they wouldn't have adored the idea of her sleeping with him right under their noses. She might be an independent woman of thirty, but to them she was still their baby. So she'd been sleeping alone in her bed, with only dreams of Nick for company. And she was aching to get back to reality—which meant it was a good thing that Jay didn't need the Marx brothers for a couple of hours.

As her father's car rounded the curve in the drive and disappeared, Nick wrapped his arm around her waist, pulling her close. "I know Lisa was on to us, but what about your parents? You think *they* figured there was something going on between us?"

She smiled. "You think they're blind?"

"I really liked them," he said. "But I could hardly wait for them to leave."

"Oh? Why?"

"When we get inside, I'll show you."

"Promise?"

"Hey, I'm never going to lie to you again, remember?"

"Never, ever?"

"Never, ever."

Carly smiled once more, then took a final glance down the drive—just to make sure her family hadn't forgotten something and turned back.

They hadn't, but a black stretch limo was pulling into view.

"Looks like someone has company," she said.

"Won't be anyone coming to see me," Nick told her.

"Me, neither."

"Good," he said, drawing her even closer.

But as they watched, the limo drove past the camp and on up to the house.

It stopped, its dark windows offering no clue as to who was inside.

The driver got out and opened the limo's back door.

A moment later, a man of about sixty emerged. He was tall, tanned and fit. His suit said "money" with quiet understatement. His expression said "displeasure," with no understatement at all.

Not uttering a word, he walked up onto the porch, eyeing them cooly.

It made Carly anxious. He looked like a man accustomed to getting whatever he wanted, and she had no idea what that might be.

Turning his gaze to Nick, he said, "Augustus Montgomery?"

"No, I'm Nick Montgomery. Gus was my uncle, but I'm afraid he died a while back."

"Then who owns Wild Action now?"

"Carly Dumont and me." He nodded in her direction, then looked at the stranger once more. "And you are...?"

"Howard Langly. I'm a business associate of Brian Goodfellow's."

For a second, Carly drew a blank. Then she realized that was Goodie. "By business associate, do you mean you're one of his partners?"

Langly gave her another cool look. "I'm surprised you know he *has* partners. He rarely mentions that Get Real isn't entirely his."

She simply shrugged. Telling Langly it was Barb Hunt who'd done the mentioning might get Barb in trouble.

"What can we do for you?" Nick asked.

"I understand Jay's been having problems with your bear—among other things."

"There's been the odd problem," Nick admitted slowly. "But if you heard the bear was to blame for any of them, it's not true."

"And the problems seem to have stopped," Carly put in.

"Well, things aren't always the way they seem, are they? And I'd like to be clear on exactly *why* so many things have gone wrong. Without knowing that, I can't be convinced there'll be smooth sailing for the rest of the shoot."

"I think this is something you should be discussing with Goodie," Nick said.

"I intend to. With Jay Wall, as well. And I'd like you two sitting in on the discussion."

"I don't think they'd appreciate that," Carly said uneasily.

"Frankly, Ms. Dumont, I don't care whether they do or not. I have a great deal of money invested in a film that's running behind schedule and over budget. But when I raise the issue with Goodie and Jay, they'll try to snow me. So I'd like a couple of people on hand who know what's been going on—to provide a little reality testing."

"I don't think we're the appropriate people," Nick told him.

"No? Well I can't think of two *more* appropriate people. Since Wild Action has a percentage of the profits—assuming there might be some—you'd be wise to make sure I hear the truth. If Jay Wall can't bring this movie in on budget, I'll replace him with someone who can."

"You mean you'd fire Jay?" Carly said.

"Can you do that?" Nick asked.

Langly nodded. "Between the third partner and myself, we hold a majority interest in Get Real. And I have the other partner's proxy, so to speak."

When Carly glanced at Nick, the naked look of concern in his eyes told her he was thinking exactly the same thing she was.

If they sat in on this discussion, and Jay ended up getting fired, he'd lay a lot of the blame on them. Then he'd bad-mouth Wild Action all the way to kingdom come.

"It's in your own best interest," Langly said.

Nick didn't look any happier, but he nodded. "I see your point. Would you like us to head down to Goodie's trailer with you? See if he's there?"

"No. Trailers make me claustrophobic."

When Langly glanced pointedly at the house, Carly said, "Nick, why don't I take Mr. Langly inside and make some coffee while you round up Goodie and Jay."

CHAPTER FOURTEEN

Hell Hath No Fury...

HALF AN HOUR LATER, the five of them were sitting in the living room—Goodie glaring at Howard Langly and Jay glaring at everyone in turn. Including Goodie.

Carly was doing her best to pretend her stomach wasn't churning, while Nick, sitting on the couch beside her, appeared so relaxed she *knew* it was an act.

"Who told you there were problems?" Goodie demanded.

"That's irrelevant," Langly replied. "What I want to know is exactly where the shooting stands."

"It's virtually finished," Jay said quickly.

Langly looked in the direction of the couch. "Is that true?"

Carly's stomach began churning faster. "I really only know about the animal scenes. But almost all of them have been shot."

"See?" Jay snapped at Langly. "We've only got a couple more to film here—one this afternoon and one at twilight. Both with these wolf dogs," he added, making a sweeping gesture that encompassed all four of them.

"Only a couple more scenes to film *here*," Langly said. "That's hardly the same as virtually finished, is it?"

Jay looked angrily at Carly and Nick, his expression saying he wished they were a hundred miles away.

Obviously Langly had been right. If he'd talked to Jay and Goodie on their own, they'd have tried to snow him.

"And then?" he asked. "When you're finished *here*?"

"Then we'll be moving on to Camp Run-a-Muck. There are a few scenes to film there."

Langly shot a glare of his own—straight at Jay. "I've read the script. I know exactly how many scenes there are at the camp. There's the one of the busload of kids arriving, the one where they get settled into cabins and our child stars meet. Then there are the ones with the counselors, the cook, the swimming coach... All in all, a *lot* of scenes before the boys decide to take off into the woods."

"Well...none of them should be time consuming to shoot. Here, it was the animal scenes that caused the delays. The shooting's been slow going because the animals don't always listen to Nick and Carly," he added, sending another black look in their direction.

This one chilled her to the bone. If she'd had the slightest doubt that Jay would blame them if he got fired, it vanished with that look.

"What about the problems before you got here?" Langly asked. "The ones in Toronto? I hear you're going to have to reshoot some of what you did there."

"That was the lab's fault," Jay told him. "It had nothing to do with us."

"Look, Howard," Goodie said. "We seem to have

had a bit of a jinx for a while, but it's behind us now. There hasn't been any trouble on the set for ages.''

Langly looked pointedly toward the couch again.

"That's true,'' Nick told him. "Recently there's been nothing.''

"And we can make up the lost time,'' Jay said. "In the end, I'll bring this puppy in *under* budget. Just wait and see.''

Langly was silent for a minute. Then he said, "I want you to take me down to the camp and introduce me around—so I can get a sense of how the cast and crew are feeling about things.''

"Introduce you as whom?'' Goodie asked.

Langly gave him a withering look. "As your partner in Get Real. Then I'll watch this afternoon's shooting. We'll talk again after that. Before I leave.''

Another chill seized Carly. Langly might be saying they'd talk again, but he sounded as if he'd already decided that Jay had to go.

CARLY CLOSED THE DOOR behind Howard Langly, Jay and Goodie, then turned to Nick. "You know what Jay will be saying about Wild Action if he gets fired, don't you?''

"Uh-huh. The only question is how badly he'd trash us.''

"And after Langly's talked to people, he'll be even more inclined to dump Jay. I mean, someone's bound to say they figure all the problems have been attempts to get back at Jay for something. And if Langly buys that, he'll decide that hiring a new director will guarantee that the problems are over.''

Nick shook his head. "Hell, can you believe we're actually worried about Jay's getting fired? Until we got dragged into that little discussion, I'd have broken out the champagne at the thought of someone taking him down a peg or two. But the way things stand now…''

"I know. So what are we going to do?"

"There's not much we *can* do. Except make sure this afternoon's shoot goes well. The Marx brothers *will* give a good performance, won't they?"

"I don't think we have to worry about that. When you tell dogs to attack a pile of meaty bones, they're pretty enthusiastic. You saw that when Jay shot the scene at night."

"Dammit, I wish that take had satisfied him. If it had, maybe they'd have been gone already and Langly would have had to find someone at Camp Run-a-Muck to sit in on their little talk.''

Carly wrapped her arms around Nick's waist and rested her cheek against his chest, trying to quell her fears. When they refused to go away, she said, "You know, there's something else making me very nervous.''

"What?"

"Well, what if the saboteur hasn't actually called it quits? What if he's merely been lying low and biding his time? And now, with Langly down at the camp being introduced as Goodie's partner… Won't his presence tempt our troublemaker to try something?''

When Nick didn't reply, she drew back a little and gazed at him. He was looking very worried, which spoke volumes.

"That chicken under the rock," he finally said. "We never did know whether or not it was poisoned.''

She looked over to where the Marx brothers were sleeping, her stomach churning worse than ever. If anything happened to them, she'd never forgive herself.

"I think we'd better wander down to the camp," Nick said. "Make sure the chef's been taking good care of the bones they'll be using."

Fresh fear began to snake around her heart. "Nick, when it came to the chicken, Raffaello was high on our list of suspects, remember? And now the bones are in *his* fridge?"

"Yeah, it could be like having the cat looking after the canary, couldn't it. So here's what we'll do. Call that butcher in Port Perry and tell him you need all the big bones he can lay his hands on. And that you need them delivered right away—by taxi, if necessary.

"Then, once they get here, we'll keep a close eye on them. And we'll get Barb to use them, rather than the ones Raffaello has."

Feeling a little less frightened, Carly made the call. As soon as she hung up, they headed for the camp's kitchen.

"What?" the chef called when they knocked.

"Just need to talk to you for a minute," Nick said, opening the door.

Raffaello looked over from where he was in the midst of slicing salad vegetables. "Yeah?"

"We've come to get those bones out of your fridge," Nick told him.

He shook his head. "Barb Hunt already had them picked up."

"So they've gone to the shoot site?" Carly asked.

"I guess."

"Well, thanks."

As Nick let the door close, she said, "If Barb's already getting the 'prey' ready, she's not going to be happy about having to redo it."

"Her happiness is the least of our worries." Nick absently ran his fingers through his hair, a gesture that told Carly he was thinking about something.

"What?" she asked.

He looked at her for a moment, then said, "Who knew Goodie had silent partners? Before today, I mean. Before he brought Langly down here to introduce him?"

"Well, Jay would have. And Barb did. And...I imagine Sarina and Garth. Beyond that, I don't know. Why?"

"I was thinking about something Langly said—that he was surprised you knew Goodie had partners, because he rarely mentions it."

"And?"

"And whoever clued him in not only knew Goodie had partners, he also knew who Langly was and how to contact him. And why did he do that if not to cause trouble?"

Carly could feel her heart thumping. "You're saying it was the saboteur who blew the whistle."

"It's certainly a possibility. So let's wander around the camp for a few minutes and see what we can learn."

They walked along one row of vehicles and up the next, not seeing anyone they knew well enough to stop and talk with. Then they spotted Royce swinging down from one of the equipment trucks.

"Perfect," Nick said. "He always seems to be up on what's what."

"Hey," Royce greeted them. "This is it, eh? The final day of shooting here. And I guess you'll be glad to see the last of us."

"Well, we'll be glad to see the last of *some* of you," Carly told him. "But present company's excluded."

Royce grinned. "You meet that Langly guy?"

"Yeah. He was at the house for a bit," Nick said.

"Oh? And were you as surprised as everyone else to hear that Goodie had a partner?"

"No, we already knew," Carly said. "Someone mentioned it to me."

"Really? Then you were one of the chosen few. Even Garth and Sarina were surprised."

"You're sure about that?" Nick said.

"Uh-huh. I was talking to them when Goodie came by. And when he introduced Langly, Sarina said, she'd thought Get Real was a hundred percent his. It was pretty funny, because you could literally see Goodie deflate."

"So almost *nobody* knew?" Nick asked.

"It sure seemed that way. But look, I've got some work to do before this afternoon's shoot, so I've gotta run."

The instant he turned away, Carly looked at Nick, her pulse racing. "Nobody knew except Jay, Barb and Goodie himself."

"That's not necessarily true. Anybody *might* have known. Even Sarina and Garth."

"But she said—"

"Don't forget they're actors. And as I've said before, they tell lies for a living. But we've got to go with the odds, which means we check out Barb first. It could be that nobody's been trying to screw Jay after all. Maybe she's been trying to stick it to Goodie. I mean, if she *is* on the unstable side..."

"Well, maybe she is. But I think you were right when you said she isn't stupid. So if she's counting on this picture to give her career a boost..."

"Yeah, but maybe she's so totally pissed off at Goodie... Oh, hell, we're not going to get anywhere by debating. Let's just find her."

They headed for her trailer and knocked on the door.

When there was no response, Carly said, "She must be at the shoot site."

"Not so fast." Nick grabbed her hand as she turned to go. "I wouldn't mind a look inside."

He pulled something from his pocket, then glanced around. The only people in sight were a couple of technicians standing a hundred feet away, facing away from the trailer.

"What's that?" Carly whispered as he stuck the *something* into the lock. His hand was concealing the rest of it, so she couldn't even see what it looked like.

"Don't worry about it," he told her, jiggling it around.

A minute later, the door was unlocked.

"Is that something you learned in cop school?" she whispered.

"No, it's something I leaned when I was a kid who fell in with bad company. Luckily, I fell out again before I got into any real trouble."

They both glanced toward the techs once more. The men were still facing the other way.

"Coming in or staying out?" Nick whispered, pushing the door open.

Images of them getting caught dancing in her head,

Carly quickly followed Nick inside. He was already opening a closet door.

"Check the bathroom," he said.

"What am I looking for?"

"Something that... Hold the phone—I think I've already found it."

He crouched down, pushed apart some clothes and peered into the back of the closet.

"What is it?" Carly asked.

"See if you can find a plastic bag."

When she did, Nick slipped it over his hand, then reached down into the closet and came up with a box of rat poison.

Carly froze at the sight of it.

"It's empty," he muttered, pulling the bag around the box. "And I'll bet I know why."

NICK AND CARLY DRAGGED Dylan out of the aviary before he'd half finished cleaning it.

"We need you to do something else," Nick explained. "There's a delivery coming from the butcher's—bones for a scene we'll be shooting this afternoon. I want you to wait in the house for them to get here, then put them in the fridge. After that, just stay in the house until we get back. Keep the door locked and don't let anyone in except us. And whatever you do, don't let the dogs out."

"Why? What's going on?"

"We'll fill you in later," Carly promised.

They stopped by the house long enough to stash the poison box and grab a couple of plastic garbage bags, then they headed into the woods.

When they reached the clearing that was being used for the 'prey' scene, Barb was there alone, putting what had to be the final touches on the deerhide-covered pile of bones.

Poisoned bones. Nick was absolutely certain of that, and it made him want to wring her neck.

She stood up when she saw them, flashing one of her Hollywood smiles and wiping her hands on the big pockets of her shorts. "I just hope this is good enough to make Jay happy. I wasn't as worried about the one I put together for the night shoot. There was so much shadow I knew it would hardly be visible. But that's what he didn't like when we saw the rushes.

"In the daylight, though... Well, with the camera focused on the dogs, there'll only be a few glimpses of this, so I guess it should pass for a dead deer. What do you think?"

"I think you're in big trouble," Nick said.

Barb gave him a puzzled glance, then looked at Carly.

"We know who caused all the problems," she said.

He smiled to himself. He and Carly made damn good partners no matter what the situation.

"Really?" Barb said. "Who?"

"We found the rat poison box," he told her.

That clearly shook her, but she said, "I don't know what you're talking about."

"In the bottom of your closet," he elaborated.

"What?" She looked slowly back and forth at them again, then focused on him. "Should I ask what you were doing in my closet? Where I come from, breaking into someone's place is against the law."

"I wouldn't push *that* angle. Not when poisoning animals is against the law, too."

She shook her head, looking more and more nervous. "Nick, if you actually found a box in my closet, somebody else put it there."

"Maybe. But a forensic lab can tell us whose fingerprints are on it. And I expect they'll find that the poison itself is on those bones you've got there."

Barb nervously licked her lips. "Look, Nick, somebody's trying to set me up here."

Taking the garbage bags out of his pocket, he wondered how many hundred times he'd heard that line. "There's only one way to prove *what's* been going on. So back off and I'll bag those bones as evidence."

"Who the hell do you think you are? A cop?"

"As a matter of fact, I used to be. So just back off."

"Like hell I will," she snapped, putting her hands on her hips and firmly placing herself between him and the 'prey.' "I didn't put this together in ten minutes, you know. And if you think I'm going to let you wreck it, you've got another think coming."

"Barb," he said quietly, "I don't want to use force, but I will if I have to."

"Oh? Well I don't want to use *this*, but I will if I have to."

For a moment, he simply stood staring at the pistol she pulled from her pocket.

It was a little semiautomatic. But not little enough that it couldn't do serious damage. And an unstable person with a gun was a dangerous combination.

When she leveled it at him, he said, "Hey, don't make things worse than they already are. Until now, you've done nothing more than cause a few problems. But if that gun happened to go off and you shot me..."

"I'm not going to shoot *you*," she said, shifting the gun so it was aimed at Carly.

His heart slammed against his chest; Carly went so pale he thought she might faint.

"I'm not going to shoot either of you as long as you do what I say. Now, just go ahead and do what you wanted to. Put the bones in those bags. Half in each."

He started bagging the bones, his adrenaline pumping like crazy. He didn't know what Barb had in mind, but the first mistake she made would be her only one.

Sticking the last bone into its bag, he turned toward her and Carly. "Now what?"

"Just leave the bags where they're sitting and back up."

Swearing to himself, he took a few backward steps. He couldn't risk trying anything when she still had her gun aimed at Carly.

"Far enough?" he asked, stopping.

"A little more."

He silently swore again. She wasn't taking any chances.

"Okay," she said to Carly when he'd moved back farther. "We're going to walk over to those bags. Slowly, one step at a time. And don't even think about getting cute.

"Either of you," she added, waving the gun in Nick's direction.

Still pale as ghost, Carly started forward.

"Pick up the bags," Barb ordered when they reached them.

Carly picked them up.

"Okay," Barb said to Nick. "Carly and I are going

to take a little walk in the woods. You get out of here and just keep your mouth shut.''

Carly shot him such a terrified look it made his gut clench harder than before.

Barb looked at him icily for a moment, then said, ''I'm warning you, Nick, don't try playing cop with me. Because if you come after us, I'll kill both of you. And when Jay discovers that the 'prey' isn't ready, you don't know a thing about it. Understand?''

His heart hammering, he reminded himself he'd talked more than one hostage taker into releasing his victim. But this time it was *Carly's* life at stake. And that made him petrified he'd handle things the wrong way.

''Barb,'' he said quietly, ''like I said before, up till now you haven't done anything really serious. But if you take Carly somewhere against her will, it's kidnapping. So why don't you put the gun away and—''

''No! I need time to think. Without an ex-cop watching.''

''But why not let us help you think?'' He paused, forcing a smile. ''After all, if two heads are better than one, then three heads...''

''I can understand how angry you must be at Goodie,'' Carly murmured.

''I doubt it. You have no idea what a little bastard he is.''

''Look, Barb,'' Nick tried, ''how about sitting down and talking—just briefly, if that's all you want. And I'll sit far enough away that I couldn't possibly try to grab your gun.''

When she said nothing for a moment, he took a long, slow breath. At least she was considering the suggestion. And if she sat down, there'd be less likelihood of her getting around to that walk in the woods with Carly.

"I've got to get rid of those bones," she said at last.

"Not necessarily. I'd be willing to cut you a deal about them." He hated the thought of letting her off the hook when she'd intended to poison the Marx brothers, but he'd cut a deal with the devil if it meant keeping Carly from harm.

"What sort of deal?" Barb said slowly.

He felt a strong twinge of relief. If she was willing to explore the idea, he was halfway home.

"We've got some fresh bones on the way. You can redo the 'prey' using those. And we'll simply dispose of these—without anyone else knowing about them."

"Why?" she asked, eyeing him suspiciously. "Why would you do that when it was *your* dogs they were meant for?"

"Because before Howard Langly leaves here today he'll probably fire Jay—unless we can prove we know who's been causing the problems. But providing proof would take more time than we've got. We'd have to get these bones to where they could be checked for poison, have that box dusted and get you fingerprinted.

"But if you were to *admit* you've been the one...Well, as I said, I'd be willing to forget that you put poison on those bones."

"Why would you care if Jay got fired? You're not exactly palsy-walsy with him."

"No, but if he got turfed off this picture, do you figure he'd have anything good to say about Wild Action? Or do you figure he'd tell people that we're the worst animal talent agency on the face of the earth?''

Barb nodded slowly. "I see your problem. But those bones... How do I know you wouldn't change your mind and tell the cops about them the minute I admitted things?''

"All I can do is give you my word.''

"You have mine, too,'' Carly put in.

Barb slowly shook her head. "I don't think I can trust you.''

"Barb,'' he said, "think about this for a minute, because you're pretty low on options. You don't want to get charged with kidnapping. And you sure as hell don't want to kill one of us and face a murder rap,'' he added, praying he wasn't making Carly even more frightened.

"But if you trust us, and it turned out you shouldn't have, what's the worst-case scenario? Only that we'd tell the cops you *intended* to poison some dogs. And that's hardly a hanging offense.''

"I didn't intend to poison them. I really didn't,'' she added to Carly. "I only wanted to make them sick so Jay wouldn't be able to get those twilight shots until tomorrow. I just wanted to delay the shooting again.''

"Why?'' Nick said softly. "I remember you telling me this film could advance your career—but only if it did good box office. So why have you been trying to make it fall behind schedule? I mean, you *know* that if Jay has to start cutting corners, the movie will suffer and...

"Well, I hardly need to get into that with someone in the business. But was punishing Goodie really worth damaging your own future?''

"My future as a set director, you mean?"

He nodded.

She gave him a wry look. "I don't *have* a future as a set director. I only got this job because I was Goodie's wife. Telling you this movie would help my career was bull.

"I'm a competent assistant—I'll always get work as that. But I'm not so stupid I don't recognize my limitations. I'm not creative enough to be in charge, and everybody knows it.

"So, since I'm not going to be Goodie's wife for much longer, I decided I'd see just how sweet revenge really is, that I'd hit him where it would hurt most. See, I've read the Get Real partnership agreement, and it's set up so that if Goodie loses a bundle on a movie...

"Oh, there's no need to go into the details, but the bottom line is that Langly and the other partner could force Goodie out. Plus, he'd have to personally make good on a portion of the loss, which would make him a very unhappy little bastard."

"But..." Carly paused, then went on. "Didn't you realize you might be hurting yourself financially? I mean, if he's just lost a lot of money, when you get to divorce court..."

Barb shook her head. "He made me sign a pre-nuptial agreement. No matter how much money he has, I won't get more than crumbs."

CARLY KEPT GLANCING uneasily around the living room while Barb confessed her sins.

Before she'd begun, Nick had emphasized that everyone was to simply listen—let her tell her story without interruptions.

Howard Langly hadn't said a word, and neither had Royce.

Carly wasn't at all clear on why *he* was here, but he'd been talking to Langly when Nick was rounding everyone up, and somehow or other he'd ended up tagging along.

At any rate, there hadn't been a peep out of either Langly or Royce, but Goodie and Jay were a different story.

Thus far, Nick had managed to cut off their outbursts by telling them they'd have to leave if they couldn't keep quiet. But she didn't know how much longer that would be effective, with both men looking ready to explode.

"So...that's about it," Barb concluded at last.

"You bitch," Goodie muttered.

"I'll see you never work in the business again," Jay snapped.

"Really?" she snapped back. "Well, let me tell you something. If I ever start having trouble getting work, I'll assume you're to blame. And I'll go straight to the sleaziest tabloids and tell them the details of what went on during this shoot—tell them about all the things that happened right under your nose and how you were too stupid to even realize someone was trying to sabotage the film. I'd make you the laughingstock of the industry.

"As for you," she added, focusing on Goodie, "you know the sorts of things I could tell about you. About your little *peculiarities*. Maybe I'd even start a Brian Goodfellow's ex-wives club and we'd write a book about you."

"Barb?" Carly said quickly. Goodie looked as if he were going to have a stroke if she went on. "Barb, what if Jay and Goodie agreed never to say a bad word about you to anyone? Would you promise to never talk about them?

"What do you think?" she added, looking over at Jay and Goodie. "Could you two live with that?"

"I think it's an excellent suggestion," Nick said. "Otherwise, it sounds as if you could all do each other a lot of damage."

"But what happens to *her?*" Jay demanded, pointing at Barb. "She can't practically ruin my picture, then walk out of here with absolutely no repercussions."

"There'll be at least one repercussion," Langly said. "She won't be getting credit as set director. But, regardless of that, I agree with Nick. The three of you can't be running around like loose canons."

Looking directly at Jay, he added, "Don't you realize how embarrassing it would be if the story got around? You and Goodie would both come off looking like idiots. And it wouldn't do much for Get Real's reputation, either, which is *my* main concern in all this."

"I can't go along with just letting her walk away," Jay snarled.

Langly eyed him coldly. "Apparently I haven't made myself clear. If you want to continue as director on this movie, you *will* go along with it."

Goodie cleared his throat. "Ahh…Jay, if both my partners wanted you off the film, I'm afraid you'd be gone."

Jay's mouth tightened into a thin line. He looked over at Barb, clearly dying to see her nailed to the wall, but he finally muttered, "All right. As long as she *swears* to keep quiet."

"Deal, Barb?" Langly said.

She nodded. Then, with a brittle smile at Carly and Nick, she got up and walked out of the house.

"Anybody know where to find a good set director?" Langly asked. "Fast?"

"As a matter of fact, *I* do," Royce said. "My fiancée's a terrific set director, and she happens to be between jobs. She could get up here from Toronto and put the 'prey' together in time to shoot the scene tomorrow."

"That would mean an extra day here," Langly said.

"Only part of one," Jay told him. "We can still shoot the twilight scene tonight."

"Carly?" Nick whispered. "Let's get out of here."

"What's up?" she asked when they got outside.

He draped his arm over her shoulders and shook his head. "I just wanted to be alone with you. I've had enough of Jay and Goodie to last a lifetime."

"Me, too. But how about Royce having a fiancée? Did you know that?"

Nick shook his head, then gave her a wry smile. "Actually, I spent a lot of time being annoyed with the guy because I thought he was interested in *you*."

"Really? And that annoyed you, did it?"

"Immensely."

"Well, it shouldn't have, because there's only one man in the world *I'm* interested in."

"Yeah? Do I know him?"

"What do you think?" she said, wrapping her arms around his neck and putting a whole lot of body language into the question.

CHAPTER FIFTEEN

Strangers in the Night

"CUT! AND PRINT!" Jay called.

"Good boys," Carly told the Marx brothers, lavishing them with hugs. "You were *such* good boys."

And they really were. The twilight shoot had gone off without a hitch, and the only way Jay could have gotten better-looking wolves would have been by using the genuine item.

She glanced over at him, hoping he'd compliment her on the take, but he was busy talking with Goodie and Howard Langly—and not looking even marginally pleased.

It made her wish for the hundredth time that Langly hadn't dragged her and Nick into the thick of things. To Jay's way of figuring, they'd sided *with* Langly and *against* him, which had him so angry at them that he might never cool down.

And if he didn't...

She tried not to think about that. But the way things stood, the odds that he'd ever say a good word about Wild Action were nil.

"Hey," Nick said, coming up behind her. "The Marx brothers were great."

"I know. I only wish Jay would say something like that."

"Well, maybe he'll have calmed down by tomorrow."

"But what if he hasn't? What if he leaves for Camp Run-a-Muck still looking as if he'd like to kill us?"

Before Nick could reply, Goodie turned away from the others and headed in their direction.

"Just wanted to talk to you for a minute," he said. "I know things got pretty tense this afternoon, but I still should have thanked you. If you hadn't figured out that it was Barb causing the trouble... Well, as I said, I should have thanked you long before this. And Jay should have, as well."

"It doesn't look like we're two of his favorite people at the moment," Nick said.

"No," Goodie admitted. "But once he cools off I'm sure he'll see things in a different light."

"I really hope so," Carly said. "Because what he says about us could have a major impact on our future business."

"I guess that's true," Goodie said slowly. "But...let me work on him a little, huh? I'll see if I can make him come around."

Carly felt like hugging him. But after hugging the Marx brothers she probably smelled like a dog, so she simply thanked him—profusely enough to make Nick laugh.

"There's not much I can add, is there," he said. "But we really *would* appreciate it."

When Goodie turned away, Carly and Nick started for the house, the dogs racing ahead. Darkness was falling fast, and by the time they reached the edge of the woods, the land stretching out in front of them lay silver in the moonlight.

"It's strange to see Attila's field without the pole lights turned on," Nick said, glancing toward it.

She nodded. This was the first night no one had been watching out for him. But with Barb gone, there was no longer any need. And no need to keep the Marx brothers under house arrest, as Nick called it, either.

"You know, I think I'll let the dogs stay out tonight," she said.

"They'd be all right?"

"Oh, sure. Gus let them do it fairly often in the summer. They like to sleep on the porch when it's this hot, and they've had so little exercise lately that they'd probably love to prowl around for a while first."

They walked a few yards in silence. Then, unable to ignore her worries, she said, "Nick?"

"Uh-huh?"

"What if Goodie *can't* reason with Jay? What if we're in his bad books forever?"

"And he spends the rest of his life slamming us, you mean?"

"Exactly."

Nick ran his fingers through his hair. "I guess we'll just have to hope there are enough people who don't listen to him. And..."

He reached for her hand, stopped walking and pulled her close. "Look, I know how much the animals mean to you, and one way or another we'll keep Wild Action afloat.

"If we end up short on clients, I'll get a job so there'll be money coming in. But let's not worry about something that might not happen. Let's just see how the future unfolds and take it from there."

When he kissed her, she told herself *not* to worry. But those thoughts she'd had at The Russell House came rushing back to taunt her, to warn her that she might not like the way the future unfolded.

If Nick had to scramble for a job—one that would pay enough to keep Attila in food, aside from anything else—and if all his contacts were in Edmonton...

Maybe, as he'd said, he really *didn't* want to live the rest of his life without her. But life had an unsettling way of throwing people curves.

THE INSTANT CARLY TURNED off the bedroom light, Nick reached for her in the bed and hugged her tightly. It made her feel as if she could never get enough of his holding her.

"Lord, I've missed you," she murmured. "Between my parents staying so long, and Langly arriving, and the trouble with Barb."

"Mmm." Nick nuzzled her throat, sending red-hot sizzles of desire through her. It seemed years since they'd been together like this, and her level of frustration had been growing daily.

"And didn't you just *love* the way Langly hung around the house with us until dinnertime?" Nick whispered, his breath warm against her skin. "Then insisted we go down and eat at the camp with him."

"I absolutely *adored* it."

As Nick began to trail kisses across her breasts, she was about to say she adored that far more—when she heard a noise.

They both froze.

"What was that?" Nick whispered. "It sounded like the back door opening."

"Did you lock it?" Carly whispered back.

"No. I thought you had."

Fear made her pulse race. "I'm not sure I remembered." By the time they'd gotten back to the house, all she'd been thinking about was being in bed with him.

"Company!" Crackers screeched from the solarium. "Company!"

For an instant, Nick tried to think of where his gun was. Then he remembered he no longer had one. He was a civilian now. He'd turned in his gun along with his badge.

"If there's really someone down there, why aren't the Marx brothers barking?" he whispered.

"They're probably off in the woods. But who do you think it is? Jay? Come to murder us in our sleep?"

"No, Jay might be a total jerk, but I doubt he's a Freddy Krueger." On the other hand, Jay *was* mad as hell at them. And hadn't Barb told them that all directors were crazy?

Barb. His imagination did a ninety-degree turn. They'd been the ones to blow the whistle on her, so maybe she'd come back seeking revenge. Maybe she was far more unstable than anyone had realized.

Adrenaline pumping, he rolled out of bed and grabbed his jeans off the floor. "I need something to use as a weapon," he said, pulling them on.

"A weapon," Carly repeated shakily. "There's Gus's rifle."

"Oh, jeez. And it's hanging right beside the back door." He told himself that whoever was down there might not spot it in the darkness, then said, "There must be *something* up here I could use."

"I don't... Wait, I have a big flashlight. For power failures." She quickly got out of bed and produced it from the closet.

When she grabbed her robe off the chair, he said, "You stay here. And if there's any shooting, crawl out the window onto the porch roof."

"Shooting?" she whispered, sounding terrified.

Nick crept out into the moonlit hall and started down the stairs, the heavy flashlight in his hand, thinking that if the guys on the job could see his "weapon," they'd laugh themselves sick.

As he reached the landing, he heard someone stealthily moving around in the kitchen—undoubtedly looking for the biggest butcher knife they could find.

He eased his way further down the stairs, then heard a tiny noise behind him. Startled, he glanced back. Carly was following him. When he waved her upstairs, she shook her head.

Giving her an angry look she probably couldn't see in the darkness, he continued on down to the main floor. Once he got there, he pressed himself against the hallway wall and began inching his way toward the kitchen, his heart hammering.

He wasn't used to going up against a gun or a rifle or even a butcher knife with only a flashlight for protection. And how was he going to play this? Shine his light on the perp and shout, "Freeze!"?

Hell, he couldn't think of any other approach, but he'd be lucky if he didn't get his head blown off.

He looked back at Carly and waved her away again, swearing to himself when it was every bit as effective as it had been the first time. The only other thing he could do was will her not to get too close to the kitchen doorway.

His gut clenching, he edged farther toward it until he was able to see that the back door was standing open. He could hear Crackers muttering under his cage cover, but there was no other sound.

Barely breathing, he waited for one. If there was even a hope of his plan working, he'd have to shine his light directly into the perp's eyes.

Finally, he heard a scraping noise near the kitchen window. His finger on the flashlight's switch, he wheeled into the doorway, flicking on the flashlight as he aimed it and yelling, "Freeze!"

Crackers shrieked. And from the counter by the window, Rocky Raccoon peered over at him.

Nick exhaled slowly, turned toward Carly and gestured her into the doorway. "Right this minute," he said, as they stood looking at Rocky, "I'm *really* tempted to make myself a coonskin cap."

She laughed, then said, "Come on, Davey Crockett. Rather than playing hatmaker, let's just put Rocky outside, lock the door, then go back to bed and pick up where we left off."

ONCE CARLY AND NICK had finished lunch, she sat down on the living-room floor with the Marx brothers to psych them up for the "prey" scene.

Nick, she could tell from his skeptical expression, still wasn't convinced they understood much English. But she *always* talked to them before they did a shoot, and she wasn't messing with something that worked—especially not when this was their last chance to make Jay happy.

"It's going to go just fine," Nick said after she'd concluded her pep talk.

She nodded, telling herself he was right. Janet,

Royce's fiancée, had arrived early this morning and gone straight to work decorating the set. And the word was that her "prey" was far more realistic looking than Barb's had been—realistic enough to satisfy Howard Langly, who'd finally climbed into his limo and left.

"Looks like we've got company," Nick said, gazing out the window. "Brock and Kyle—without a chaperon, so we'd better keep an eye on them."

When the boys climbed onto the porch, the Marx brothers hurried over to the screen door, tails wagging furiously.

"Come on in," Nick called.

"We just wanted to say goodbye to the animals before we left," Kyle explained as the screen slammed behind him.

"Well, the dogs are obviously glad you did," Carly said.

The boys hugged the Marx brothers and stroked Blue. The other cats decided to hide behind the couch.

"Can we go into the kitchen and see Crackers?" Brock asked.

"Sure." Carly followed along a few feet behind them, trying not to make it *too* obvious that she was watching their every move.

"Company!" Crackers called, dancing along his perch.

"Can he jump on my shoulder again?" Kyle asked.

"Mine, too?" Brock said.

She nodded. "Just don't take him outside this time."

Crackers happily climbed back and forth from one boy's shoulder to the other's until Nick glanced at his watch and said, "I'm afraid we've got to go now, guys. It's time to take the Marx brothers to the set."

"Can we stay in here and play with Crackers while you're gone?" Brock asked.

"No, I think he's had enough excitement for the moment," Nick told him. "But have you said good-bye to Paint and Brush yet?"

When they shook their heads, Carly said, "They're in their field. Here," she added, reaching into the fridge. "Take a couple of apples for them. But they're not saddled, so don't try to ride them."

"Our moms already said not to," Kyle told them. "They said if we were stiff for tomorrow's shoot, Jay would kill us."

After ushering the boys out of the house, Carly leashed the Marx brothers—just in case the smell of the bones was too tempting. Then she and Nick walked them through the woods to the shoot site.

The cameras and klieg lights were in place, ready and waiting, and the "prey" was a lot better than Barb's had been.

"Okay, showtime everyone," Jay called, spotting them. "Now, you know what I want, Carly. Have them start to savage the 'prey' when I cue you, and let's do this in one."

She nodded, her heart in her throat as she told the dogs to sit, then unleashed them. If they screwed up the first take, Janet would have to construct her 'prey' all over again.

"Okay," Jay said. "Bells!"

The smell of the bones had the Marx brothers' noses twitching, but they held their sit.

"Clear the eyeline...and roll it."

Carly didn't take her eyes off the dogs until the

soundman called, "Speed," and the production assistant said, "Scene ninety-eight—Take one," and clicked her slate.

At the sound, Carly looked at Jay.

"Action!" he said.

"Volcano!" She whispered the code command for "attack."

The Marx brothers dashed forward and wholeheartedly attacked the 'prey.'

She hardly breathed until, at last Jay called, "Cut! And print! Great take!" he added to everyone in general. "And that means it's a wrap here. So let's get everything that isn't already packed ready to roll."

When he turned and started talking to Goodie and Royce, without a glance in her direction, she got a sinking feeling in the pit of her stomach.

"Dogs!" she called. *"Off!"*

Reluctantly they backed away from the bones. "Good boys," she told them. "Now you head straight back to the house, because I left special treats for Dylan to give you."

"They were perfect," Nick said, appearing beside her as the Marx brothers started off through the woods.

"For all the good it did us." She looked at Jay again. "You know, he isn't going to say a word to us before he leaves. He's just going to keep on sulking—probably forever."

"Carly? Nick?" Goodie called. "That was terrific," he said, hurrying over to them. "But I thought I'd better check on something with you. Jay wants Royce to shoot some video footage of him with Attila before we leave. I mean, he'd stay outside the fence, so there's no problem with the two of them going along to his field, is there?''

She was tempted to say that yes, there was a problem with it, simply on general principle.

But before she could say a word, Nick said, ''Just remind Jay not to yell.''

''Oh, he's clear on that after all this time.'' Goodie looked over at Jay and Royce and called, ''It's fine.''

As the two men started off, Goodie fell into step with Carly and Nick. ''I'm still working on Jay. So, hopefully, before we take off, he'll stop being such an ass.''

Carly nodded, but at this point she wasn't holding out much hope. And she wished Goodie had gone with Jay and Royce. He walked far too slowly for her liking. She wanted to get back to the house as fast as she could, because the thought of a good, therapeutic cry held a lot of appeal.

When they finally emerged from the trees, they could see Royce and Jay in the distance. They were already by Attila's field, Royce with his eye to the camcorder's viewfinder.

For half a second, Carly didn't realize anything was wrong. Then she took in the big picture and her heart began to pound.

Kyle and Brock were inside the field, standing frozen—about a hundred feet from Attila. And he was staring straight at them.

''Oh, jeez!'' Nick whispered.

''There won't be any problem as long as they don't yell or run,'' she whispered back. ''But hurry. I'll go into the field. You get to Jay so he doesn't do anything stupid, then talk the boys slowly over to the fence.''

"What are you two whispering about?" Goodie said. Then he looked toward the field again and saw the boys.

"Run!" he shouted. "Boys! Run and climb the fence!"

Panic threatening to overwhelm her, Carly took off on the dead run, Nick beside her. But inside the field, the boys began to run, too.

Attila lowered his head and flattened his ears back.

"Attila! *Sit!*" she screamed.

But she was far too far away to make him listen. He pawed the ground once, then charged.

"Jay!" she shouted, her heart pounding even harder. "Jay, scream at him! Distract him!"

For a fraction of a second, Jay hesitated. Then he screamed, "Attila! What the hell are you doing! Stop! Stop right now! You're a horrible bear. I'll cut all your scenes if you don't stop!"

Attila skidded to a halt and stood glaring in Jay's direction.

"Keep it up!" Nick shouted as they ran on. "Yell some more!"

Jay began screaming again.

Attila snorted. Then he growled. And then he charged at Jay.

"Attila! *Stop!*" Carly shouted, her lungs burning. *"Stop!"*

This time she was close enough to be heard. And, miraculously, the bear slowed his pace. Then he stopped.

On the far side of the field, the boys were climbing the fence.

"Good boy, Attila!" Carly called, the utter terror

that had filled her draining away. "Good boy!" Totally out of breath, she slowed to a walk.

Nick jogged the rest of the way, and by the time she reached the fence he was standing with one hand on Kyle's shoulder, the other on Brock's, and was talking with Jay and Royce.

Jay said something to the other men, then turned to the boys. "Whatever possessed you to go into that field?"

Kyle and Brock looked at each other nervously, then Kyle said, "We were sayin' goodbye to all the animals. But when we got to the field we couldn't see Attila."

"We thought you musta taken him somewhere," Brock said, looking at Nick. "And we climbed the fence 'cuz we wanted to wade in the pond. But then, when we were walking across the field, Attila came out of that thing." Bryce pointed at the hibernation 'cave.'"

"We'd *never* have climbed the fence if we knew he was in there," Kyle added.

"Well, you're just lucky Jay was so fast off the mark," Nick said. "By thinking to yell the way he did, he saved your lives."

Carly glanced at him, wondering if he hadn't heard her tell Jay to start yelling.

He met her gaze and held it. For a second, she didn't know what message he was trying to give her. Then it dawned on her. If they made Jay look good, maybe he'd do the same for them.

"You're a first-class hero, Jay," she said.

"Boy, you sure are," Goodie agreed, finally reaching the rest of them. He was puffing so hard that his words were barely audible.

"What did you get on video?" Nick asked Royce.

"I'm not sure, exactly. I just kept rolling. But there's got to be some of everything—Attila charging, the boys running, some of Jay. And the audio of his yelling, of course."

"What a publicity angle, eh, Jay?" Nick said. "Once you edit that, it'll make a terrific promo piece for the movie."

Goodie gleefully clapped his hands. "It will, you know. Hell, Jay, I'll bet we can get you on 'Oprah' with it. And maybe even a segment on 'Sixty Minutes.'"

"Siskel and Ebert might use it, too," Carly put in. "It'll just be such a great bit of docudrama—a movie director risking his life to save a couple of child stars."

Jay eyed her for a moment, looking as if he couldn't quite believe what was happening. "I didn't *exactly* risk my life," he said slowly.

"Oh, Jay, don't be so modest. You don't expect us to believe you forgot that isn't an electrified fence, do you? Why, we all know that if Attila hadn't stopped, he'd have been right on top of you."

Jay went pale. Then his color began to return, and the way he puffed up his chest almost made her laugh out loud.

"No, you're right, Carly. Of course I didn't forget. But what sort of man *wouldn't* risk his life to save two wonderful boys like Brock and Kyle?

"Royce?" he added. "Is there any footage left on that video?"

"A little."

"Good, because I want you to shoot an ending for the docudrama right now, while we're all still looking a little the worse for wear. Everyone except Brock and Kyle clear the eyeline.''

When Carly, Nick and Goodie moved back, Jay dropped to one knee and gave the boys a warm smile. ''Kids, when I say, 'Action,' you run over and give me a big hug for the camera.

''Okay, Royce, roll the film…and action!''

The boys raced over and flung their arms around Jay. He gave them each a hard hug, then turned his gaze toward the camcorder—and darned if he hadn't managed to produce a few tears.

He gazed in Royce's direction for a long second, then slowly wiped his eyes.

''Cut!'' he said a moment later. ''Good scene, kids.''

Pushing himself up from the ground, he strode over to where Carly and Nick were standing. Resting one hand on each of their arms, he said, ''Well, I've got to give credit where it's due. The idea of a docudrama was positively inspired. I don't know how to thank you.''

Goodie cleared his throat. ''They'd probably figure your recommending them to other directors would be a good way.''

''Well, that goes without saying,'' Jay said, positively beaming at them. ''And the next time *I* need animals for a film, we'll be working together again.''

Carly smiled at him, thinking, ''Never in a million years.''

WHEN CARLY AND NICK got back to the house, Dylan was still there.

''I was just on my way home,'' he told them. ''All

the animals have been fed, I cleaned the aviary and I gave the dogs their treats.

"So...I was kind of wondering. Now that the filming's finished, will you be needing me anymore? I mean, even once I'm back at school I could still work on the weekends. And maybe a couple of hours after school most days."

Nick nodded. "There'll definitely be lots of work for you."

"Hey, great! And if there's a *real* lot, Jonathan said to tell you he's available, too. He really got a kick out of baby-sitting Attila."

Carly barely heard Dylan's words. Nick's were still echoing in her mind—causing a chill to settle around her heart. Nick knew that she and Gus had managed with just the two of them. So if he was intending to stay on, they wouldn't really need help.

Did that mean...

Almost afraid to be alone with him, to hear what he was going to say, she ushered Dylan out and waved goodbye. Then, her heart thudding, she turned to Nick.

When he smiled at her, she tried to imagine what it would be like if she couldn't see him smile every day—and decided it would be unbearable.

"Didn't I tell you we shouldn't worry about something that might not happen?" he said. "Jay's so damn happy with us... Carly? Is something wrong?"

"I don't know," she said slowly. "When you told Dylan there'd definitely be lots of work for him..."

"Uh-huh?"

She gave an anxious little shrug. "Well, I wondered if that meant you'd decided to go ahead with your plans. To go back to Edmonton and start up your agency.''

''Hey,'' he murmured, stepping closer and putting his arms around her waist. ''The agency was my dream for a long time, but being with you has become far more important. Besides, I've worked with partners for years. I'd probably miss the company if I was on my own. Whereas, if I stayed on as a partner in Wild Action, I'd have you for company. Assuming that plan's okay with you.''

''Oh, Nick, it's so much *more* than just okay. But you're sure you'd be happy here? Working with the animals?''

''I'd be happy doing just about anything with you. And I've gotten pretty fond of the animals.''

The last whisper of anxiety faded from her heart. ''But if you're staying,'' she murmured, ''why do you think there'll be so much work for Dylan?''

Nick smiled again. ''Because I figure you and I will be spending a lot of time doing other things.''

''Oh? What other things?'' she teased.

''Well, just for starters...'' He cradled the sides of her face in his hands and proceeded to demonstrate.

''You know what?'' she whispered when their kiss ended.

''What?''

''I think we'll be keeping Jonathan employed, too.''

EPILOGUE

WHILE NICK FIDDLED with his tie, Carly absently eyed the embossed invitation that was tucked into the corner of the bedroom mirror.

You are cordially invited
to attend the Canadian premiere
of Two for Trouble.

Saturday, May 21st, at the home of
Mr. and Mrs. Nicholas Montgomery.

Drinks: 6:30 -7:30
Showing: 7:30
Champagne reception to follow

Dress: Black tie optional

"That's as good as it's going to get," Nick said into the mirror.

Carly smiled at him. "Did I ever tell you how gorgeous you look in a tuxedo?"

"Oh, I seem to recall you mentioning it on our wedding day." He captured her hands and drew her to him. "Happy?"

"How could I not be? I love my husband to bits, we've got almost too much work to handle and this morning's reviews of the L.A. premiere were great.

All I need to be positively ecstatic is for Siskel and Ebert to give us two thumbs up.''

"That's what it would take, is it?" Nick drew her closer yet and kissed her—his kiss so long and hot that it left her breathless.

"Actually," she whispered, "I think another of those is all it would take."

Before he could follow through on the suggestion, Lisa stuck her head into the doorway. "Hey, you two lovebirds had better move it. The first of your guests are coming up the drive."

They hurried downstairs just in time to greet Royce Chalmers and his fiancée.

"Go on into the solarium and get yourselves drinks," Nick told them. "We set up the bar in there so Crackers wouldn't feel left out."

As the rest of the guests began arriving, the Marx brothers got more and more excited—until Carly finally put them outside. "But don't run off or you'll miss the movie," she warned them.

A little before seven-thirty, she and Nick shepherded everyone out to where chairs were set up on the lawn facing the porch, where the VCR and the big-screen TV they'd rented were stationed.

Right on time, Dylan brought Attila up from his field. Once he was settled in at the back, between Nick and Carly, Lisa turned on the TV.

"First," she told everyone, "we have a short tape of last night's premiere in L.A. Goodie had it flown up for us this morning."

When she pressed Play the screen came alive with a Hollywood moment. First, Brock and Kyle arrived at the theater—both boys a couple of inches taller than they'd been last summer. Then Sarina and Garth emerged from their limo, waving like royalty.

Jay had one of Tinseltown's hottest starlets on his arm, while Goodie was accompanied by Barb Hunt's successor, the fifth or sixth Mrs. Brian Goodfellow.

Once the celebrities had filed into the theater and the doors closed behind them, the tape faded to black.

"And now our feature," Lisa announced, changing tapes.

Excitement bubbled inside Carly as the credits rolled. Then the action began. First the city scenes, followed by the ones shot at camp Run-a-Muck, and finally the part they'd all been waiting for.

Nick reached around Attila and took her hand as the bear made his first appearance. When he saw himself on the big screen he sat up straighter—wriggling his nose and trying to smell the movie bear's scent.

"No, that's *you*," Carly told him.

Then it was the Marx brothers' turn in the spotlight, and everyone broke up when they wolf-howled right along with their on-screen howling.

"What do you think?" Nick whispered. "Is it a two thumbs up?"

When he leaned behind Attila and kissed her, happy tears filled her eyes.

"Oh, Nick," she murmured as he leaned back. "My entire life is a two thumbs up."

EVER HAD ONE OF THOSE DAYS?

TO DO:

☑ late for a super-important meeting, you discover the cat has eaten your panty hose

☑ while you work through lunch, the rest of the gang goes out and finds a one-hour, once-in-a-lifetime 90% off sale at the most exclusive store in town (Oh, and they also get to meet Brad Pitt who's filming a movie across the street.)

☑ you discover that your intimate phone call with your boyfriend was on company-wide intercom

☑ finally at the end of a long and exasperating day, you escape from it all with an entertaining, humorous and always romantic Love & Laughter book!

ENJOY
LOVE & LAUGHTER™
EVERY DAY!

For a preview, turn the page....

Here's a sneak peek at
Colleen Collins's RIGHT CHEST, WRONG NAME
Available August 1997...

"DARLING, YOU SOUND like a broken cappuccino machine," murmured Charlotte, her voice oozing disapproval.

Russell juggled the receiver while attempting to sit up in bed, but couldn't. If he *sounded* like a wreck over the phone, he could only imagine what he looked like.

"What mischief did you and your friends get into at your bachelor's party last night?" she continued.

She always had a way of saying "your friends" as though they were a pack of degenerate water buffalo. Professors deserved to be several notches higher up on the food chain, he thought. Which he would have said if his tongue wasn't swollen to twice its size.

"You didn't do anything...bad...did you, Russell?"

"Bad." His laugh came out like a bark.

"Bad as in *naughty.*"

He heard her piqued tone but knew she'd never admit to such a base emotion as jealousy. Charlotte Maday, the woman he was to wed in a week, came from a family who bled blue. Exhibiting raw emotion was akin to burping in public.

After agreeing to be at her parents' pool party by

noon, he untangled himself from the bed sheets and stumbled to the bathroom.

"Pool party," he reminded himself. He'd put on his best front and accommodate Char's request. Make the family rounds, exchange a few pleasantries, play the role she liked best: the erudite, cultured English literature professor. After fulfilling his duties, he'd slink into some lawn chair, preferably one in the shade, and nurse his hangover.

He tossed back a few aspirin and splashed cold water on his face. Grappling for a towel, he squinted into the mirror.

Then he jerked upright and stared at his reflection, blinking back drops of water. "Good Lord. They stuck me in a wind tunnel."

His hair, usually neatly parted and combed, sprang from his head as though he'd been struck by lightning. "Can too many Wild Turkeys do that?" he asked himself as he stared with horror at his reflection.

Something caught his eye in the mirror. Russell's gaze dropped.

"What in the—"

Over his pectoral muscle was a small patch of white. A bandage. Gingerly, he pulled it off.

Underneath, on his skin, was not a wound but a small, neat drawing.

"A red heart?" His voice cracked on the word *heart*. Something—a word?—was scrawled across it.

"Good Lord," he croaked. "I got a tattoo. A heart tattoo with the name Liz on it."

Not Charlotte. Liz!

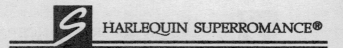

HARLEQUIN SUPERROMANCE®

WOMEN WHO *Dare*

*They take chances, make changes
and follow their hearts!*

WHERE THERE'S SMOKE... (#747)
by Laura Abbot

Jeri Monahan is a volunteer fire fighter in her Ozarks
hometown—and Dan Contini, former navy officer, is the
fire chief.

Jeri's a natural risk taker—and Dan's a protector, a man who
believes women shouldn't be exposed to physical danger.

Jeri's a woman who wants it all, including marriage—
and Dan's a divorced father embittered by his ex-wife's
unfaithfulness.

There are a lot of sparks between Jeri and Dan—and a lot of
problems, too. Can those sparks of attraction be fanned into a
steady fire?

Find out July 1997 wherever Harlequin books are sold.

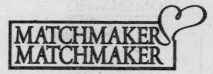

SHOTGUN BABY (#750)

by Tara Taylor Quinn

FBI agent Con Randolf is desperate to claim his abandoned infant son—a child he didn't know he had. Yet as far as the state is concerned, Con doesn't have much to offer a child—he has a risk-filled job and he's single.

Con doesn't know a single woman who would marry him—or whom he wants to marry. But he does have a best friend—Robyn Blair—who could benefit from a *temporary marriage of convenience.*

Watch as the sparks fly this August 1997.
Available wherever Harlequin books are sold.

MOI897

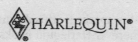

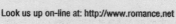